Gravity

Gravity

LAUREN RUNOW

INDIE SOLUTIONS

Photo taken by Ryan Bates Photography
Cover Images © Adobe Stock – pressmaster and jeliva
Cover Design © Designed With Grace

Designed with GRACE

For every band I've ever loved,
Thank you for feeding my soul.

Books by
LAUREN RUNOW

Unwritten
Rewritten

Black Widow

The High Road (free novella)

Gravity

Chapter 1

Pulling me down. Feeling the weight
Living for tomorrow not knowing if it will be too late.
The life, the people, hell—my own sanity
I need her to keep me grounded like she's my personal gravity.

- Trevin Allen

Lily – Age 12

"**C**ome on, Trev! We have to get home, now!" I turn to scream behind me as I ride up the hill, watching the sun slowly fade away into darkness.

He knew we'd gone too far back in these hills on our bikes, and no matter how much I told him we needed to turn around, he wouldn't listen. Now we're still at least a mile from home and losing sunlight by the second.

"I'm going as fast as I can, but it's kind of hard to push this thing with a popped tire," he nags back at me.

"Well, whose fault is that? I told you not to do that jump," I yell, looking over my shoulder.

The boy is crazy. Anything he can fly his bike off of, he will. I went around a steep rock, but not him—he went right over it and bent the rim, shredding the tire in the process.

Grunts of frustration come from behind me as I stop and turn in his direction. His irritation level is evident as he reaches down to pick his bike up from a different angle, hoping it would be easier to carry. The sight of him struggling has me off my bike, walking it back to where he's standing.

"Here." I push the handlebars toward him. "You pedal and I'll ride between your legs. We'll just leave yours here and come get it tomorrow. No one's going to mess with it all the way out here."

Without a second thought, he drops his bike, grabbing mine with a huge smile. "Good idea. Hop on."

I straddle the metal bar, looping my fingers around his forearms and resting my butt and legs up high on the middle bar. The position is extremely awkward, and I'm already regretting my suggestion.

Memories of when we met at eight years old fly through my head as we take off down the street together.

"Hi, I'm Trevin. What's your name?" A boy sneaks around the fence to where I tried to hide from him.

"Lily," I shyly state, not daring to meet his gaze.

"Lily—like the pad?"

"Excuse me?" My head shoots up.

"You know, lily pad, like what frogs jump on in a pond."

My glare in his direction makes him laugh before he continues. "So, Lily Pad, did you just move in?"

"My name is not Lily Pad, just Lily…and yes, we moved in yesterday."

"Okay, well, can I call you another name then? Maybe Turtle? You looked like one the way you were peeking your head out behind the fence."

"No, you can call me Lily."

"Okay, Lilllllyyyy…" he drawls my name out, making a point. "Come on, grab your bike. Let's go ride."

"I don't have a bike…" My voice is low, embarrassed by not having one, but even if I did, I don't know how to ride one.

"You don't have a bike?" He seems shocked by my revelation.

"I lived in San Francisco. You don't really ride your bike in the street there."

"That's crazy! Well, come here then…you can ride mine, or I have a scooter if you want."

"Um, I…um," I stutter, not sure what to say.

"It's cool if you don't know how. I'll teach you."

"Uh, okay, I guess so."

Perched on the bike, he holds the seat and runs down the street next to me while I try my best not to fall. The wheels wobble and I almost lose control a few times, but he catches me before I hit the ground. My heart pounds with adrenaline pumping through me, the joy of riding overruling the fear of falling.

"Come on, Lily Pad. Try to stay upright."

I glare at him over my shoulder, and he laughs in response as he pushes me forward again, telling me to pedal faster. Following his instructions, my little feet push as hard and quick as they can to pick up speed.

I'm so focused on trying to maintain my balance and breathe at the same time, I don't realize I'm doing it all by myself. It's not until I hear him screaming from behind me, celebrating my success, that it dawns on me he's no longer by my side.

My attention is thrown off when I see him so far away and fear instantly sets in. The bike starts to sway from side to side and panic takes over. I remove my feet from the pedals, slowing my speed down by running them along the ground yet still straddling the bike. My gaze finally lifts, only to see a huge wall of bushes, and in the blink of an eye, I slam right into them, scraping every inch of my body as the branches bring me to an automatic stop.

"Lily!" I hear Trevin scream as he runs down the street after me.

I try my hardest to fight back the tears threatening to fall, not wanting him to see me cry.

"Are you okay?" he asks, moving branches away and pulling on my arm to help me up.

"Y–yeah," I stutter.

"Good because that was awesome!" He celebrates, throwing both hands in the air and jumping up and down. "Man, I wish I had my parents' camera. You should've seen yourself going into those bushes!"

Remembering his excitement from my crash years ago, and knowing how reckless he is on his own bike, I can't stop worrying about riding with him now. Fear of falling and breaking something takes hold of my chest. That cannot happen. I have a dance recital coming up and I can't miss it.

"Here, just sit on my lap. That way, I can see over you and you'll be more comfortable than you would be sitting on that bar."

"But I'll crush you," I whine, not looking at him.

"Really? You're the tiniest thing alive. Have you looked at me recently? I'm the biggest guy in our class. There's no way you could crush me."

I turn to see his face painted with pride. Even though he says it's not a big deal, deep down he loves the fact he's the "cool kid" in class. His hair is always in the latest style, spiked up in front and cut close in the back—the same cut other boys want but their moms won't let them have. He's the only guy I know who cares about his clothes. Trevin only wears plaid button-ups or skater-looking shirts with jeans and his Chucks. He's also the only kid in the class who can ride a skateboard and can even do tricks on it. The other guys try, but for him, it just comes naturally.

Most of the girls in our class are jealous we're so close, but I don't get all girly and giggly like they do when he's around. They talk about the butterflies in their tummies and their flush faces when they see him. He's not just Trev—no, he's Trevvvviiin, all long, drawn out, and dreamy-like when they say it.

Sitting back on his lap, I lean against his chest and adjust my legs so they're in a more secure position. "Is this okay?" I ask.

He laughs. "Yeah, now hold on."

I turn and our eyes meet for a brief second as a small smile forms on his lips. They're so close to my face I can feel the warmth of his breath on my skin, and instantly, my chest tightens.

Looking forward, I maintain a death grip on his arms, unsure of what's wrong with my chest. I take a deep breath to try to calm the fear seizing my ribs. I mean, it must be fear I'm feeling. I've seen this boy jump off the craziest cliffs, and here I am, trusting him to ride my bike to safety—with me on it.

Yes, that must be it. Fear.

Surprisingly, he maintains a normal pace, and after a few yards, the ache in my chest subsides, replaced with a feeling I can't explain. The cool breeze floating through the summer night relaxes me while his warmth wraps around my body. Without realizing it, I drop my head to the left, sinking into him, and making this ride even more comfortable.

His breathing picks up, and I can hear the sudden shakiness in my ear and feel his heart starting to race as the steady beat taps my back. He isn't pedaling fast, but I guess having to exert enough energy to propel both of us must be tiring. The farther we go, the rougher and deeper it gets.

We make it back to the house just as darkness completely takes over the night, and I lift my head off his shoulder when he pulls up in front of my driveway. Once he stops, I climb off the bike and turn to face him. The streetlight above cast shadows over his face, but I catch a glimpse of his eyes when he tilts his hat up, and then…I feel it.

The butterflies other girls talk about.

My eyes meet the street when fear of the unknown takes over my body.

The silence in the air starts to sting and the hum from the lamplight above us begins to mock me. Awkwardly, I wait for him to move, to say something, but neither of us do anything. Stunned, in this frozen state, I desperately want to curl into a ball and hide. This is not us—we don't sit quietly or not interact, especially Trevin. He always has some silly remark or an ease about him that has amazed me since we first met.

The sound of my parents running out from our house breaks my thoughts. "Lily, you're in big trouble, young lady. Do you see how dark it is?" my dad sternly makes his point.

I glance at Trevin, our eyes meeting for a brief second before I turn around, apologizing to save my life. "I'm sor—"

"Mr. Pace, I'm so sorry." Trev cuts me off. "This was my fault. My tire broke on my bike, and we finally had to leave it back in the hills or we would have been home much later. That's why I'm riding Lily's." He jumps off the bike and walks it up to my garage where my parents are walking toward us.

Both of my parents want confirmation, looking first at me and then back at Trevin.

"We're sorry, but there was nothing we could do. We have to go back to get his bike in the morning. I rode on…" I pause as I feel heat rise up my face, suddenly embarrassed and unable to make eye contact with either of my parents. "I…um, I rode on the handle bars."

The urge to look at Trevin takes over, and when I glance his way, our eyes meet, but he quickly looks away and back toward my parents.

"Okay, Trevin, well, I'm sorry about your bike. I'm glad you guys made it back safe. Your mom is worried sick as well. Go on home now. Have a good night," my dad says to Trevin while taking the bike from him before walking it into the garage.

Trevin turns in my direction, those butterflies taking flight again in my stomach. Our eyes lock on one another for a second too long before he turns and walks to his house.

My mom's soft laughter takes me out of my butterfly-induced state when she wraps her arm around my shoulders. "Well, well, well. It's about time you two noticed each other," she teases.

I shake my head in instant denial. "What? What are you talking about?" I shrug out of her embrace, mad at her comment.

"Uh huh…" She laughs as she walks away, back into the house. "Glad you're home safe, Lily," she calls over her shoulder, leaving me sitting in the dark garage—alone with my butterflies as thoughts of leaning against his chest fill my mind.

After getting ready for bed, I crawl under the covers and hear my walkie-talkie beep. "Hey, Lily Pad, you there?"

Our bedrooms face each other, but there's a good forty feet between our houses. A few years ago, his mom got him walkie-talkies for Christmas, so he instantly ran over to my house to give me the second one, and it's been here ever since.

I grab it from the dresser and open up my blinds so I can see him while we talk. "Yup, I'm here. Just about to get in bed. What's up?" I say as we glance at each other, back-lit by the lights in our rooms.

"Hey." He smiles, tilting his head up in acknowledgment.

"Hi," I respond as the butterflies return to my tummy—stupid butterflies. "Are you in trouble?"

"Nah, thanks for stepping in to tell them about your bike."

"No prob. I just didn't want to get you in trouble."

"How about you? How mad was your dad?" I'd never say his dad had been an overly friendly guy, but lately, I've noticed things aren't going very well around his house. His dad has been very different—more distant than

5

he has been in the past. But every time I ask Trevin about it, he changes the subject. I love his mom, though. She's the sweetest lady, always offering us something to eat and taking us wherever we want to go. She's even come to some of my dance classes and has volunteered as an instructor.

I hear him take a deep breath before he answers. "He's not home yet," is all he replies. I look at my alarm clock and wonder where his dad could be after ten o'clock.

Weird…

We sit in silence, where normally our conversations carry on forever. There's not much to say tonight, and the nervous sensation in my stomach makes it hard to even breathe.

"So…um, do you want to go get your bike in the morning?" I finally think to ask.

Before he can answer, lights sweep across his house, signaling his dad pulling into the driveway.

"Um…uh—I've got to go. Night." Trevin abruptly throws the walkie-talkie down and runs to turn off his light.

I can't help but wonder what that was about. I whisper, "Night," more to myself since I can see he's no longer paying attention to me. I get up to turn my bedroom light off and hop into bed, snuggling under the covers and getting comfortable with my pillow.

Just as my eyes close, muffled yells awaken my senses. Looking for the source, more of the angry sounds fill my room. I realize it's coming from the walkie-talkie that has fallen between my bed and the wall.

Finally securing it in my hand, I quickly turn down the volume since the yelling has turned into screaming. I peek out my window, trying to get a glimpse of what's going on. In his rush to go to bed, Trevin must have tried to hide the walkie-talkie making the talk button lodged firmly against something keeping it activated.

The light flicks on, and I see a large figure standing in his doorway. The voice booming through the walkie-talkie gives his dad away before I can see all of him. "What the fuck did you do?" His voice so intense it cracks under its own pressure.

Trevin sits up in his bed, squirming as far against the back wall as he can go, putting distance between him and his dad. "It was an accident. I swear."

Helplessly, I watch my friend cower in the corner, fear lining his voice as he shields himself from the onslaught of words being thrown at him.

"What did I tell you?" his dad screams in response. "There's no such thing as an accident. If you weren't such a dumbass, or a total fuck up, this kind of shit wouldn't happen."

"Dad, I'm sorry. I didn't mean to." Trevin's hands go up in front of his face, trying to defend his actions.

"How about I sell that damn baseball glove of yours to pay for a new wheel? Seems that's the only thing you care about anyway."

"No, Dad. Please don't. I'll pay for it, I swear. I'll go mow lawns to earn the money, I promise. Please don't take my glove."

My eyes trace his dad's steps across the room, terrified of the repercussions Trevin was about to face. Never in my worst nightmare could I have foreseen his dad lifting his fist and throwing a punch at, what looks like, Trevin's face.

The man's voice sounds possessed, like a demon taunting him. "Damn right you will."

My stomach constricts as my chest screams for the air my body's refusing. I can't believe I'm witnessing this. There was no way this could be happening. Not to my best friend.

Thankfully, his dad turns and storms out of the room, leaving Trevin alone. I hear his muffled cries through the walkie-talkie as he covers his face with a pillow.

Unable to move, choking on fear, I stare into his room, knowing things will never be the same between us, or his family.

A few minutes later, his mom walks into the room and quietly shuts the door behind her. The second the latch clicks she rushes to Trevin's side. "Oh, baby, are you all right?"

The walkie-talkie picks up her audible gasp when she sees Trevin's face. She quickly grabs for him, drawing him to her chest and rocking back and forth in a protective embrace…like any mom would when her baby's hurt.

"I'm so sorry, honey. You know he doesn't mean it. He's going through a hard time. I promise this will never happen again. Here, let me look at you." She pushes him back enough to inspect his face, her fingers gently caressing the skin on his cheeks. Their interaction is comforting, even to me, but nothing about this is right.

My heart is broken.

Visions of Trevin scrambling away from what he must have known was coming caused me to toss and turn all night. The sound of his father's fist when it hit him, the loud whack that resounded through the walkie-talkie, played over and over in my head. I couldn't make it stop no matter what I did. Now that it's morning, I'm still sick to my stomach, and I don't have a clue what to say or do.

As I lay in bed, watching a rerun of *The Wonder Years*, I hear the walkie-talkie come to life. "Hey, Lily Pad, you awake?"

The butterflies take flight in my stomach when his voice dances around my room. It's not the first time he's checked in with me in the morning, and it's definitely not the first time he's called me Lily Pad, but somehow, everything has changed. My feelings for him, our friendship, his family…it's all different. One thing overrides all the other uncertainty that I can't deny—his voice sends chills down my spine, making the butterflies' wings beat faster. I don't know whether to smile or throw up from nervous sensations overwhelming me.

Swallowing my fears and filling my lungs, I choose to pretend nothing's different. "Only if you don't call me Lily Pad," I tease while looking up to the ceiling, inhaling a steady breath.

His laughter filters through the other end. "No chance. Let's go get my bike."

I shake my head, not able to fight the annoyed smile taking over my face. This stupid nickname hasn't gone away since the day we met.

"Okay, give me fifteen minutes and I'll be down."

"Cool, see you soon."

I spend ten of the next fifteen minutes staring at the mirror, lost in thought. A tingling sensation burns through my veins and my chest squeezes, remembering the way his father treated him last night. Finally, I gather the courage to move and go face my best friend.

I find my mom sitting in the kitchen, drinking her coffee. "Mom?"

"Yeah, baby," she says, looking up at me sincerely.

I never realized until this moment just how lucky I am to have the parents I do. Both my mom and dad would do anything for me at any time. Shoot, they moved their entire life out of the City so I could have a more normal childhood.

I contemplate talking to my mom about what I saw, but I honestly don't know if there was anything she could do. I'm certain about one thing—I don't want them looking at Trevin or Julie any differently, so I decide to keep his secret safe in my heart.

"I'm going out with Trevin to get his bike," I say, having completely changed my mind.

She knows I'm hiding something—she reads me like a book. Facing me, seeing the look in my eyes, the hesitation in my face, she knows. "Is everything okay?"

"Yeah, I just wanted to say I was sorry about last night," I kind of lie. I mean, I am sorry, but that's not what I really wanted to say.

"It's okay. We understand things happen sometimes. Just glad you guys were safe. I must admit, knowing you were with Trevin eased my mind. I know he cares a lot about you."

I smile, knowing how important my best friend is to me. I know he'll do anything to protect me. Now I just need to figure out how can I protect him.

"Thanks, Mom." I give her a bigger hug than normal before walking to the front door.

When I open it I find Trevin already sitting on the steps with his back to me and a baseball cap on his head. The mere sight of him spreads a smile across my face as the butterflies return in full force.

Without saying a word, I sit next to him, close but barely touching, staring out at the street in front of us. "What's up?" I say in greeting.

"Not much." He bumps my leg with his.

I turn to face him, and my heart sinks at the sight of a swollen black and blue eye. There's a small cut an inch above the bruises he's trying to hide under the hat. His chest rises as he takes a deep breath but doesn't say a word when he releases it. He's trying desperately to mask the shakes overtaking his body.

I lean over, lifting his hat slightly and, without saying a word, kiss his eye softly then place my hand over his on his knee. We sit silently, saying all that needs to be said through that touch before he stands and pulls me up along with him, heading out to get his bike.

Chapter 2

The music is alive
Running through my veins
Fueling me, feeding my drive
Like a speeding car flying through the lanes.

- *Trevin Allen*

Lily – Age 13

"**M**y parents are making me learn an instrument," I whine to Trevin as we walk home from school together.

"Why are you bitching? I'd love to play the guitar, but you know there's no way my dad will ever go for it. I wouldn't even dare ask. He's threatened way too many times to pull me from baseball as it is."

He's right. Baseball is his life and his father hangs that over his head all the time. I'll never understand what's happened to his dad in the last twelve months, but he's become a horrible man. The way he treats Trevin is awful—the yelling, throwing things…and I know he's hit him more than once. There have been bruises to prove it. But we don't talk about it.

"I know, but what will I do with an instrument?" I respond, kicking the rocks down the road in front of me. "I'm a dancer, not a musician. If I hear them tell me I need to be *well rounded* one more time, I may scream. I just don't care about the flute or the clarinet like I care about making the high school dance team."

"Yeah, those are pretty dorky instruments. The piano's cool. How about that?"

"Yeah, I guess." I shrug. "I just don't want to. Then they'll make me practice all the time, and it's just boring."

"Hey, I've got an idea. Why don't you take guitar lessons and then you can come home and teach me? We can practice together."

I see the excitement in his eyes, and I can't help but laugh. "You really want to learn to play the guitar?"

"Hell yeah I do. Haven't you listened to the rock music that's coming out lately? It's awesome. I'd love to be like them someday. Can you imagine me playing with bands like Offspring or Stone Temple Pilots? I can totally see myself on stage ripping chords with a crowd going wild." He stops on the sidewalk to do his version of air guitar.

I can't help but laugh at him. "Okay, fine. I'll pick the guitar, but that means you *have* to practice with me."

"This will be awesome! I promise you won't regret it. You just have to start listening to better music now."

I slap his stomach with the back of my hand. "What's wrong with my music?"

"Well, I must admit it's gotten better since you stopped listening to New Kids on the Block—thank God—but this country kick you're on is almost worse." He feigns a look of irritation, but I know he's just giving me a hard time.

"Hey, they play guitar in country music."

"Yes, but we"—he points his finger back and forth between us—"will not be learning any country songs."

"Hey, this is my thing. I'll learn country songs if I want to. I'd love to play *Don't Take the Girl*," I smile all dreamy eyed for my new love, Tim McGraw.

"Not that sappy song. No way. Forget about it. If I'm going to make learning an instrument fun for you, we'll play some Green Day, Soundgarden or Bush. The list is endless, but it won't be Tim McGraw."

I roll my eyes. "Whatever, see you later." I hit his shoulder as I walk up to my door.

"But we're on, right? You're going to learn guitar and teach me?"

"Yeah, yeah, we're on." I wave him off with a grin.

"And you're coming to my game tonight, right?"

"Have I ever missed one?" I tease.

A smile fills his face. "Great. See you tonight, Lily Pad."

My glare just makes him laugh as he runs toward his house.

First guitar lesson and I'm already regretting it. My fingers hurt from holding the strings down, and I don't have any rhythm or coordination—strumming alone is hard for me. My teacher instructs me by saying, "Move the pick up…down…up…down…up, down, up, down."

Sounds easy enough. Wrong. I'm all over the place and can't keep up with him at all. My fingernails get in the way and I've never been so happy to see a clock hit four thirty in my life—my first lesson is finally over. I thank my teacher and walk out to Trevin, who met me downtown after baseball practice to walk me home.

"So? How was it?" he asks with excitement written all over his face.

"Horrible. My fingers hurt and I can't hold a tune for the life of me."

He laughs. "Come on. You can't be that bad. Let's go…if we hurry up, you can show me some things before my dad gets home." It seems we're always avoiding encounters with his dad, and we for dang sure never want to upset him. My heart aches for my friend's situation, but there's not much I can do other than try not to get him in trouble.

Watching Trevin's face light up at the sight of the guitar reminds me of why I'm doing this. The way he holds it in his hands like it's a precious baby, coddling the neck and body, playing with the strings, it's like he's amazed that something like it even exists. He plays baseball like his life depends on it, and I can tell just by the way he's holding the instrument he has the same passion for music.

After pulling a pick from my bag, I go over the chords I learned today. I show him the best I can how to hold the pick properly and the method for strumming the strings. While I didn't seem to be able to grasp any of it, Trevin is a natural. I'm annoyed with how flawlessly he picks up on the techniques and sounds just like my teacher. Both making it seem effortless.

"See, I'm just not musically inclined," I say with frustration as I sit back on my heels.

His laugh makes me glare at him. "It's okay. You'll get it. So what does this thing mean?" he asks, pointing at the sheet.

I go over the difference between chords and tablature, and it instantly clicks in his brain. Now he's helping me understand. "I'm supposed to be teaching you, and now you're the one teaching me." I'm flustered by the entire experience.

"Don't worry—you'll get it, too. You have me to help you, remember?" he teases.

"What do we have here?" His mom comes out from the house and walks toward us.

"Hi, Mrs. Allen." I jump up to give her a hug.

We've gotten close over the years. She used to dance before she had

Trevin, so she comes to all my performances and has even started helping out as an instructor more recently.

"Lily's learning how to play guitar. Check this out." He strums the few chords I just taught him. "She's going to teach me to play, too." The excitement in his eyes shines brightly as he beams at his mom.

Silently, I watch pain reflect in her expression, and I try to imagine what's going on in her head. Her anguish centers around his dad, and the bruises he's left behind are a testimony to her torment. The marks on her arms mimic fingerprints, and since I haven't seen any more bruises on Trevin, it's obvious she's taking the brunt of his anger.

Trevin and I never spoke about that night. He doesn't know I saw the entire thing go down, much less heard it word for word, and I've never felt the need to tell him. It's none of my business, and if he doesn't want to talk about it, then neither do I.

When his mom looks at me, she blinks away the tears as she thanks me for teaching him before quietly turning around to go back inside.

A week ago, I would have done anything possible to get out of learning the guitar, but now, after seeing his face and then hers, I know in the end it will be worth it, and for them, I'm happy to do it.

Trevin

Music has been my escape from my screaming father for the last few years, and I'm so excited to finally get the chance to learn the guitar.

At night, I lay with my Discman playing music through my earphones as I imagine being them someday. Baseball is my passion, but music is my dream. If I concentrate long enough, I can see myself performing for thousands of screaming fans who get as much happiness from my tunes that I do now listening to my favorites.

I spend the majority of my time at home, alone in my room, hiding from my dad, so when I walk in from being outside with Lily, I'm surprised to see my mom sitting on my bed with a CD and my Discman.

"Oh, hey baby." She pauses as she wipes a tear from her eye.

"Mom, what's wrong?" I walk up to her, looking at my Discman and the CD. "What's that?"

"I'm just...I–I'm really happy that Lily is teaching you to play guitar. I know music is important to you and I'm...I'm just happy for you right now. I'm sorry we can't put you in lessons."

I shrug. "It's okay, Mom. I get it."

"Well, here, I was going to leave you a note with this, but we can listen to it together now. Here, come sit next to me."

I do as she asks, picking up the CD case that shows seven very hippy-looking guys on a street and Lynyrd Skynyrd written above them. I've heard of the band but can't name any of their songs off the top of my head.

"Lynyrd Skynyrd?" I ask as I flip over the case to look at the back.

"I know, they're a band from my era and not the *cool* stuff you listen to today, but there's a song I want you to hear. When I found out I was pregnant with a boy, I played this song over and over again, praying you would become a simple man."

I look at her, confused, and she smiles, walking to my small boom box to play it there instead so we can both listen to it. "The song is called *Simple Man*. Just listen to the lyrics. This could be a good first song for you to learn to play."

A slow guitar riff starts the song and catches my attention as I listen to a man sing about his mom wanting to sit down and talk with him.

My mom looks at me with tears in her eyes.

"Mom..." I plead with her to stop looking all sappy.

Her sniffles make the words hard to hear, but she wipes her eyes again and tries to quiet down. "I know. I'll stop, just listen."

I sit in silence as the lyrics talk about his mom preaching for him to follow his heart, being satisfied and content in his life—a simple man.

Even though it's got a slower beat, I still dig the lyrics, especially with my mom sitting next to me, as though she's part of the song. I understand her need to share this with me, and it's cool she's trying to talk to me in a way she knows I'll connect with—music.

She doesn't want me to turn out like my father but doesn't know how to ensure our horrible home life doesn't define my future. He's an abusive drunk who's not even a dad to me. I'll never comprehend why she stays. Without him, we would have such a better life. But I'm no one to make that decision—I'm just a kid. She's the one who will have to do something about it.

She tries her hardest to shield me from him. I overhear her begging him to be quiet so he doesn't wake me, and pleading with him to lower his voice so I don't hear him degrading her. I'm well aware of exactly what kind of man he is, and I know for a fact I don't want to be anything like him.

She grabs my hand as the song ends, crying again.

"Mom..." I'm annoyed and look away from her.

"Baby, just promise me. Promise you'll learn to play this song and remember it for years to come. I want you to grow up to be something you love and understand," she says, quoting the song. "It's important to me. Your father isn't being the role model you need him to be or setting an example to show you how it should be done. But I want to make sure you turn out to be a good man, a simple man, no matter what you've seen or lived through."

"I will. I promise."

"Okay, baby. I love you," she whispers against my head as she leans in to kiss my forehead like she has a million times before.

"Love you too, Mom."

Chapter 3

One kiss is all I need.
One kiss and I'll be freed.
One kiss was all we agreed.
One kiss is all I need.

- Trevin Allen

Trevin - Age 14

"**A**ren't you getting tired?" Lily yawns as she rolls over on her bed, looking at me stretched out on the floor.

She had dance class tonight, and since my mom is her instructor, I got to go just to hang out and watch. I know firsthand how tired she must be, but I really don't want to go home. Not yet.

"Nope. Don't tell me you are? It's not even that late." I glance at the clock to see it's just now ten pm. I sigh and meet her stare, silently begging her with my eyes not to kick me out.

Throughout summer break, I've hidden at her house for as long as she lets me. For hours, we sit, just like this, idly passing the time—talking about nothing, laughing till our sides hurt, playing my guitar, or just listening to music. These nights have been my favorite part of the summer. When school starts next week, I won't be able to hang out like this anymore. I'll be stuck at my house, listening to the never-ending screaming from my father, or being punished for things I didn't do. I swear he creates shit in his mind just to make my life a living hell.

"It's okay. How are things going?" Her eyes are glassy and the edges rimmed with red. The evidence of her being tired keeps showing up in the form of numerous yawns. I'm selfish, but being here with Lily is my only solace. She knows well enough my home life is shit. I don't need her to clarify what she's asking about.

I don't answer her, just shrug and reach up to the stereo, turning the Bush CD to track five to play *Comedown* before I go sit right next to her bed so we're only a few inches away from each other. The mellow flow of the song hits my soul as I lean back against her bed, closing my eyes, enjoying the escape being with Lily and listening to music provides me. It's my safe haven.

Even though the TV is on, the sound is muted so only the blue hue filters through the otherwise dark room. I turn back to find Lily with her eyes closed, asleep on the edge of the bed. I've seen her practically every day since we were eight years old, but today, her soft features, curled up like this, brings a small smile to my face.

Lately, I find myself thinking more and more about her, but not only as a friend. I notice little details about her that haven't caught my attention for years, but now, they're glaringly obvious. Every time I look at her, it's like I'm seeing someone new, not the girl I grew up with and have known for years. And not the silly nicknames I call her, either. For the first time, I'm actually seeing *her*—Lily. I've liked other girls in our class, but not like this.

My heart beats erratically, slowing down, speeding up, and my palms start to sweat when I stare in her direction.

With her eyes closed, I can look at her and take in every detail of every feature. No matter how hard I try to force my eyes away, they stay glued to her, and I can't figure out what's going on inside me.

A small strand of her hair has fallen over her eye, and before I can think, my hand is up, moving it to the side, giving me a better, unobstructed view of her face. The bracelet she gave me when we were nine comes into view on my wrist, which fuels my fire more.

"Are you nervous, Trevin?" she asks as she slides into the car, getting ready to leave for my baseball game where I'm pitching tonight.

"Me, nervous? Come on. I got this." My pride-filled response earns a laugh from her.

"Well, here, I made you a good luck charm. Hold out your right hand." Lily motions for my arm, wiggling her fingers.

I do as she asks, and she wraps a thin piece of string around my wrist. I cock an eyebrow in her direction, giving her a funny look. "A bracelet? Come on, Lily Pad, I'm a guy."

"Yes, and even boys need good luck charms. I made it with boy colors just for you."

Giving it a second chance, the blue and black braid turns out to be a pretty cool design. It's thin and barely noticeable. When I glance back in her direction, she's got this huge grin on her face as she secures it to my wrist.

"Okay, I guess it's cool. Thanks," I say, never taking my eyes off her.

Every time it breaks, I've had her make me a new one as soon as she could. Glancing over to her desk, I see the making of one already started. She's getting smart and making them when she has time so I always have a backup ready and never have to be without it.

Her eyes flutter open and gaze into mine as we stare at each other, both of us completely silent. The CD is on shuffle, and the low guitar sounds of *Glycerine* fill the loud silence, making the tug between us stronger, pulling us closer together.

My hand is still on her hair, and I hesitate to slowly move it more to cup her cheek. A need I've never felt burns through me as I inch closer, desperate to feel more of her. My stare drifts from her eyes to her mouth, and instinctively, her soft tongue sneaks out, licking her lips briefly before slipping back in, tucked away, looking like she's not sure whether to speak, stop me or meet with mine for the first time.

My chest constricts the closer I get to her. I don't have a clue what I'm doing, but happiness fills my heart when I realize she isn't doing anything to stop me. Complete opposite in fact. Her arm tucked in front of her gradually slides to the side, removing the only barrier between her body and mine.

When the lyrics sing, "Couldn't love you more, you got a beautiful taste," I watch as her eyes move to my lips, and I can't help but wonder what hers taste like.

I'm so close I can't stop now. This is it. The thought of kissing her has crossed my mind before, but never has there been this desperate need that's taking me over now. This might be a horrible idea—it could all go horribly wrong, changing everything about us, but I have to taste the lips I've stared at the majority of my life.

I'm centimeters away when my tongue sweeps out, wetting my lips, preparing to meet with hers for the first time.

"Trevin." The warmth of her whisper brushes against my mouth.

"Shh…" I answer as we meet, connecting softly at first, experimenting with the sensation of her sweet, supple lips against mine.

I pull back briefly, checking her response. Greeted with a small smile as she draws in a shaky breath, I lean in again, opening my mouth wider and sweeping my tongue against her lips.

Without any hesitation, she welcomes me in, and goddamn, I accept her invitation without any thought. Everything about her lips—the way her tongue dances with mine, her fantastic taste—feels right. In this moment, even with everything else wrong at home, my life is perfect. Nothing else matters but her sweet body I'm dreaming of pulling into mine.

Wrapping my arm around her back, I lean in, and bring her closer to me. Deepening our kiss, we shift to sneak in a breath and further open up to each other.

My desire to feel her, hold her, be one with her grows and I can't stop myself from leaving the floor to join her on the bed. Instantly, I regret trying to progress what's happening between us when her hand meets my chest. Stopping me in my tracks and breaking away from my lips.

"Trev…" she whispers, looking up at me.

Reality sinks in, and when I realize what I just did, every ounce of happiness washes away. Internally, I kick myself for kissing my best friend.

What the hell am I doing?

"I'm—shit…Lily, I'm sorry."

My feet are underneath me in seconds, carrying me out of her room, then her house, and across her lawn to mine. The night sky covers me in a blanket of darkness as I struggle to stop my intense, ragged breaths. My arms tingle with the rush of blood flowing through them as feelings I don't understand course through me. I don't know what came over me or why I'd kissed her.

But she kissed me back.

The moment I crack the front door, my dad's voice reverberates off the walls—yelling at my mom has become a normal occurrence in my house. There's no telling what's upset him this time, but I've learned not to get involved. I used to, but my mom said every time I did it just made the situation worse, so for her sake, I stay out of it. Instead, I head straight to my room, shutting the door to try to eliminate the noise from my home and the chatter inside my head.

I face the window, and the frame is filled with an image of Lily sitting on her bed, staring at the wall. I know she can't see me with my light off, but I can see her clearly. She picks up the walkie-talkie three times, hesitating with each attempt before bringing it to her mouth like she's going to say something. But she drops it again before the crackle ever comes through on my end.

She was just as affected by that kiss as I was, but we can't do this. I refuse to risk our friendship. Lily is the only positive in my life, and I can't lose her. I've watched my friends ruin friendships with girls they've tried to date—it never ends well. I need to end this now, fix it before we become an us.

Holding the walkie-talkie in my hand, I take a deep breath and press the button down to lie. "I'm sorry."

She jumps at the sound of my voice and instantly jerks her head to look in my room to see if I'm watching her.

I am.

She stares into the darkness, looking to see if I'm there, so I hold the button down again, trying to assure her. "I'm here...I shouldn't have done that. I'm sorry, Lily."

I never call her by just her name. There's always some silly nickname, but right now, nothing fits. Just her. Just Lily.

"No, Trev, I'm sorry," she whispers.

"Please don't let this change anything between us. I need you, Lily. I promise, I'll never let it happen again." My heart pounds, waiting for her to accept my apology and promise she'll never leave my side.

"Uh, oh...okay. Um..."

"Goodnight, Lily." I interrupt her when the static from the connection disappears and I can tell she's let go of the button.

I said what I needed to say. I don't want to make this even weirder than it is, so I turn off the walkie-talkie and close my blinds, removing the temptation to look in her direction again.

Lying in bed, I'm unable to stop the recurring thoughts of the way she felt as I absently rub my fingers along my lower lip. I know I need to put an end to this now, but I can't deny, deep down, I never want another pair of lips to touch mine again.

Only hers.

Chapter 4

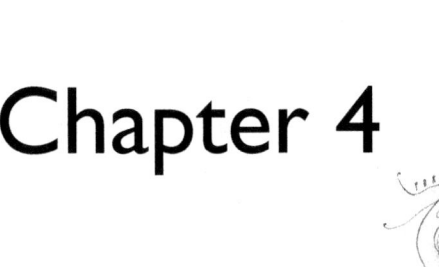

Loss, if I only knew
Loss, can I pull through?
Loss, my chest open wide
The devil reaching in to pull me aside

- Trevin Allen

Trevin - Age 15

Tonight is the night. Varsity baseball state championships. As a sophomore, I made varsity as the starting pitcher. Coach says I have a real shot at a college scholarship, which is the only chance I'll have of getting out of here. There are no other options since my dad's made it very clear he won't pay for me to attend any type of college, even a community college. He's such a prick, and I can't wait until the day I can leave his house and be done with him forever.

Figures, with this being the biggest event of my pitching career, my dad decides to make his first appearance—ever. I'm convinced he's just coming to throw me off my game, destroy my concentration, and justify him believing I'm the loser he always tells me I am.

The team rides together on a bus, along with the dance team, which Lily is a member of. We've never had them or the cheerleaders accompany us, but since this is the state championship, they're coming to show their support.

She's up front with the other girls and I'm near the back with the guys, but that doesn't stop us from talking over rows, teasing each other back and forth.

At the game, I'm in the bullpen warming up when I hear him. "Hey, shithead. Don't fuck up tonight. Everyone's watching." I cringe at the sound of his voice and turn to see my dad stomping up to the fence with a smug look on his face. My mom grabs his arm, trying to pull him away. "Get off me, woman! Who do you think you are?" There's a slight slur to his words, and I wish I could blame his actions all on alcohol, but the truth is he's just an asshole.

My head drops as I roll the ball around in my glove, practicing different holds while focusing on my breathing. When I finally have the nerve to glance up, I see him headed toward his seat. My mom gives me the same *I'm sorry* look I've gotten most of my life.

By the way my father's acting, you'd think he was here to cheer on the other team. He's not the supportive, *you've got this* kind of dad. No, he keeps chanting, "Don't fuck up."

Other dads have said a few words to him, but if they're smart, they'll keep to themselves and not bother him or it will just make it worse. I'm already mortified enough and just trying to keep my focus on the batter instead of the asshole I hope one day to find out isn't my biological father.

Thankfully, after a few innings, he calms down somewhat and changes his harsh chant to an awful glare with sporadic words right when I need to concentrate the most.

After a while, my coach comes to the mound in an effort to calm my nerves. "I'm sorry, Trev. I had no idea he was this bad."

I shake my head, turning away from him, embarrassed. This is the first time my teammates encountered him. The sideways glares sting, but I try to ignore them.

"Hey." My attention snaps back to the coach in front of me who's trying to help me make my dreams come true. I kick the dirt on the mound while he talks. "Don't listen to him. You've got this. I have faith in you, and I know you can make this happen. Just focus and do your best," he encourages me while slapping my back.

I thank him and get back to the game, striking out the next two batters.

It's not until the ninth inning that my team gets their first hit. I cringe every time my dad makes a snide remark when each kid struck out or didn't make it on base. But when it came to me, he was particularly vulgar. By far, the worst part is all the other family members and classmates witnessing firsthand what my life is really like. However, the one that cuts the deepest is Lily.

She's not clueless. I know she has an idea of how bad things are, but we've never actually spoken about how abusive he truly is. Thankfully, he's never hit my face again, but he's taken more than a few whacks with his belt against my bare-skinned back. It didn't take him long to figure out people ask questions if the bruises actually show, so he's mastered the fine art of hidden reminders. Marks no one else sees, yet we're unable to forget.

Now it's the bottom of the ninth. We are up one to zero with two outs. This is it. I take a deep breath, calming my nerves while I look at my catcher who's calling my pitches.

I dig my foot into the mound, take a deep breath, wind up, and throw. "Strike one!" the ump yells out.

While the crowd roars, my dad sits, giving me a death stare. Ignoring him, I pick my next pitch, wind up, and throw. "Strike two!" The words reverberate in my head. I need one more.

With the ball in hand, I turn my back to the stands and the batter. I can't focus with him staring at me like that. Deep breath in then slowly let it out.

I turn around to choose my pitch, wind up, and throw. "Strike three!"

"Yeeeeeeessssss!" I scream out as the emotion overloads my brain and my body, falling to my knees. The entire team clears the bench and the field, all joining me on the mound, celebrating our success. I'm hoisted onto the shoulders of a few senior players as everyone jumps around.

I make the mistake of looking toward the stands, only to see my mom trying to stop my father from walking away, ignoring our win, and actually appearing pissed off. I should have expected this, but for some reason, it hurts more than if he had punched me straight in the face. Maybe it's the embarrassment of it being in front of my peers, or that regardless of what I do, he's never proud—whatever it is, this bruise will never heal.

After her futile attempt to stop him, our eyes meet before she turns her head, ashamed to even look at me.

The entire team lines up for the trophy presentation, and the stands erupt again when we're announced as State Champions.

With the exception of my asshole dad, today is quite possibly the best day of my life. Unable to imagine it getting much better, we walk off the field and there stands Lily. She's always the one cheering me on...my true champion.

"You guys did it!" she hollers, unable to stand still. With one big jump, she latches onto my neck, hugging me tighter than she ever has.

Lost in the moment, I pick her up, swinging her around, finally able to celebrate with someone who's important to me.

Somehow, my dad still manages to ruin the moment when I glance over just in time to see him shove my mom against the gate. Leaving her alone, he storms out the back of the stadium.

I carefully put Lily down on the ground before walking toward them.

"Trevin." Lily grabs my arm to stop me.

"Lily, I can't let her go home with him like this. Not alone anyway." The pain radiating from her eyes is a stab to the heart, but I need to go protect my mom right now.

"Hey, Coach," I yell, standing only a few feet away. "I'm heading home with my mom, okay?"

He turns, fully looking at me now. "You sure about that, Trev?"

"Yeah, I'm sure. She doesn't need to be alone."

He nods before clapping me on the shoulder and shaking my hand. "Good job tonight. You made the team proud."

"Thank you." I start to run toward my parents before turning back to Lily. "I'll call you later, okay?"

She offers me a weak smile and nod, and then I'm back running to the gate to reach my parents before they leave.

Everyone is still celebrating, leaving us alone in the parking lot, and with the way he's been acting tonight, I just want to get home quickly without him causing more of a scene.

My mom stands by the car, leaning against the driver's side door and putting up a fight with my dad when I walk up. "Richard, I don't think you should drive. You're drunk and it's not safe," she pleads with obvious fear in her eyes.

I'm proud she's actually standing up to him. This is the first time I've ever seen her do anything like this.

"Shut up, bitch." The words slur and he raises his hand as though he's going to hit her, but thankfully, doesn't. "Get your ass in the car."

"No, Dad!" I yell. "Let her drive." I don't know where my assertiveness comes from, but when I continue, I issue a threat I wasn't sure I was ready to follow through on. "Or I'll go have Coach call the cops, and then they can pull you over and haul you off to jail."

His nostrils flare when a deep growl releases from his chest, and then he stomps to the passenger side. My mom's lips push together in a shy thank you when she looks my direction and reaches for me, giving me a brief hug. "I'm proud of you, Trevin. You did great tonight." She kisses my cheek before I hop in the backseat behind her, glad I was able to defuse the situation for once.

There's no music streaming through the speakers. The only sounds filling the air around us are of my father grunting and the tires spinning on the asphalt. With no streetlights and only a few cars passing by, the roads are dark, leaving only the headlights of our old beat up Buick to light the way.

Tension is thick in the air. In a feeble attempt to calm the emotion, my mom speaks up. "Honey, aren't you proud of Trevin tonight?"

He glares in her direction, not saying a word but squints his eyes when he looks back at me, giving me a look of death. The scowl on his face could have frightened the meanest of men.

"Don't you think so, dear? I still can't believe they won the state championships!" My mom's tone overflows with pride.

"That doesn't mean shit. All this baseball shit is pointless. It's not going to get you anywhere," he spits out, glaring over his shoulder at me.

My blood starts to boil. I've had enough, and everything is about to finally spill over.

"You know he'll always be the same useless piece of shit he is right now." He sneers in disgust, and I finally pop.

"Really, *Dad*, like you? Is that what you mean? Because you know what, I could be a ball player. Coach says I have a good chance at a college scholarship."

"Yeah right, college my ass. You ain't going nowhere. You'll end up being a shithead loser, probably living in my house forever, still trying to get in that little girl's pants next door."

I sit up, as close as I can to the front seat to get in his face. "What did you say?"

"Okay, okay, calm down. Let's just stop all this nonsense," my mom says, only making the situation worse rather than trying to eliminate it.

"What did you say, bitch?" My dad grabs a fistful of her hair and brings it down to the middle of the bench seats. The sudden attack catches my mom off guard and her hands yank the steering wheel down when her head hits the seat, causing the car to swerve. A force I've never felt swings me through the air, throwing me against the door as we slide to the left, then right, and before I can grab ahold of anything, the car starts a barrel roll.

Pain radiates through my head as it smacks the roof of the car, then slams into the window, shattering it. I close my eyes in an effort to block the glass from doing any more damage. My upper body collides with the headrest of the driver's seat, and my seatbelt starts to play tug-of-war with my body as the force throws me around the car.

Instantly, a white-hot, searing pain radiates from my right shoulder and rips through my body. Seconds later, everything goes black.

An eerie silence surrounds me when I pry my eyes open. Nothing but stars cover the night sky. Thoughts of where I am, or if I'm even alive, cross my mind briefly. I mentally try to focus on every part of my body before trying to move. When I wiggle my fingers, all I can feel is dirt and something wet seeping in through my uniform. Realization strikes me hard when the memory of my body breaking open the panel that held my seatbelt and being thrown from the car flashes through my mind. I try to shift, but the stabbing pain shooting down my right arm stops me instantly.

After a few failed attempts, I'm finally able to sit up, shaking my head before I look around for the car and my parents. Behind me, the car rests upside down on its hood and my dad climbs out, stumbling to the ground.

But there's no sign of movement from my mom. Using every ounce of strength I can muster, I stumble to my feet, bracing my right arm. Even the smallest change in position sends a screeching pain from my shoulder to my fingertips, but I have to get to my mom.

He sees me trying to make my way back to her and walks straight toward me, holding out his finger as though he's going to scold me. "Listen, Trevin, and listen good. Nothing happened in that car just then. A deer ran out in front of your mom and she swerved to miss it."

"But—"

"Don't you fucking *but* me, you little prick. This is what you say or I'll make sure you never leave the house again. You hear me, fucker? I'll lock you in your room and make your life a living hell. You got that?"

He's fucking serious. He wants to blame this all on mom and a damn deer!

Pushing my protest aside, I focus on more important things—my mom. Only a few feet away and I still haven't heard or seen anything from her. He didn't even bother to check on her before he set out his plan to threaten me, making sure he didn't get arrested for any wrongdoing.

I shove past him and approach her side of the car. Screams fill my lungs but nothing comes out, and my brain doesn't know how to function by putting sound to my vocal chords.

All I see is blood. And the smell is pungent—metallic.

A crimson color covers her face, pooling down her arm, and even worse, the thick substance pours off the glass sticking out of her neck.

Instinctively, I reach up to try to stop the bleeding before I remember the agony in my shoulder. The tearing sound rings in my ears and crippling agony rips through my arm, finally allowing screams to exit my mouth in the most excruciating pain I've ever felt.

I fall to my back as red lights and sirens fill the darkness. Shock takes over my world, and I struggle just to keep my eyes open.

"Hello, I'm Matt, I'm a paramedic. Do you know where you are?" A man's voice hits my ears as he checks my vitals, bringing me back to the now. "Stay with me here."

"Yes, we were in an accident," I try to respond.

"Do you know your name?"

"Yes, it's Trevin, Trevin Allen."

"Trevin, you've been in an accident. I'm here to help you."

"I know, my mom…she's still in the car." I try to sit up, but he places his hand on my chest in an attempt to keep me down.

"We know. My partner has her. Let's focus on you right now. Can you move your legs?"

"Yes, I can, but my right arm hurts like hell." With clenched teeth, I moan as pain rips through me again when I try to lift it.

"It's okay, don't move it. Let me stabilize you and we'll get you to the ambulance. Is the other man your father?"

I don't answer, just grit my teeth and nod.

"We have someone else tending to him, but he seems to be doing okay. He's here though, so don't worry. I want you to focus on your breathing—in through the nose, out through the mouth. Do you hurt anywhere else?"

"No, just my arm."

"We have another paramedic behind you, and both of us are going to lift you to the gurney once I stabilize your arm, okay?"

I nod, dropping my head to the ground, focusing on my breathing to manage the pain and calm my racing thoughts.

Not too long afterward, they lift me up and roll me over to the ambulance where I'm greeted by a police officer. "Son, can I ask you a few questions before you go?"

My jaw flexes as I grind my teeth in an effort to keep quiet, laying my head down, trying to ignore the pain and the questions.

"Your father here says a deer jumped out in front of the car, causing your mom to swerve off the road and hit the ditch."

I still don't say a word, just nod in response.

He pats my leg. "Don't worry, son. This kind of thing happens all the time. Those deer jump out of nowhere. Even the most experienced of drivers get into accidents. Sometimes, there's just nothing anyone can do."

But there was something I could've done. I was here to protect my mom, yet I seemed to make the situation worse, and now...

"But my mom. Where's my mom?" I ask in a complete panic.

The cop looks at Matt, the paramedic, who looks down, not answering my question. But his face says it all.

She's gone.

Her life is over, and it's my fault.

Chapter 5

Hate, disgust, but mostly fear
That's what I feel whenever you're near

- Trevin Allen

Trevin - Age 15

My life has been shit since that fateful day. My mom died in that car and my dad lied to the police, and got away with it.

It all came back to me. I was the only one who could put him away forever for killing my mom, and believe me, the thought crossed my mind a few times. I wanted his life to end like hers did—painfully.

Keeping his secret was killing me, eating me alive, but the alternatives didn't prove to be any better. I wasn't convinced telling anyone the truth would even make a difference since he wasn't actually driving. I honestly don't know what the laws are regarding *causing* an accident that killed someone. And I worried about where I'd go if they did arrest him. I have an uncle on my dad's side who lives in Colorado, but I haven't seen him since I was five—they might send me there, or hell, even worse would be foster care. One thing is for sure: they'd take me away from Lily, and right now, she's the only reason I was still breathing. Unwilling to risk losing her, I keep his secret. I'll sacrifice anything to keep her in my life.

My dad didn't give my mom a proper funeral. Just acted like nothing happened and went on with his pathetic, drunken life. I was in the hospital for two weeks and he barely came by to say hi. I underwent two surgeries to repair my shoulder, and now I'm sitting in my doctor's office with Lily by my side, because my dad couldn't give two shits about my life.

As the months tick by, the countless hours of physical therapy don't seem to help, and my chances of ever playing baseball again slip further and further away.

The doctor walks in with the results from my latest MRI. I wrap my fingers around Lily's, waiting for my fate. "Well, Trevin, I'm afraid I have bad news."

My chest tightens and I know this is it. I'm done.

"I'm sorry, son, but your shoulder doesn't seem to be repairing the way we hoped, and I just don't see you ever pitching again."

Lily grips my hand tighter as I drop my head back against the chair, completely deflated. My mother's dead, I can no longer play ball and my home life gets more destructive by the day, leaving me afraid to even sleep sometimes.

I have nothing to say in response, so I stand up and leave his office without looking back. I hear Lily apologize to the doctor and run after me, but I don't stop. I need to be alone.

"Trev, please stop, wait for me," she pleads from behind.

"Lily, just go home. I need to be alone right now." I turn in the opposite direction of the bus stop we would take to get home and start walking. To where, I have no clue.

Thankfully, she respects my feelings and lets me be. I walk around for the rest of the day until darkness fills the sky and my feet eventually lead me back home. I stop out front, staring at my front door, not wanting to walk through but having no place else to go.

My dad's car is gone—typical. After my mom passed away, he found out she had a life insurance policy she'd taken out shortly before the accident, and he's been living it up ever since. He hasn't gone to work all week, and when I do see him, he's either drunk or high. The fact he's partying with money he collected from my mother's death makes me sick. He practically lives at the bar, with zero thought about the lowlifes and sluts he brings home, having sex with random women and partying with strangers until the early morning. I wake up to multiple people passed out around the house with no clue who the hell they are, and I can't remember the last night I slept well.

I glance over to Lily's place, only to see her walking toward me. Without saying a word, she encloses her hand around mine, resting her shoulder against me, and wraps her other hand around my upper arm. As the years have passed, I've gotten a lot taller, yet she seems to stay the same size. I stand a good foot over her and her shoulder rests perfectly on the curve of my bicep.

Every time she touches me like this, either to comfort me or looking for security of her own, shocks of electricity flood my veins. I try like hell to ignore them. I don't want a girlfriend right now—all I need is my best friend.

"Trev," she finally whispers.

"Shh, don't say anything. I know," I say, cutting her off.

She doesn't respond, just stands silently with me, comforting me in this small way.

After a while, she breaks the silence. "Are we still on for tomorrow?"

I chuckle, shaking my head before looking down at her as she cranes her neck up to stare into my eyes. "Yeah, I guess."

Tomorrow is my sixteenth birthday. I should be ecstatic—this is an important day for any teenager. A car. A driver's license. Anyone else my age would be jumping up and down, but I couldn't care less. My mom's gone, my dad's a drunk, and I'd rather ignore the day all together. But Lily has other plans. No matter how much I fight it, I know she'll make the day better.

She stretches up on her tiptoes to kiss my cheek. "Goodnight, Trev."

"Night, Lily Pad." I kiss the top of her head before walking toward my front door.

The emptiness of our lifeless house hits me hard, but honestly, it's better than having to face my drunken father. I run straight up to my room, shoving my door closed and turning on my music to blast Deftones.

Lily finally gave up on music lessons about a year ago and gave me her guitar. I keep it hidden under my bed and only play when I'm alone in the house. I never know what my dad might do in a drunken rage. He's destroyed everything else in this house, but if he touched my guitar, I might have to finally hurt him back.

He's taken my baseball dreams, and with it, any chance of college; I won't let him ruin my music dreams as well.

I've gotten pretty good and can keep rhythm with the song to play along. Music heals my soul and gets me through each day. Other than Lily, it's the only thing that's kept me sane since the death of my mom.

I play late into the night and click it off only when I'm ready to go to bed. My dad's still not home, and the fact that he's having a late night out is the best part of my night.

I've been asleep for some time when my dad bursts through my door and into my room, flipping the light on and yelling at me to get up from a dead sleep.

"Come on, Trev, get up! I have a surprise for your birthday!"

His excitement scares the shit out of me. More so than his anger.

"What are you doing? I was sleeping," I respond, confused.

"Not anymore. It's your sixteenth birthday, and it's time you became a man. Now get up and come downstairs."

Oh no. I have no idea what he's up to, but the idea he's going to make me a man scares the piss out of me. I don't have a clue what that means. Maybe he's kicking me out and that's why he's so damn chipper.

I throw on some lounge pants over my boxer briefs and walk downstairs without a shirt or socks on. Arriving in the living room, I'm greeted by my father standing between two women dressed in the raunchiest, most revealing clothes I've ever seen.

"They're hookers!" he exclaims in the happiest voice I've ever heard from him. "I got one for each of us."

Hookers? Is he serious right now? He bought me a hooker for my birthday.

"Ohhh, you weren't kidding, Dick. I call dibs on him," I hear one of them say as she walks out of his arms and wraps hers around my lower torso.

I've always found it ironic that my dad goes by Dick. His real name is Richard, but if a nickname ever fit someone to a T, this would be it.

"Um, I… Um…" I stutter, having no clue what to say or where to put my arms as she rubs all over my bare chest.

"See, girls? I told you he was still a virgin. He spends all his time with the princess next door—she sure as hell ain't putting out. Fucking pansy ass. I knew I'd have to pay to make you a man," my dad spits out.

There's the dad I know.

"I thought we were going to party first?" the girl still standing in his arms whines.

"Yeah, I think this one needs a drink," the girl wrapped around me says to my father as she slides her hand over my dick.

I flinch, shocked by her forward movements. No one but me has ever touched me there, and as I stand here, I'm still not one hundred percent sure if this is a dream or reality.

My dad laughs at my response to her hand between my legs. "Come on, you little shit. Be a fucking man. Let her touch you. Enjoy it for fuck's sake. She's costing me a fortune." He walks into the kitchen and comes back with a bottle of Jack Daniels and pours us all shots. "To my stupid ass son, who has to have his dad pay someone to get his dick wet."

The girls both holler in response as they take the shot back, but my dad and I are caught in a staring contest, and I'm not backing down. "Happy birthday, Trev," he says in the most condescending way possible before downing the shot himself.

Taking a deep breath, inhaling the scent of the whiskey as the air fills my lungs, I look at the shot and take it back. It burns all the way down my throat. I cough when the fiery trail lines my esophagus, through my chest, and fills my stomach in a blazing inferno.

They all get a hearty laugh at the display of how young and inexperienced I truly am. The girl wraps her arms around my torso again. "Oh, this is going to be fun. I'm Candy by the way."

"Candy." I laugh. "Really?"

"Yeah, sugar. Just wait till you see how sweet I am."

Everything about this feels wrong, but I'm a sixteen-year-old boy and my thoughts are clouded by my ever-growing urge to bring any and all attention to my dick. Here it is, right in front of me. She's offering it up with no work on my part. I'd be stupid to turn this down.

My dad watches my mental epiphany and starts laughing when a smile creeps over my face.

This is what he considers father-son bonding? I need another shot.

After the third shot of Jack, things are feeling good and my nerves start to fade. For the first time, I'm actually talking and laughing with my dad, but I try not to focus on why.

More importantly, for the first time since my mom died, I don't have that ache in my chest that feels like someone's sitting on my throat, blocking all the air to my lungs and twisting my insides to oblivion.

I hate to admit it, but I'm actually happy.

Things take a turn when the girls stand up, creating a center stage by the coffee table, and start to strip each other. Watching hookers put on a show in my living room with my dad sitting next to me is awkward as hell, but my dick is still hard as a rock. I can't help it, though. I've seen porn and looked at *Playboy*, but having it live, right in front of me, is a totally different experience.

My dad's laughter to my right catches my attention. He leans over, whispering, "Close your mouth, son." The smell of alcohol on his breath is awful and almost breaks my enjoyment of the scene in front of me.

Heat fills my face and my cheeks blush as I snap my mouth shut, embarrassed to be sitting next to my dad while experiencing this for the first time.

Individually, the girls take each of us by the hand and walk us upstairs to our own bedrooms. "Have a good night, Trev." My dad's maniacal laugh echoing down the hall pulls me out of my lust-induced haze and totally kills the buzz I have going on from the alcohol.

When Candy clicks the door shut, my heart thuds against my chest. I look up to see her falling against the wood with a sexy smile on her face. As she pulls down the straps of her bra, I should be thrilled, but something's not right—it's all off kilter. This is my chance. What every guy dreams about.

But Lily is at the center of my thoughts.

I've never thought about having sex with her—I mean, not really. She's my best friend. She's cute, but when I picture my first time, I've never pictured her—yet here I am, about to lose my virginity and all I can think about is that she's not Lily.

I shouldn't be doing this.

"Oh, honey, you're nervous." Candy smiles as she tiptoes up to me, standing between my thighs with me on the bed. Her hands cup my cheeks. "Don't worry, sugar. I'll be gentle."

She leans down to kiss me, but I instantly turn my face to the right so she kisses my jaw. The thought of kissing this random stranger makes me sick to my stomach, I truly don't want anyone else's lips to ever touch mine. Only Lily's.

"Wow, not even a small kiss for me, sugar?" she whines.

I shake my head. "Look, sorry. This is a bad idea." I go to stand up, but she stops me.

"Oh dear, you have a girlfriend don't you?" A look of disappointment crosses her features.

"No, actually I don't," I respond, pushing her completely away from me so I can stand up and start to walk toward my door.

"But there's a girl you like?"

Even though I don't answer, I stop in my tracks, because up until a few minutes ago, I would have said no. Now I'm not so sure.

She wraps her arms around my waist from behind, running her hands down my pants and grabbing my dick, rubbing up and down. No matter how hard I fight it, I'm instantly hard just from her touch.

"See, sugar? Don't worry. I understand. Let me blow you at least. I mean, I've already been paid; you might as well take advantage."

The thought almost drops me to my knees. I can't say no. I've dreamt about having a girl's mouth wrapped around my dick so many times. A shiver travels up my spine and she laughs at my reaction. She turns me around, pulls me toward my bed, pushing me to lay down. Before I know it, she's stripping me of my pants and licking my dick from base to tip. Shaking, I take a deep breath and focus on my air intake, trying not to look as I feel the warmth of her mouth wrap around me and take me all the way in.

Holy. Shit. Fuck. Goddamn!

I drop my head to my pillow, trying not to cum instantly. Who knows when the next time will be that I'll have this opportunity—I want this to last, so when I have regrets later, at least I can say it was kind of worth it.

The instant her hands join her mouth and run up my length just behind her lips, I'm done for. She giggles as I cum instantly but sucks me back down to finish me off.

"Well, sugar, that was the easiest money I've ever made. How was that?"

I look away, ashamed.

"Hey, don't sweat it, sweetheart, I've had grown men cum just as fast. Maybe now when you're with the girl you actually want to be with, you'll last a bit longer. Are you sure you don't want more?"

She stands up, jiggling her tits back and forth, but I just shake my head, turning over in my bed to face the wall.

"Okay, your loss. Thanks for the easy money."

And just like that, the first girl I've ever been with walks out of my room, never to be seen again. As I lay in bed, confusion stirs through my brain. The euphoria from the shots I took and the load I just blew bring a sense of calmness to my life that I don't think I've ever felt before.

Even though I know all of this is wrong, it also feels right knowing it didn't mean anything and that woman just walked out of my life right after. Since it wasn't Lily, I realize I'm totally fine with that fact, so I flip onto my stomach to enjoy the remaining alcohol still running through my body as I drift off to sleep.

Chapter 6

A simple man I am not
But Lord please, I beg for one more shot

- Trevin Allen

Trevin - 16th Birthday

The harsh pounding reverberating in my skull is never ending. When I peel my eyes open, the piercing light through my window shoots lightening bolts of pain directly to my brain.

I want nothing more than to fall back asleep, but the walkie-talkie is alive this morning with Lily on the other end. She leaves me no choice but to get up and act like nothing's different, because there's no way I can tell my best friend my dad bought me a hooker. And I sure as hell can't tell her I couldn't do anything with the chick because she invaded my thoughts.

The mere idea makes my head hurt worse.

"Birthday boy…wake up…" I hear her sing through the crackling speaker.

"I'm up, I'm up," I respond as clearly as I can while holding my head in pain.

"Great! Get dressed. I'm taking you out!" She's way too happy this early in the morning. Glancing at the clock, I realize it's noon and definitely time to get my ass out of bed. I pray my dad isn't lurking somewhere in the vicinity.

If only my luck were that strong. As soon as I walk out of my room, my father's belittling voice greets me like a fist to the face. "I can't believe you didn't fuck her, you pansy ass! Are you gay or what?"

"No, I'm not gay." I stand up for myself.

"You just chicken shit then? I pay for a woman to fuck you and you don't," he screams in my face. "It's that little girl next door, isn't it? Is she giving it up to you?"

"Don't talk about her like that!" I scream back.

"Ha! You're a pansy-ass when it comes to that chick and you don't even get anything in return. I'm embarrassed to call you my son." He spits the words in my direction before walking away, retreating to his room.

More frustrated than I have been in a while, I storm outside, ready to take off anyone's head that messes with me. Unfortunately, Lily is the first person I see.

"Hey, birthday boy, you ready?" The sun catches her hair in the most perfect way, resembling the angel she's become.

"I'm not in the mood." I shouldn't be taking this shit out on her, but the bite in my tone makes her cringe just a bit.

"Okay…want to talk about it?" she says as sweetly as she can while rubbing my back.

Just the feel of her touching me makes my skin crawl. I feel guilty for what happened last night. I'm not committed to her, so I don't have a clue why it bothers me, but it's eating at me, and now I'm not sure what to do.

When I sit down on the curb without responding, she joins me and takes my hand. Her thumb caresses mine while she silently tries to soothe me. "It's going to be okay. Whatever it is, I promise, I'll be here."

And I believe her. In this moment, I know everything will be okay, because just like every day since we were eight, she'll be here with me.

I finally give in as a slight smile forms on my face. "What do you have planned today?" I ask while nudging her body with mine.

"Okay, don't be mad." Her radiant smile prevents me from ever being angry with her. "I don't exactly have anything planned, but that's my plan. I thought we could have a day like we did last summer. Doing nothing but lying around in my room listening to music and just hanging out."

Instantly, my arm goes around her shoulders, bringing her into me. "That's perfect. There's nothing I would rather do today."

She leans into the hug, wrapping her arms around my waist. The warmth of her body next to mine lessens the tension I walked out the door carrying. "Okay, good. Come on, let's head up to my room."

Memories of last night flood my brain—my reasons for not letting the hooker kiss me. I promised myself last summer no other lips would ever touch mine, and I still mean it. At some point, I hope I'm able to have her again, but I know now is not the time. I push my thoughts away, strolling into my best friend's house for a perfect day of nothing but her.

After the last few months, this is exactly what I needed. I sat on her floor as she laid on her bed and we listened to music and talked the day away.

Anytime I'm with her, none of my other problems exist. The only thing that matters is the smile on her face and the fact she makes me feel whole again. She grounds me, tethers me to reality to keep me from floating away.

The day's fading into evening, but there's one more thing I want to do, and I finally get the courage to ask Lily to go with me. "Thanks for today. I needed this, but I'm hoping you'll come with me somewhere?"

She sits up without hesitation. "Sure, where are we going?"

I assist her all the way up and we walk out of her room hand in hand. "You'll see. I just need my guitar first."

"Mom?" Lily yells, trying to locate her mother.

"Yeah, honey." We enter the kitchen to see her standing at the kitchen counter.

"Is it okay if I take the car so Trev and I can…" She looks at me, questioning our destination since she has no clue where we're going. "…go get ice cream?" she finishes to my surprise.

Her mom looks at me, then back at her, noticing both of us have odd expressions on our faces. She laughs and her eyes twinkle. "So that's what you kids are calling it these days? Well, I guess I should say it's about time for you two."

I choke on my own spit, making me cough when I catch on to what she's implying. Her parents have always leaned toward the hippy side and are very open about a lot of things, but I'm shocked she just insinuated we were talking in code for having sex.

"Mom…" Lily's cheeks burn bright red. She covers her face, embarrassed. "I can't believe you!"

Seeing her blush like this reminds me of the good girl she is. This is why I couldn't do anything with that hooker last night. I want—no, I *need*— someone innocent like her.

Even though I love watching her squirm, I finally speak up to ease her bashfulness. "I didn't tell Lily where I wanted to go yet, but maybe afterward we'll see about some ice cream." I wink, making Lily hit me in my stomach in response. I just couldn't resist.

She grabs my hand, pulling me toward the front door and shaking her head as she says goodbye to her mom.

Her mom fights the smile threatening to take over her face, but before we make it out the door, she stops us. "Trevin." She brings me in for a hug. "Happy birthday."

I give her a soft hug, thanking her in return. I'm not just grateful for Lily, but for her family as well now that my own mom is gone.

I'm able to sneak in and out of my house without my dad noticing, and I hop into Lily's car already running in the driveway.

Gravity

She turned sixteen a month ago, and her parents are pretty cool about her taking their car. I can't imagine what it would be like to have parents like hers. I used to have my mom to balance the harshness that is my dad, but now I have to fend for myself. I'm just not sure how long I can last with him.

"Okay, where to?" Lily says with the sweetest smile on her face.

"Can you take me to see my mom?" My voice is barely above a whisper.

Without saying a word, she reaches out to intertwine her fingers with mine. We hold onto each other until she has to release me to park at the cemetery.

"Do you want me to come with you?" The hesitation is visible on her face.

I reach for her hand again, needing her for courage just to open the door. "Please?" is all I can get out before I take a deep breath and reach for the handle.

With my guitar in one hand and Lily's held tightly in the other, we walk together in silence to my mom's gravesite.

It's a simple flat headstone. The cheapest my dad could find. One day I'm going to replace it with a proper headstone that an amazing woman like her deserves.

My knees give out and my eyes well up with tears as soon as the grave marker comes into sight. I plop down on the ground, wondering why she had to die.

My fingers trace the letters of her name and "Loving Mother." That she was. She put up with a lot she didn't deserve—all to make sure I had a roof over my head and food on my plate.

I made her a promise years ago, and tonight I'm going to fulfill it. Reaching behind me, I grab my guitar and sit cross-legged in front of her grave as I pick out the beginning chords to *Simple Man* by Lynyrd Skynyrd.

No one has ever heard me sing, and even though Lily's sitting behind me listening, I begin to feel the lyrics from the bottom of my heart, holding nothing back and pouring my soul into the song. "Mama told me, when I was young."

My eyes stay closed as I sing for my mom, imagining her here in front of me, smiling because I learned her favorite song—just for her. When I get to the lyrics that talk about finding a woman, without thinking, I open my eyes. Turning slightly to Lily sitting beside me now and looking directly at her, I sing, "And you'll find love."

I see the tears well up in her eyes and spill over, so I close mine again, focusing on the song for my mom.

I make it through the entire song before completely breaking down, dropping my chin to my chest and crying the tears I've held in since the day she died.

Lily's arms wrap around me. She doesn't say a word, just holds me, putting me back together after I completely fall apart.

Right here and now, I promise myself I will be a Simple Man. For my mom, I will try my hardest to be the best man anyone would want to love, especially the girl holding me right now.

Chapter 7

Dirty girl, different every night.
Dirty girl, don't think you're right.
With your warm body and fake tits
All I want are your long licks.

- Trevin Allen

Trevin - Age 17

Never in my wildest imagination would I have believed my dad getting me a hooker for my sixteenth birthday would have brought us closer together. That night, over a year ago, convinced him I was finally a "man" and has begun including me in all his activities, including any alcohol and drugs he can get his hands on.

The first time he sent me on a drug run was the scariest day of my life. He thought since I was still a kid, the guys wouldn't fuck with me…but, yeah, let's just say he was totally wrong.

"Trevin, don't be a shithead. No one will mess with you. You're a kid for fuck's sake. Me, on the other hand…" He shakes his head, looking around like someone's standing right outside the door getting ready to bust him. "Just take the money." He forces the cash in front of my face. "And walk back there; they're waiting for you."

I stare at my dad, who's sitting in the front seat next to his current dirty slut. There's a new one every couple weeks, so I don't bother to keep track of them anymore. Disgust seeps from every pore as I stare at the two of them. I can't believe I'm about to do this. I can't believe I'm stuck in this mess, but most of all, I can't believe I'm here because of my dad.

Letting out a loud huff, I grab the money and open the door to his new Cadillac Escalade, bought with the money from my mom's death. It's past midnight, and he has me walking down a dark alley toward the back door of a chop shop on the shady side of town. Any normal father would beat their child if he found out they were back here. But not my dad. He would beat me if I didn't go back here.

By the light of the moon, I see a door to the right and knock in the manner I was instructed to do so. The door swings open and I'm met by a grizzly man. His dark beard and leather jacket make him far more intimidating in the dark. "What the fuck you want, kid?"

I swallow hard, puff out my chest and pretend to be someone I'm not. "I want the goods. I got money." I pull it out from my back pocket. "You gonna give me some or not?"

"How about not, kid—get lost."

He starts to shut the door, leaving me standing in the alley, but visions of facing my father empty handed flash before my eyes, and I put my hand out, willing to do anything to not have to withstand his wrath tonight.

"Look. I ain't a kid and you have something in there I want, something I already ordered. Now, are you going to stop me or am I going to call your boss?"

The guy lets out a deep laugh, and I watch as his large belly rumbles through the shadows. "You're not PD?"

"Fuck no. Just me," I state with a tip of my head, trying to be hard.

"Okay..." He gets close enough I can smell the stench of beer and cigarettes on his breath. "Then prove it."

"What? You want to frisk me? I'm not wearing a wire."

"Na, kid. Something better. I wanna watch you do a line. You ain't chicken, are you?"

My palms instantly start to sweat, but I clench them together, grind my teeth and nod, pushing my way past him, ready for whatever he's got.

Motorcycle and a few car parts lying around fill my vision before a group of guys head my way with one of them slapping a tire iron against his open palm.

The bearded man slams the door shut, making me jump slightly before he lets out a small laugh. "This kid here wants to buy from us. I say he's PD. He says he's not, so why don't you cut a line for him to prove it."

One guy nods without saying a word and walks to the cupboard, grabbing something before heading back to a table to prepare my first high.

Without hesitation, I pull the chair out, turning it to sit backward, straddling it as I ready myself for what's going down.

Before long, he slides a mirror my direction with a wicked grin on his face. I grab the rolled up bill instantly and lean down to snort my first line.

The sting burns my eyes and I can't help but cough from the powder hitting the back of my throat, but I did it. My throat goes numb and my body temperature rises. The job is done, so without a word, I reach for the money in my back pocket, hand it to the guy in exchange for my dad's eight-ball and stand up. I'm ready to get the hell out of here but try to act badass and maintain my composure. The sound of grown men laughing at my reaction as I walk out the door brings tears to my eyes that I quickly blink away. I don't know whether to be disgusted with what my life has become or pity myself.

The term scared shitless might have run through my head a few times that night. I'd never done anything illegal, much less any type of drug, and had just taken my first drink a few weeks before, which knocked me on my ass. At the time, I had no idea what the coke would do to me. Now though, it's something I've done more times than I should ever admit.

We'd become the trash of our town. Whenever I'd leave the house after my mom died, I would hear people whispering behind my back, expressing their sorrow over what had become of me in my mother's absence. I was a replica of my father, and people were reluctant to make eye contact with me. They believed I didn't give a shit she was gone—just like he didn't. That, coupled with my dreams of playing baseball going up in flames, and I really don't give a shit about anything. I quit fighting him in favor of joining him—the path of least resistance. If anything, it's made my home life more tolerable.

My friends have all vanished and the only thing left in my life is my guitar, and of course, Lily, though sometimes even I wonder why she stays around. We don't hang out like we used to, but I still see her at least once a week.

My grades are slipping more than they should, but without a parent at home who gives a shit, it makes it hard to stay motivated. I started hanging out with a group who would rather get high than be at school. And when they're here, the assholes drink from their 7-11 cups full of alcohol right on school grounds during our passing periods.

None of us give a fuck if we get caught. Shit, my dad would high-five me rather than yell at me if we did. So completely twisted, but it's a hell of a lot easier now than it was when he yelled at me all the time.

I'll never forget the first time he got me high on weed. It was like all the pain within me melted away and I was floating above the home that I called hell.

The only reason I haven't dropped out of school completely is because of Lily. I can't let her believe I'm a complete fuck up. Besides, the best part of school is anytime Lily walks by me between classes. It's also one of the few times I can count on seeing her, and it makes the days stuck in these halls bearable. Between periods, she stops, not turning but rather walking sideways, straight into my arms. We stay like that, in a soft embrace, until the bell rings and we go our separate ways.

The two of us are quite the sight to be seen. Her friends give her constant shit for stopping to have contact with me, but that doesn't stop her. Imagine me with my pierced lip and spiked black hair in contrast to her All-American high school look. I'm always dressed in tight black pants as opposed to her preppy jeans and flip-flops. Or my studded belt and black leather jacket with safety pins running up the arms and a white flag pinned to my back for my favorite band, the Misfits, against her Abercrombie and Fitch floral tank top and her hair long with soft curls. My favorite, though, is cuddling up to her in her dance team uniform with her hair braided to the side—the only thing hanging to my side is the chain on my belt attached to my wallet.

Nothing of me remains the same that she grew up with, other than the thin black and blue bracelet she gave me, and I've worn it every day since I was nine. It's a reminder of who I really am—a visual ground wire—a tether to Lily. She swore it was my good luck charm, but to me, it's a piece of her I get to keep connected to me at all times. Funny how it matches my look now more than it did back then.

To say we don't match is an understatement, but that never stops her. Like clockwork, between second and third period, then again between fifth and sixth, she walks straight into my arms, pushing through my group of lame ass friends and stays there, not saying a word, just leaning against me like she enjoys the feeling I offer her. And believe me, it's mutual.

Just like every other day, here we are, between second and third period, and she's making her way straight to me until her friend Morgan stops her. "Are you serious right now? Do you have to stop every time you see him?" I watch the judgment form on her friend's face and morph into disbelief when Lily answers.

She smiles, staring straight into the girl's eyes. "Yes, he's my gravity. I'm pulled toward him, and there's nothing I can do about it."

I laugh and wrap my arms around her as her friend walks away in a huff.

I can't help it when I whisper in her ear, "I like being your gravity for a change."

She smiles as the bell rings and hugs me tightly before walking off to her next class.

The day drags on and I'm dying to get out of here, but I know I can't leave until after our time together between fifth and sixth periods. As I approach my locker, Brent calls to me. "Let's bail. My dad has a sack and I'm ready to get lost for the rest of the day."

"Yeah, just give me a few minutes," I respond as I lean back against my locker and wait for Lily.

"Really, fucker? You're just going to wait on this chick? I'll never understand your feelings for her. She doesn't put out, you've never gotten a thing from her, yet you sit here all pussy whipped, waiting with your dick tucked between your legs."

"Shut the fuck up. You know it's not like that."

"Yeah, whatever. I'll be in the car when you get your balls back," he mocks, walking away with the rest of the guys just as Lily walks up. It's rare that my friends aren't present for our brief interactions. With the opportunity to actually talk to her, I ask, "How's your day going?"

"It's okay. Samantha's having drama with Kyle, so there's been a lot of emotions flying today."

I shake my head, not caring at all about her friend's boyfriend-girlfriend drama, which makes her laugh.

"I know you don't care, but you asked." She hits my chest before snuggling in closer.

"I know. Sorry I did." I lean down and kiss the top of her head. Her familiar scent fills my nose and warms me inside. It's a moment of contentment, happiness, with her and no one else.

We sit in a comfortable silence. I lower my lips to the top of her head, kissing her before inhaling her sweet shampoo, loving the way her scent calms my inner turmoil. Sadness knocks me from my high when the bell rings again. "You're not leaving are you?" She looks up, still wrapped tightly in my arms with concern written all over her face.

"Yeah, they're waiting for me in the car...unless you want to go get ice cream together?" I ask, wiggling my eyebrows, using her mom's sexual innuendo. It's become my favorite joke between us, next to her nickname, of course.

"Trev..." she scolds. She's prim and proper and I'm crass and outcast.

"Lily Pad..." I tease back. She hates it when I call her that, which is why I always will. Just for fun. Her face proves why I love messing with her, and I laugh in response until she shrugs it off, knowing it's a losing battle.

"Just be careful, okay? And I'll see you tonight, right?"

"Wouldn't miss it. Oh, here." I hand her a piece of paper that's folded down to a small rectangle, then kiss her forehead before heading in the opposite direction of my classroom and straight to the parking lot.

We head to Brent's house. His dad's a dealer and sometimes throws down a few sacks of green bud for us to enjoy for free. A few girls came over to party, and we're all sitting around his living room, high as fuck and not giving a shit about anything.

Tracy, a girl I've seen around a few times, comes to sit on my lap. "Hey, Trevin."

"Hey, Trace, make yourself at home." I smirk in response.

"Thanks, I think I will. Why don't you take me into the next room."

Well fuck, no guy's going to turn that down. "After you." I grin as she moves off my lap, pulling my hand as we slip out of the room and into Brent's bedroom.

"I've heard about you," she teases as she pulls me close to her, placing her hands on my chest.

"Yeah, what have you heard?" I say playfully.

"That you don't kiss." She leans up to try to reach my lips, but I turn them to the left so she gets my cheek.

"Well, you've heard right," I tease.

She sticks her bottom lip out. "Not even me?"

"Sorry, baby. Not even you."

"Then what are you doing back here?" she asks, trying to flirt and be as sexy as possible; it's working, a little.

I grab her, pulling her into me. "Well, that's up to you. You're the one who wanted me back here." Her hands wander as she slowly starts to undo my buckle. "Yeah, you want what's in there?" I nudge her to continue.

She nods as she bites her lower lip, looking down at my cock when she pulls it out of my boxer briefs. Without hesitating, she drops to her knees right in front of me. Fuck, I love being a guy. It's amazing what girls will do to try to please me, and I don't have to do a damn thing in return. I've gotten more blowjobs than I can even remember, but I still haven't kissed anyone else. I have no desire knowing one day, I'll have Lily the way I want her.

I'm not a scumbag—these girls always come on to me. I don't mislead them; I'm very open that I won't do anything more. For some reason, that seems to turn them on. I don't know why, maybe it's the thrill of the hunt, or trying to be the one girl to beat out the rest. I think they all silently hope they'll be the one to change me and finally get the first taste from my lips, but it will never happen. I'm not complaining one bit though.

I move Tracy slightly to the side so I can sit down on the bed and enjoy the feeling of this chick's mouth wrapped around my dick that much more. No, she's not Lily, but she'll do the job for now.

Lily

After I sit down and my teacher starts his lesson, I pull the paper Trevin handed me out of my back pocket. I've grown to love these notes. They're so much more though—they're poems or lyrics he's written. I know I'm the only person he shares them with, and it helps me know that the real Trevin, the boy I've known since I was eight, is still in there.

When I unfold two sides I see his writing:

My Lily Pad, shy like a little turtle.
One day we'll get ice cream,
Just hope she's not a fertile myrtle.

I laugh out loud, cupping my hand over my mouth to silence my laughter. His silliness has no boundaries. Morgan glances my way, and when she sees the note in my hand, she shakes her head.

"Seriously, Lily, what is going on with you two?" she whispers so the teacher doesn't hear her.

"Nothing, you know that."

"Liar. Your face lights up every time you read his notes. What do they say anyway?"

I hold it close to my body, like I'm protecting it with my life. This is my thing with Trevin, and I don't share it with anyone, not even Morgan.

"See, you won't even show me. Lily, you never talk about other guys. I've never even seen you check out anyone else. Why don't you two just do it already," she spits out before turning her attention back to the teacher. I can't tell if she's truly irritated or just worried about me. She doesn't understand Trevin—none of my friends do. They don't see the boy I know—my best friend.

My lips tilt into a smile as I think about his ice cream comment, but it fades fast when the reality of what Morgan is saying hits me hard. She's right. And so is Trevin. I am shy, almost to a fault. I don't put myself out there or even talk to other guys…but they don't talk to me, either. Just him.

Glancing down at the note, flipping over the other folds, I see there's something more inside.

I'm so different, I hardly know who I am.
The only thing that keeps me going is knowing she gives a damn.
I'll wait for the day, till I feel her fire.
Knowing deep down she's my only desire.

And there it is. That's why. He's enough. He's all I need. I see no point in wasting my time with other guys who will use me or hurt me when Trevin's… *everything*. Even if it's only as my best friend.

As I get ready for my big dance recital, I peek out from behind the curtain to see what the crowd looks like. I'm on the school's dance team, but I still perform with the same studio I did growing up. I'm lucky enough to become an instructor, and tonight is my last performance in the company as a student. To close out my time with the studio, I'm doing a solo routine to end the night before they announce my new role.

My nerves settle only to be replaced with a happiness that raises my heart to feel like it's floating away. At the back door, I see Trevin walk in by himself, looking like a lost puppy. It's not the single red rose he's carrying that brings a tear to my eye, though—it's his outfit. I don't know where he even got the brown slacks or a light green button-up top, much less the plaid tie. His shirt is more wrinkled than it should be, and his tie is not quite straight, but just the fact that he dressed up for me puts a huge smile on my face. This look is so far in the opposite direction of his everyday attire that I ponder what prompted the change.

The lights dim, drawing my attention away from my best friend as the music starts signifying the beginning to the show, so I head back to help the younger girls get ready before my final performance.

When it's over, my parents come backstage to congratulate me, and my mom informs me I have a *visitor* waiting outside. The way she says visitor tells me she's talking about Trevin, and makes me wonder how many scoops of ice cream she thinks we've had together. She's constantly teasing me about our relationship, and I know she is just as amazed as I am to see him dressed so differently.

When I walk out to greet him, he's standing against the wall, holding the rose in his hand and looking down at the floor.

"Look at you," I tease, bringing him out of his trance.

He looks up and I watch as his eyes light up when he caresses my body from head to toe with his gaze. The contemporary costume leaves little to the imagination with the low-cut neckline and thin spaghetti straps. It fits like perfection from my shoulders to my waist before the skirt billows out in sheer fabric that stops just below my knee. The slit up the side of the skirt adds just a hint of sex appeal and allows my legs to move freely. I'm filled with pride at Trevin's approval. Then, I see that look in his eye—the one acknowledging he sees me as more than just his best friend.

His lips curl up into a sexy smirk as he holds out the flower, never pulling his eyes away from mine.

"Thank you for coming." My voice is timid, as is my reach for the beautiful flower. I can't help but cast my gaze down toward the ground, unsure of what to do with his lust-filled eyes.

His fingers curl around my wrist and he pulls me into him, bringing me right where I belong. Wrapped in his arms, pressed against his chest, my hands run over his wrinkled shirt, and I can't help but giggle.

"Whose shirt?" I ask.

He looks down, smiling a goofy smile. "It's Brent's. We had a hell of a time figuring out how to tie this thing." He reaches for his tie, trying to make it straighter.

"Well, you look very handsome." I can hardly contain my excitement over Trevin going to these lengths for me.

His face lights up, and for a brief moment, we stare at each other, our eyes locked together like magnets.

Kristy, one of the younger girls I instruct, comes bouncing up to us. "Ms. Lily, is this your boyfriend?"

Both Trevin and I instantly separate and I reach down to pick up the tiny ballerina, who thankfully, broke our spell.

"No, Kristy. *This* is my best friend in the *whole* world." I exaggerate "whole" like I'm her age again, emphasizing like it's the only thing that's important. "Can you say hi to Trevin?"

I'm surprised by the hurt look in his eyes when I glance up, but he blinks it quickly away before putting his hands back into his pockets and smiling brightly at the golden-haired child on my hip. "Nice to meet you. I loved your performance tonight."

"You saw me?" She shines like the sun high in the sky from Trevin's comment.

"Of course I did. Your green dress stood out from the white, blue, yellow and orange dresses. I take it you were the star of the show."

He glances in my direction and winks at me with a slight smile pulling on his lips.

Kristy bounces in my arms, overwhelmed with excitement. "My mommy said the same thing!" She jumps down from my arms and runs straight to her mom's leg, pulling on her shirt, and I watch the little girl tell her mom with exaggerated animation what Trevin said.

The dance Kristy was in was a representation of the sun rising. The younger girls were in the back, dressed in green, swaying as the grass while the older, more experienced dancers were the sun. Most people wouldn't have paid attention to the tiny three and four-year-olds in the background—they're lost as living scenery, only there to give them experience being on stage. Trevin noticing her melts my heart…and hers.

Someone calls my name, so I turn to Trevin. "I've got to run. Thanks for coming tonight. And for getting dressed up."

Both of his hands reach out, grabbing my waist and pulling me into him. "You looked beautiful up there. I wouldn't have missed it for anything."

I feel his light tug, bringing me even closer to his body as he places a soft kiss on my forehead. "Night, Lilies."

My eyes squint and question him at the sound of a new nickname. He does nothing more than laugh and walk away. I'm utterly confused by our interaction and how it felt different than it normally does. Hopefully now though I might finally live down the Lily Pad nickname.

Chapter 8

Forever.
It's not just a word.
Forever.
When will my voice be heard?

- Trevin Allen

Trevin – 18th Birthday

Lily has me standing outside at noon on my birthday, which is really early after the night I had partying with the guys. She's only told me she has a surprise for me and I needed to be ready.

"Okay, I'm here. Now where are you taking me?" I ask as she walks outside to meet me.

"It's a surprise, but if we're going to make it, we have to go now. You never know what traffic's going to be like getting into the City."

"Are you kidding me right now?"

"Nope. Oh, I forgot, though—you'll need your electric guitar. Come on, go grab it and let's go." She waves me in the direction of my house, indicating my need to hurry.

Her excitement is contagious as she jumps up and runs to her mom's car while I retrieve my guitar. It's become my pride a joy since she gave it to me a year ago for my seventeenth birthday. She saved her money for over a year to be able to buy it for me—it blew me away then, and it still does now.

Once we arrive in San Francisco, we head to the infamous Fillmore. The place was made famous in the sixties after every big band played there. I've dreamed of seeing a concert here, but I'm not sure why we're here at one thirty in the afternoon.

"Surprise!" she yells out as we reach the front door.

"Uh, okay. I'm confused. What are we doing here?"

"Sony Records is holding auditions, and I got you a slot!"

Holy Shit! "Are you kidding me right now?"

Her face lights up with the biggest smile I've ever seen. "Nope! I saw a flier when I was in town a few weeks ago visiting friends. I took the flier and sent them a demo I taped when you played in my room over the summer. You're on at two, so we made it just in time. Come on." She grabs my hand and pulls me into the venue, her excitement evident in her demeanor.

We enter a narrow hallway that opens up to a large room with a stage on the far end. A bar lines the back wall and you can see the upstairs peeking through the cutouts in the walls that are lined in every psychedelic concert poster ever made from the sixties. What I would have given to see the Grateful Dead or Jim Morrison play in this venue…

A man walks up with his hand stretched out to greet us. "You must be Trevin Allen."

I switch my guitar and offer my right hand to the man. "Yes, I'm Trevin, and this is my friend, Lily."

"Nice to meet you two. We're almost ready for you. Go on and head backstage to get set up. You're next in line."

I look at Lily wide-eyed with a huge grin on my face. She giggles as she leans up to kiss my cheek. "Go knock 'em dead."

The guy on stage before me is good but not great. I've never played for anyone but Lily, but after seeing this guy's skills, the confidence inside me threatens to overflow. Chills run up my arms as I walk backstage to get ready.

"Okay, next to the stage is Trevin Allen," I hear them call from the huge, open room.

After taking a deep breath, I grab my guitar and head on stage for the opportunity of a lifetime. The first face I see is Lily's, standing in the background—her hands are cupped around her mouth, but she can't hide the smile behind them or her excitement as she bounces on her toes in anticipation. Seeing her there instantly calms any nerves threatening to creep up. A quick glance around shows the majority of the place is empty. The judges occupy a table they set up a little ways back for optimum sound quality.

"Whenever you're ready," the man says.

Without hesitation, I wrap the strap around my neck, holding it tightly to my body as I begin to play Jimi Hendrix's, *All Along the Watch Tower*. I figure since we're in the Fillmore, there can't be a better choice to channel my inner guitar god.

My fingers fly over the strings and up and down the neck of the guitar as I keep my focus only on Lily. Having her here transports me mentally back to her room, playing a concert just for her instead of auditioning for one of the biggest record labels in the world.

Happiness rips through my feet, coursing through my body, and out of my fingers as I begin to dance around, feeling the music in my soul, putting on a show with everything in my being, and never skipping a beat or missing a note. I'm in absolute heaven, and I know this is what I'm meant to do, who I'm meant to be.

I belong on a stage.

Sadness threatens to tighten my throat as I play the last of the notes, not wanting this opportunity to end so soon. The guitar strings fade away as I look up into the eyes of two men sitting completely silent. Fear quickly sets in. I instantly start replaying the entire audition in my mind, wondering what I did wrong. I hadn't missed a single note; I was spot on. But here they sat, quiet as mice, not saying a single word. They just stare at me, completely bewildered.

And I wait.

My fears disappear as one of the men slowly starts to clap in pure amazement as he stands, moving from behind the table and approaching me. "That…that was unreal. How old are you?" He reaches out to shake my hand.

"Thank you. I'm eighteen. Actually, today is my eighteenth birthday," I reply, looking him straight in the eye and giving him a firm handshake.

"Well, Trevin, thank you for coming out and spending time with us on your birthday. We will definitely be in touch."

The other guy, who had occupied the seat next to him, finally speaks up as he walks toward the stage, reaching out to grab my hand as well. "Definitely," is all he says as we shake.

"Cool, thanks guys." I jump off the stage and run straight into Lily's arms. Picking her up, I swing her around, feeling truly free for the first time in my life.

We spend the rest of the day in the City, walking down the pier, being silly tourists, and taking pictures with the man who's painted solid silver standing still like a statue. I love how comfortable the two of us are together. Other than when she's up on stage during a dance recital, she's more of an introvert at school and around her friends, but I bring her out of her shell—like nothing's changed since we were eight years old.

On the way home, I can't take my eyes off her face. Every few seconds, the streetlights give me a glimpse of just how beautiful she is. My life would be nothing without her and I'm beginning to think I'm ready to let her know how I feel. How I've felt for years.

One week later...

"Get the phone!" my dad screams from downstairs.

I've been trying to ignore him—and the female's moans and screams—for the last half hour, but nothing I do can drown out the nausea going through me.

My fucking dad. I swear. I'll never know why I was given this piece of shit for a father or who I pissed off in a former life that's retaliating against me now. I guess it's cool that he lets me do whatever I want, but fuck, sometimes it's just too much. Nobody wants to hear their parent going at it with some random bitch on their living room couch. That's just gross.

It's past eleven at night, and the only phone in the house is in the kitchen. It rang over and over again for the last five minutes, but I couldn't care less about answering it because that means I would have to walk by my old man and whatever whore he's got with him—no thank you.

"Trevin, get the goddamn phone!" I hear him scream again.

Frustrated, I slam my pencil down on the poem I'm writing and stomp downstairs, trying to avoid seeing random body parts or anything else that might make me want to hurl in my mouth.

"What?" I answer, one hundred percent pissed off and not even pretending to hide my irritation.

"Yeah, is Trevin there?" a man with a slight British accent replies.

"You got him—who's this?"

"Boy, I'm about to make your dreams come true. This is Arnie. I'm with Sony Records and I just saw your audition tape from San Francisco last week. Stone Cold's lead guitarist just left the band and they need someone immediately. What do you say? You up for the ride of a lifetime?"

Tightness overwhelms my chest and the thought of air becomes foreign as I stand, frozen, trying to process what was just said. Stone Cold, *the* Stone Cold that I listen to every day. The one I fucking love with every part of me wants me to play for them. I'm in awe, dumbstruck by the notion that one afternoon, one audition, can bring my dreams to life.

Arnie laughing over the receiver brings me back to the present. "You still there, dude?"

I look up, just in time to see my dad flip the whore he has on the couch over and stick his disgusting, old-ass dick in her nasty, disease-ridden pussy.

Without bothering to look away, I answer, "Fuck yeah. I'm in. When do you need me?"

"Glad to hear it. A car will pick you up at your house at five tomorrow morning to take you to SFO where you'll hop a flight to LAX. I'll be there myself to pick you up. Can you be ready to leave in that short amount of time?"

"I'm already ready," I answer without hesitation.

"Great. Oh, and Trevin, strap your boots on tight, boy, your life just changed forever."

He hangs up his end before I can respond, and after slamming down the phone, I look up to see my dad again, only this time, he's calling me over. "Hey, son, I'm ready to blow here, but this little piece wants more," he says, slapping her ass as he rams her hard. "You want in?"

He's got to be fucking kidding. I'm not sticking my dick anywhere near anything that has touched his, much less the nasty-ass broad calling over the edge of the couch to me.

"Oh yeah, please come fuck me…" The words fade off into a grotesque moan that repulses me instead of turning me on.

I shake my head without responding and call Lily's pager, entering eleven—my code. Then I walk straight up to my room, find an old duffle bag, and slam a few clothes inside. Grabbing my guitar, I turn back to take in my room for what will hopefully be the last time ever.

I stop, glancing at my mirror to a picture I have of my mom and me together at the baseball field. It was taken a couple of weeks before she passed away. The other two pictures are of Lily and me—one when we were younger and one taken about a year ago. I reach for all three, shoving them into my back pocket as I walk down the stairs, past my dad without saying a word. I leave the house I once called my home, never to look back. There's only one place I need to be tonight.

I sit in front of her house, silently begging for her to be awake and to have heard my page, but I can't help the slight fear setting in.

This is it.

Everything I've ever wanted, but it dawns on me this could be the last time I see Lily. It washes over me faster than I realized what was actually happening. I hear the lock click behind me and the door slowly opens, revealing Lily in small boy shorts and a tight tank top that doesn't quite sit on her waistline, and she's obviously not wearing a bra. The sudden rush of cold air from outside instantly turns her nipples hard, and my dick responds in seconds.

"Hey, Trev, everything okay?" she asks in a sleepy voice, her eyes squinting, trying to adjust to the streetlight outside.

After a deep breath, trying to calm my nerves, I reply. "Can I come in?"

She opens the door wider. "Of course. Just be quiet; my parents are asleep."

She turns to walk back toward her room and I quietly follow her blindly to the room I've been in thousands of times before. Her sweet little ass sashays up the steps as I watch the words *Love Pink* sway from side to side, screaming at me in the dark.

I've been with other girls but held fast to two rules: no lips will ever touch mine that aren't hers, and Lily would be the first person I would ever have sex with. I knew the time wasn't right, so I've waited. Waited for her. Waited for us.

The moment we enter her room, I turn to close the door quietly behind me. Before she can sit down, I grab her hand, pulling her toward me, slamming our bodies together. Without a second thought, I push my lips against hers, letting go of her fingers to cup her head between both palms as I kiss her. I kiss her the way I did a few years ago, like I've wanted to do every day since—holding nothing back.

She doesn't fight. She doesn't resist. No. The second my lips touch hers, her mouth opens, inviting me in, sweeping her tongue against mine and pushing her body closer to my own.

Patiently, I walk her backward, one step feels like forever, but I want to enjoy this. Savor every second of my first, and possibly, my last time with the only girl I will ever love.

Our lips haven't parted since I walked in the door, but we both pause when the back of her legs touch the side of her bed.

This is it.

She knows what I want.

She can feel my desire bulging in my pants. I pray she won't stop me, but I feel her hesitation as her lips slowly pull away from mine.

"W–wait...Trevin." Her hands push up to my chest, not pushing me away, but keeping space between us.

I pull back slightly and look into her eyes, grabbing her hands, holding them close to my heart. "Please, Lily. I'm leaving. Tonight is it. I just got a call and *the* Stone Cold *wants me* for their guitarist. This is my—"

"Trevin!" She cuts me off. "Are you serious right now?" She jumps up and down, holding onto my hands tighter.

I can't help but smile at her excitement. "Yes, they just called and—"

"Is this from the tryouts in San Francisco?" She interrupts me again. "So what's next? You're leaving? For where? What about school? What about—"

It's my turn to interrupt her. "They're picking me up at five in the morning. But I can't go. Not without being with you first. I've wanted you for so long, and I promised myself that you would be my first."

Gravity

My lips move back to claim what I've always felt was mine just as her hands wrap around my neck, pulling me down toward her bed.

Once she's on her back, I push myself up, staring directly into her chocolate brown eyes as I sweep her soft, brown hair away from her face. "You'll always be my gravity. You're what I need to stay grounded, no matter where I go, no matter what happens. Remember that. Only you."

I place one soft kiss on her lips, then her cheeks, moving down her neck as my hands slowly glide under her tank top, pulling it up, and sliding it over her head. Our eyes meet once again as we stare at each other, not saying a word but knowing nothing needs to be said.

My lips reunite with hers as my hand brushes over her breast, cupping it, indulging in the feeling of her soft skin against my rough fingers.

Pulling my lips from hers, I lean closer to her ear and whisper, "I've wanted this for so long." My fingers travel from her breast and down into her boy shorts.

With an arch of her back, she invites me in and whispers my name in the sexiest moan I've ever heard. "Trevin…"

The want and need in her voice will be my undoing. I know, without a doubt, she wants me as badly as I want her. For the rest of my life, I'll wonder why I waited so long to do this. But I try to push away that thought in favor of enjoying what's happening now.

Her hands slide down my torso and pull the hem of my shirt up. I pause my own exploration to allow her to remove it completely. Bare chest to bare chest, skin to skin, I lower myself, feeling her exposed body softly against mine for the first time.

Every second, every inch of her, carving memories into my mind. My arms wrap around her, holding on tightly for fear I might float away if I let go. My tongue explores hers, dancing together in harmony. All I can think about is holding her tightly, trying to register this feeling in the back of my brain for the rest of my life. I need to be able to recall this memory at any given time regardless of where I am.

When I feel her hands reach between us to pull on my belt strap, every ounce of self-restraint flies out the window. Excitement floods my veins, knowing not only does she want this, but she's willing to get the party started by making the first move—the point of no return.

My lower back lifts slightly, giving her room to finish what she's started. Only in my wildest dreams did I truly believe she would be here, doing this with me. I never believed she'd be bold enough to touch me the way she is. We've never talked about other guys just like she never asks me about other girls, but right now, I pray to God this is her first time, too.

Our lips continue their exploration, our tongues communicate in the silence, as I feel my zipper slowly being lowered. When it finally stops moving, the pressure that built up is released as my cock springs free. To my ultimate surprise, Lily reaches in and grabs ahold of it like she's never going to let go.

A moan starts deep in my chest before it escapes my lips, breaking our kiss as I try to hide the excitement threatening to shoot out of me. Unable to stand it any longer, I make my way down her beautiful body. When I reach her shorts, I slowly start to shimmy them down her legs until they're completely off and I drop them on the floor beside the bed. My hands run up her soft legs, memorizing every inch until I reach where I really want to be. Where I've dreamed of being for so long.

Trying to hide the tremor in my hands, I take a deep breath and run my fingers along the inside of her thigh, then against her pussy for the first time. The sound of her quick inhale sends chills down my spine and rushes blood straight to my cock.

My fingers part her lips, circling her clit, and moving lower to feel her wetness seep out. I dip my fingers in slowly, keeping my eyes on her—loving the way her back arches off the bed in ecstasy. She's ready and my dream is finally coming true.

I stand tall before her and remove my own clothing before I look down at my best friend, the girl I will always love, who will always hold a place very deep in my heart. Our eyes meet and a slight smile curves her lips as her hand reaches out to mine, entangling our fingers, pulling me down, back to Earth, back to her.

Without breaking eye contact, I nestle on top of her, between her legs, and pause, waiting for acceptance, searching for any sign of doubt. But there is none.

All I see is her.

The unconditional love she's always offered me. The way she accepts every part of me exactly as I am. My tiny piece of perfection. The portion of my heart that wanders the earth on the outside of my body. She sees me—the raw, unedited version of me…and she still loves me.

My lips are pulled down to hers as I slowly start to enter her for the first time. Her body tenses and I wrap my arms tightly around her, cocooning her as I make my final thrust inside.

There's no lingering doubt. This is her first time. I swallow her winces of pain, wishing I could take away the discomfort so she could enjoy this the way I want her to. Kissing her as softly as possible, I try to show her what she means to me, what this moment means to me.

We lay together, united—giving her time to adjust to me. When I feel her body loosen, and her legs wrap around my waist, I slowly pull back before moving back in and whispering, "It will always be you." I kiss her lips softly while I begin to make love to the only woman who will ever own my heart. Breaking away only to whisper, "Are you okay?" in her ear.

She sighs and I feel her nod, saying yes. Her lack of verbal response worries me, so I pull back, needing to see her eyes. What I didn't expect was to feel myself tipping even more in love with her at this very moment.

Instantly, her mouth finds mine again and we both find our rhythm, pushing, pulling, tugging, moaning, loving one another like we should have many times before now. For the last decade, we've loved each other silently, never voicing the words—today, we seal it physically.

I want this to last forever. I try to focus on every part of her, locking it into my memory. My fingers run through her hair to remember how soft it is. I lower my nose to her neckline to breathe in the scent of the cucumber melon lotion she wears. And finally, I bring my mouth to hers, to taste her sweet lips on my tongue one more time.

Breaking the kiss, I place my forehead against hers and slow my movement, rolling in and out at an even slower pace. I pulled back thinking if my lips weren't attached to hers I could last longer, but I was so wrong.

When she stares up at me, her eyes are so sweet, so expressive. I hold her gaze as I continue moving in and out of her. The tender smile that spreads across her face tells me exactly how much I mean to her, too.

Being able to see her lying so beautifully underneath me, a spot I've dreamt about for so many years, sends my heart racing, and any remaining control I had went out the window.

"Lily," I whisper.

Now it's her turn to say, "Shh…" Her lips reach up to silence mine, and I cum for, what feels like, the first time ever. Never have I experienced the pleasure she just brought to me, the depth of emotion, the joy in the release.

Afterward, we lay in each other's arms. I was afraid things would be awkward, but it wasn't at all. Once she got back from the bathroom and we put our clothes back on, we just laid together like we always had. Cuddling with one another on her bed, talking about me leaving and how excited she was for me to get this opportunity.

We didn't exchange words about us or what just happened. There was nothing to be said. We both know we just changed everything yet nothing at all. She'll always be mine, and whether I'm here or not, I'll always be hers.

With every emotion running through my mind, and the anticipation of the journey I was about to start, there was no way I could sleep. Instead, I sat and watched her all night long.

Five in the morning came too soon. The swarm of light that fills her room notifies me of a car pulling up in front of my house. I lower my mouth to gently kiss her lips, waking her to say goodbye.

"Good morning, Lilies. Sorry to wake you, but I have to go."

With sleep in her eyes, she turns to me, sadly saying, "You're leaving now?" Her brow furrows and her face exudes sadness.

"I am. Wish me luck, okay? I'll call as soon as I get situated." I turn to crawl out of her bed.

"Trevin..." Her arm reaches up to stop me.

I turn to look at her, but she doesn't say anything. I lean in to kiss her lips once more, not knowing exactly what she wants to say, but knowing the emotions that are threatening to overtake me, and hoping she feels the same way.

As I pull apart from her kiss, I place my forehead onto hers, whispering, "Me too."

Taking a deep breath, I grab my things and walk out of her room, moving on to better things in my life and praying to God that somehow, she'll find a way to be there, too.

Chapter 9

Why did you push me to be my own?
Why did you love me enough to care?
Now I'm here all alone
Floating in the middle of nowhere.

- Trevin Allen

Lily – Age 18

Graduation day wasn't the same without Trevin. I always expected us to walk across the stage together, having our picture taken with those silly gowns and throwing our hats into the air. Thankfully, part of his signing deal was he had to finish high school, and since he was only a few months out, he was able to get a tutor on the road and finished everything in time to technically graduate with us—even though he wasn't here.

No, he's on the road somewhere. He's called a few times, but our conversations have been rushed since his schedule has him traveling constantly or it's packed with practice, photo shoots, and performing. He was Stone Cold's new golden boy, and the fans are eating him up.

I'm constantly replaying our last night together. I've gone through all the emotions an eighteen-year-old girl could have. First it was amazement over not being a virgin anymore, and I'd given it to my best friend. Then fear when I realized how stupid we'd been not using a condom. Then relief when I started my period a few days later. I had no clue what the time frame was of when I could get pregnant, so I studied up and got on birth control. Why, I don't know—it's not like he's here to need it. I guess as a just-in-case kind of thing. Then, I just went to simply missing him. He's been here, with me, every day since I was eight years old, and now he's gone.

The last six months have been long and lonely without him, but he called the other day saying he wanted me to come to LA. I can't wait to see him and finally figure out what's actually going on between us.

He purchased the ticket and indicated I'd be staying with him while I was there. Even though we've never spoken about that night, or our relationship status, every thought of starting right where we left off fills me with excitement. I think I'm going to be sick sitting here waiting for this flight to land.

Trying to push my way through the long line to get off the plane, I lightly jog my way down the tarmac, wanting to jump into his waiting arms. As I exit the area, I look around, but he's nowhere to be seen. Instead, I see an older man holding a sign that reads "Lily Pad" on it. I thought for a second, years ago, he would drop the name, but no such luck. I just gained an additional nickname instead.

I walk up, shaking my head at his sign. "Of course he would put Lily Pad on there, but that's me. My name's Lily." I reach out my hand to greet the man in front of me.

"G'day, I'm Arnie. Trevin's sorry he couldn't pick you up and was even more sorry you got stuck with me. But he demanded if he couldn't pick you up himself, it had to be me over some roadie." He laughs at his own joke, and I can tell he's a sweet man, putting me at ease.

"I'm sure you'll be fine. Where are you taking me?"

"I'll be dropping you off at his place so you can get settled."

We drive for about twenty minutes, not talking about much, just listening to the radio as Arnie thumbs out the beat on the steering wheel and hums the tune. We pull up to a house that sits on the beach, and I'm instantly in awe. He said the house he was staying in was pretty cool, but I think he was downplaying it just a tad. This place is gorgeous!

Arnie lets me in and leads me back to his room, where we both assume I'll be staying. The room is bare of anything on the walls or dressers except for three pictures. I walk up to his mirror where a picture of his mom and two pictures of Trevin and me sit nestled into the frame.

Turning around, I smile at Arnie who gives me an appreciative grin in return and says his goodbye. He indicates Trevin shouldn't be much longer and insists I make myself at home.

All the other band members live on their own, but he shares this house with some of the head sound crew and road managers. A total of four guys live here, but you'd never know by the looks of it. I guess they have a maid—I know they didn't clean for my arrival.

After taking a tour, I step outside to a view I've only dreamed of. Their place sits right on the water with a long deck wrapping around the back. The thought of slipping into my swimsuit, laying out and relaxing takes over, and I run to change, excited to soak in some sun while I wait for my own rock star to come home.

About an hour after I laid down, I hear the glass door slide open and I turn, excited to see if it's him. Hard eyes stare back at me, scanning my entire body, slowly engulfing every inch without shame. I let him take me in, sitting still, waiting for him to get his fill as I enjoy the look of hunger taking over his face.

When his eyes finally reach mine, we stare, frozen, watching each other. My lips finally separate as I whisper, "Hi."

He walks up, taking each step like he owns the world and everything in it, including me. I already see a difference in him. In just these few months, he's changed. More sure of himself—cocky. Which I must admit, is damn sexy.

I want nothing more but for him to swoop me up, take me to his room, and start off exactly where we left it. But I'm more than surprised when he stops short of touching me and stuffs his hands deep into his pockets. "I'm glad you were able to relax. Sorry I wasn't able to pick you up."

He's got to be kidding me right now. Where's my best friend? "Um, it's okay. How have you been?" I reach my arms to wrap around his neck and hug him tightly, inhaling the CK One cologne I've always loved on him.

I get less than a tight hug, I barely get a light, friendly tap, and suddenly, I'm spinning in a world of confusion.

"What's up? Why are you acting like this?"

He stands up straight, like he's surprised I noticed anything was off. "What do you mean?" He goes to sit down on the chair next to where I was like nothing was weird between us.

With no clue what to say or how to react to his attitude, I say, "So…what have you been up to?"

"We were at a photo shoot that ran over. Things have been fucking crazy." He sits back, lying his head down, letting out a sigh of exhaustion.

"But you're enjoying it, right? I mean, I see you everywhere. Still crazy to see your photo on the cover of a magazine at the grocery store." I smile.

He laughs in return. "Yeah, pretty crazy to me, too. It's all just happened so fast. Still trying to take it all in."

"Have you talked your dad?"

"Fuck no. He's tried but everyone knows I don't want any contact with him. Fuck him."

I grab his hand the way I always have. "I'm sorry. I didn't mean to bring it up."

He looks down at our hands, slowly removing his from beneath mine and starts to get up. "Come on, let's get something to eat. I'm hungry." He stops short, standing tall and looking down at me with a crazy look in his eyes. "Can you cover yourself before we go in?" The tone of his voice and the sneer in his question stings.

I turn to grab the towel I was laying on. Before I can say anything, he walks back into the house, not waiting for me—leaving me lost in my thoughts, starting to regret coming here in the first place.

When I finally gather all my things and walk back inside, three guys and two girls greet me. They all stare my way like I have an alien head growing out of my neck. Self-consciously, I pull my things closer to my body, covering more than I had before, saying, "Hi, I'm Lily…"

I look around the room, but Trevin's nowhere to be found.

Finally, one of the girls jumps up. "You're the girl from the photo that in Trevin's room."

"Y–yes, that's me," I stutter, not sure what to say and sad to hear this girl has been in his room enough to notice the small photos on his mirror.

"Hmmm," she says, eyeing me up and down in question.

Everyone else offers a semi-friendly hello as I walk by, heading toward Trevin's room. He's sitting on his bed, slumped shoulders, looking down, playing with the bracelet I started making him when he was nine. Remembering I'd made him a few more to make sure he had backups while he was here, I grab them and walk up to him. Separating his legs and squeezing between them, I see if I can start this whole *hello* thing over.

"I made you your next batch," I tease as I hand him the bracelets.

He grabs them from me as his arms wrap around my waist and he settles his head against my chest, not trying anything but holding onto me tightly. I let him—shoot, I need him to hold me just as much as I feel he needs to.

We sit like this for a few minutes, not saying a word until he backs up, taking a deep breath and lightly pushing me to the side so he can stand.

"So, what do you want to eat? Should we see if the guys want to join us or go out by ourselves? I haven't ventured out much, so I'm not really sure where to take you."

Wow. What the hell is going on? Something is off, and I truly feel like this was a mistake to come here. This back and forth is a whiplash of emotional overload. He's the one who invited me. I didn't ask to come.

"Up to you. I'm okay with whatever," I reply, sitting on his bed, completely deflated.

"Okay, well, I'll go talk to them. Go ahead and get dressed. I'll be out here when you're ready." He leaves the room without so much as a glance over his shoulder.

What. The. Hell?

I take my time getting dressed again, volleying with the notion of just leaving altogether. Trevin and I have been friends most our lives and it has *never* been like this. This is painfully awkward. Something's up, and I just wish he would talk to me.

When I enter the living room, the guys are engrossed in a pre-season football game and the girls are vying for their attention. One in particular is sitting very close to Trevin, who's staring off into space—lost in thought. I watch as he closes his eyes, taking a deep breath, and letting it out slowly.

Jealousy creeps up my skin like a nasty bitch when I realize one of the girls has her hand resting between Trevin's thighs. When he finally notices my presence in the room, he stands, dropping the girl's hand like he didn't even know it was there and walks toward me.

"You ready?" he asks as he eyes me up and down once more.

I smile, still hoping I can start this visit over. "Yeah, what did you have in mind?"

"The guys suggested a place down the road. They're all going to go. Should be fun." He shrugs, but I get the feeling he doesn't believe what he's saying.

I haven't seen him in six months, and it hurts he's invited these people I don't even know to join us. It's like he doesn't want to spend any time alone with me, avoiding it at all costs.

But I didn't invite myself here. He called. He wanted me here. He even paid for my flight. So I don't understand the cold shoulder. If he didn't want me here, he shouldn't have bothered asking.

Dinner was exactly what I expected when he said everyone was going. I sat, barely speaking to anyone, and no one really talking to me. I've never felt so uncomfortable in my life. I'm the outsider. The "normal" person in this rock-star world he's entered. Even the two girls with us look the part—I definitely don't. They have on their slutty skirts that barely cover their bottoms and short tops that leave little to the imagination, while I'm wearing a white, corduroy jean skirt and a printed tee from Aeropostale.

Once back home, they all talk about getting some beer and hanging out, but I'm not up for it. I've never been a drinker, and I don't plan on starting now. Thankfully, Trevin agrees and follows me back to his bedroom.

"Sorry, I've had a long day with the flight and everything. I think I'm just ready to crash," I say as I reach into my bag to pull out my pajamas.

"No worries. I'm beat, too."

"Where am I sleeping?" I ask, not looking at him but purposely searching through my cosmetics bag for my toothbrush and toothpaste to avoid his face.

When he doesn't answer, I glance up to see him sitting on his bed, slumped and staring down. I have to fight the urge to go to him—to comfort him. It's the only thing I know, it's the way we've always been. But it didn't get me anywhere last time, and I'm not putting myself out there again.

Hearing me sigh, he looks up. "I thought we could just share this bed… if that's okay with you."

A pinch of hopefulness creeps in and I fight the urge to smile. "That's fine. I'll be right back." I try to maintain my composure as I head into his en-suite bathroom.

After I finish my business, Trevin and I switch places, so I crawl into his king-size bed only to hear the shower start. I turn to my side, completely defeated by the day and ready to just sleep this awful feeling away.

I don't hear him come out of the bathroom, but I smell the freshness from his soap. The bed dips down when he crawls in, but he stays to his side so I make no notion of acknowledgment that he's here with me. With a small shake of my head in disbelief, I pretend to be asleep, curling up even more, pushing all thoughts out of my head and trying my hardest not to cry.

I hear rustling around before I feel the touch of his hand on the skin that's exposed between my shorts and tank top. It's soft, still callused around his fingertips, but his touch does the same things to me it always has. I don't acknowledge it though, just let him leave his hand there, keeping my eyes closed and my back to him.

A few minutes later, he moves closer, wrapping his arm completely around me but not bringing his body to mine. I remain still, unsure of what he's doing or thinking—I refuse to keep putting myself out there only to be denied. He tugs me slightly, pulling me onto my back and I let him. I don't look his way or acknowledge him, but at the same time, I don't stop him, either. His arm wraps around me tighter, pulling his body closer to mine so we're in full contact.

We lay like this for what seems like an eternity—me on my back and him on his side with his arm draped across me. My heart pounds deep in my chest and my pulse races with him so close, but he doesn't make another move. My entire being responds to him the way it has for the last ten years. The pull is undeniable—it always has been, but he's fighting it so I am, too.

Just when I feel like this is it, he just wants to sleep holding me and isn't going to make another move, he gets even closer. My body now fully engulfed by his, I turn my head to face him but stay on my back. Our mouths are inches apart, but it's so dark, I can't see anything; I just feel his minty breath blow across my lips.

My pulse races in crazy anticipation of his next move. I wait for him to kiss me, wondering if he wants to have sex with me again, though I question his reason for acting so strangely and pushing me away. The thoughts pummel me, leaving an emotional mess in their wake.

I should be pissed at him for acting the way he has today. But just as everything inside me tells me to move away from him, my heart begs for him to take me in his arms and make love to me again.

With questions flying around in my head, my heart feels like it's going to explode. I want this so badly, but at the same time, not in exchange for the way he's treated me today. Confused, I lie frozen, fighting an internal battle in my head.

The longer I think, the more I realize he hasn't budged. We've been lying, inches apart for God knows how long, doing nothing but holding each other. The longer we lie here, the faster my pulse races. I realize I don't care what will happen or what happened today, I just want *something* to happen.

I'd only have to move an inch for my lips to touch his. He's made no further advance, and I wonder if I should be brazen enough to take what I want. He's already turned down my advances twice, and I wasn't sure I could handle it again. Trevin rejecting me is like a knife to the gut.

Just when I feel like my heart is going to explode from waiting, his lips crash into mine as he slides his body to cover me. I give in to him immediately, no longer fighting the internal struggle but loving the relief my heart is finally getting. His hands explore my body, and this time, they don't stop. The hunger I saw in his eyes when we first saw each other, I now feel all over my body as he searches for more, devouring every inch of me in a slow, methodical manner.

Clothes are pulled from my body as I reach to pull down his boxers. Before I know it, he's at my entrance. With a brief hesitation, he enters slowly, holding me tightly with his head buried in the crook of my neck.

His breath is ragged, strained, as he pulls in and out, clutching me like he's holding on for dear life. I feel his need and completely surrender my body to him, giving him everything he needs and taking what I love in return. Him.

Meticulous in his movements, he slowly pulses in and out of me, kissing my neck, my cheek, and my lips, but never looking me in the eye. The first time we had sex, our souls united, we never slipped from each other's view, our eyes were locked on one another. Now he doesn't say a word. Just breathes, deep and strong, holding me tightly as his body trembles through our reunion.

I'm lost in emotions. This time doesn't hurt as bad physically, but emotionally, I'm being ripped apart. He's so loving yet so distant, leaving me in a mass of confusion. The way he holds me like he can't get enough, but the fact he hasn't said anything or won't look at me speaks volumes about his desire for this to actually be happening.

I try to focus on the feelings he's showing me with his body instead of his actions he's taking away with his mind. Before I know it, I'm completely lost in sensation. The tingle grows lower in my belly and my heart starts to beat uncontrollably. His pace picks up, intensifying the feeling as my body ignites from below, freezing my movements in time as a rush flows through my body I've never felt before.

My head falls back and my eyes roll beneath the lids uncontrollably as he continues in and out until that one final slam inside me where he freezes from what I can only imagine is his own release. My body clings to his, clenching around him from the inside uncontrollably as the tingles slowly subside from my entire body.

We both lay there, not moving, not saying a word, just holding each other as our breathing turns to normal and reality creeps back in.

Without looking at me or saying a word, he slides off me and walks to the bathroom. I feel his cum seep out of me, but I don't care. I roll over with my back to his side, cover myself and curl up, totally lost in my head, wondering what the hell just happened.

I feel him crawl back to bed, wrap his arm around me and we fall asleep without a word between us. Slowly, tears slip from the corners of my eyes that I try to ignore and hide from him.

When I wake up the next morning, he's already out of bed, so I walk to the bathroom to take a long, hot shower. I need some time to think about yesterday, but mostly, last night. I have no clue what is going on with him or with us, but this is definitely not what I expected when he asked me to come see him.

I take my time getting ready, and each second that ticks by is a second he doesn't come to check on me, making thoughts of going home start to overwhelm me. I finally get up the nerve to head out, ready to say I should leave if he shows any signs of the way he acted yesterday.

When I walk to the kitchen, I see him standing at the counter. His shirt is off and his head is down, not moving—he stands eerily still. No one else is here and the house is quiet. I accidently hit the stool that sits at the counter and watch as Trevin jumps slightly, startling him from his trance.

Slowly, he turns around and I see the pain in his eyes before he wipes them away and puts a smile on his face. "Good morning." He reaches to grab me a mug. "Coffee?" He holds it out in offering.

My eyes rake over his body, and that's when I notice the tattoo that covers the left side of his chest, directly over his heart. He pauses as I take in the inked guitar with a lily coming up from the hole, breaking through broken strings with the word *forever* worked into the lines of the flower. When I look back to him, he quickly turns around, reaching for a shirt sitting on the chair and slips it on without saying anything else.

The sight of the tattoo gives me hope. I know it's for me. Whatever's going on with him must be overwhelming. I know deep down he cares for me, loves me even. I just hope I'm strong enough to let him.

Chapter 10

I wanted her here, I wanted her near.
But when my eyes fell to her curvy waist
I felt that fear, I felt that hidden tear.
I just pray my two worlds someday will interlace.

- Trevin Allen

Lily - same day

I'm glad I decided to stay. Trevin seems to be more himself and we spent the day walking around Los Angeles, him acting like a silly tourist and trying to make me be the same.

Just like last night, everyone is at his house when we get back, and even though he walks in like nothing's happened today, my heart sinks. I dread the same Trevin I had last night sneaking his way back into our wonderful day.

Unfortunately, I was totally right.

The minute we walk through the door, he drops my hand and walks to the other side of the room. He takes a seat on the couch and one of the guys throws him a beer. I sit next to him, not interrupting his conversation, and even though he makes room for me, he doesn't make a move to touch my knee or wrap an arm around me like he'd done earlier.

The night drags on and the distance between us grows until it's a wide valley. When he's across the room, the same girl who questioned me yesterday sits down next to me. She's smiling, but deep down, I feel a mean girl moment coming on.

"Hey, I'm Melissa by the way. So, how long have you known Trevin?" she asks with a plastic smile on her face. She's as fake as the huge tits popping out of her shirt.

"Since we were eight years old," I answer nonchalantly, trying not to engage her in more conversation than necessary.

"Wait, so that's you in both of those photos on his mirror?"

I take a deep breath, trying to calm my disgust at the thought of her being in his room. "Yes, that's me." I pause to prove my point. "In *both* photos."

"Yeah, he's told me all about you two. Pretty amazing really."

I look at her, thinking I should smile, but in my gut, I don't like where this is going. "Oh, yeah? What's he told you?"

"All about you two." She smiles snidely. "I can't believe you guys can share a bed and have never touched each other or done anything. I sure don't have friends like that, especially a guy who looks like Trevin. He's so hot! How do you do it, girl? I can't keep my hands off him and try to get in his bed every chance I get." She eyes me up and down as she pauses, licking her lips before saying, "But obviously, he wants different things from me than he does you, and honestly, I get it now that I see you."

I've never felt my heart beat through my throat till this moment. She's been with Trevin. I don't want to know what he's done or if he's slept with her. I want to slap the smug look off her painted face. *Now that she's seen me—* nothing but blind fury sets in.

I can't open my mouth for fear of throwing up all over this nasty girl. There's no way he could possibly be attracted to someone like this. I feel myself start to panic, and thankfully, she grabs my hand before I do, asking, "But tell me, has he really never kissed anyone?"

Wait. What? "Excuse me? What do you mean?" I shake my head in confusion.

"No matter what I do, he won't kiss me. I've never seen him kiss any girl he's been with, and he says that's his only no go."

I look over to where he's sitting and we catch eyes. He looks at Melissa, then back at me. I witness the old Trevin battle the new one. After a moment, the Trevin I know loses the war when he looks down with his shoulders slumped. He gets up to walk to his room, obviously mad about something.

I look at her, saying, "I wouldn't know, remember, we don't have *that kind of relationship*," before getting up to follow him back to his room.

When I walk in, his back is to me, looking at my photo tucked in his mirror. He looks up and our eyes meet in the mirror before I walk up, wrapping my arms around his waist. I try not to think about what Melissa just said and focus more on the fact he'll only kiss me.

He touches his hands to mine, hugging my arms briefly before pulling my fingers apart and moving me away from him. He walks toward his door as though this isn't open for discussion.

Rage fills my veins as I yell, "What's up with you, Trev? You can't invite me here, ignore me one minute then make love to me the next. Or what? Am I just another notch on your bedpost? How many girls have you had in that bed besides me?"

He turns around, shocked to hear me call him out. He's never seen me go off on anyone, especially him, but I've finally had enough—this reserved girl is bursting out of her shell and he's my target.

Trevin just stares at me, without saying anything, so I continue, "This isn't what I expected when I came here. So why, Trevin? Why am I here? Obviously you have your choice of females to be with. Melissa was all too happy to tell me all about it."

"What did she tell you?" he snaps back, walking up too close to me, invading my space. As if he has anything to be angry about.

"She mentioned trying to get in your bed any chance she gets. Says you're with multiple girls all the time."

He looks down in shame, not denying my claims.

"And you talk to her about me? *Me!* Why are you talking to anyone about me? What we have"—I move my hands back and forth between us—"is no one's business."

"I've only told her how much you mean to me." He reaches out to grab my waist but keeps his eyes focused on the ground.

"Liar! You're a freaking liar, Trevin." I throw his hands off me. "If you told her how much I meant to you, then why would you lie and say we were *just friends*? Why would you tell her we share your bed together but nothing ever happens between us?"

"Fuck, I don't know. I don't know what *is* happening between us. I'm so fucking confused. I thought having you here would help, but it's only made everything worse."

"Worse? Did you really just say that to me?" I push him to the side and stomp over to my bag, packing to get the hell out of here.

"That's not what I meant, Lily Pad."

"No, don't you dare freaking call me that."

He grabs my hand from the strap of my bag. "Stop, Lily, just listen to me."

I stop, mainly because in the past ten years we've known each other, he hardly ever used my real name.

"Everything's happening so fast. I don't know what's up or down, right or wrong, but I do know that even though I'm living my wildest dreams, something doesn't feel right. Then the second I saw you, I knew—it's you. Not having you in my life, but I don't know what to do about it."

"But I *can* be in your life," I exclaim, holding his hands together.

He lets go. "No. You can't. Not right now." He walks to the mirror and looks at me through the reflection, hurt written all over his face.

"Then take me home. I don't want to be here anymore." I grab my bag, pick it up and walk toward the door. When he doesn't stop me, my heart shatters.

I make my way to the front door, open it wide, and strut to his car that's parked exactly where we left it after our dream day spent in the city of stars. Funny, now those stars are shattering my dreams.

He joins me at the car and unlocks my door without saying a word. The silence is painful as he drives me to the airport, and when I open the door to get out of the car, he doesn't stop me.

No. He lets me get out of the car and walk through the sliding glass doors to the ticket window. He doesn't say goodbye, he doesn't apologize—he offers me no explanation, just kills any hope that might have remained.

It's not until I bend down to gather my things and walk toward my gate that I see him standing outside the doors, just staring at me, with his feet apart and hands tucked deep into his pockets.

We lock eyes for a moment before I blink and walk away from him, away from here and leaving him standing there outside as tears stream down my face.

Chapter 11

I didn't think I needed you.
I didn't think you cared.
I didn't think you'd see it through
I didn't think I'd be so scared.

- Trevin Allen

Lily - One Month Later

"**W**ait, you're actually coming to the party?" Morgan says in disbelief.

"Yes, I am. Why are you so surprised?"

"Um, mainly because you never go to parties. I must say, I don't know what happened when you went to see Trevin, but I sure like the new Lily that came home." She jumps up and down. "Oh, this is going to be fun."

She's right. She doesn't know anything that's ever happened between Trevin and me. Even though she's my closest friend, I've never spoken about my trip over a month ago.

That's right. It's been one month since I left Trevin standing outside the airport, and I haven't heard a peep from him. Nothing. Every day my heart breaks more, but I'm ready to say *screw him* and have some fun tonight. He has his new life so it's time for me to have mine. I start college in just a few weeks, so there's no better time.

I've always been the shy girl, the good girl. I have my group of friends, but I rarely go out with them. Not tonight, though. I'm ready to have a good time, maybe even drink, and forget all about Trevin.

Morgan helps me pick an outfit of hers to wear and does my hair and makeup. When I look in the mirror, I don't see anything I'm used to, but I'm trying to forget the old me—and this is step one.

A few of our friends moved into their own place and are hosting a party tonight to celebrate. An hour later, the door opens to a scarcely furnished apartment with an old couch and milk crates used as coffee tables. Red solo cups already litter the area and loud music blares through a rickety speaker, making it hard to hear anyone next to me.

I recognize most of the people as we walk in from school. Danny, a guy I had English with, smiles and gets up to greet me. "Well, well, look who's here. Good to see you, Lily."

"Good to see you, too. Is this your place?" I respond, giving him a quick hug hello.

He opens his arms out wide, proud to say, "Sure is. Can I get you a drink? One of the other guy's brother stocked our liquor cabinet, so I can get you anything you'd like."

"It's okay. I'm fine," I reply until Morgan steps in.

"Um, no, she's not. We finally got her to come out—she needs a drink."

I tilt my head to her, smiling. "Fine. Morgan, surprise me then."

"You got it!" she says and bounces away, leaving me with Danny.

"So yeah, it is a special occasion to see you at a party. What, now that Trevin's gone you're starting to venture out?"

I look up, giving him a skeptical glare. My brows pinch together slightly. "What does that mean?"

We're both yelling over the music, so he leans down, pulling my hips—and face—close to him. "I mean, now that he's gone, do you think I finally have a chance to show you a good time?"

"I'm confused. He and I were just friends."

He laughs, pulling me in tighter. "He made it very clear to every guy in school that you were his and no one was to lay a hand on you—or even try to."

I pull back to look more clearly at him, shock written all over my face as to what he's saying. I've had a few guys flirt with me in class, but it never turned into anything. Any guy I somewhat dated throughout high school, I met elsewhere, and Trevin hated every one of them.

I guess I never thought about why I didn't date guys from my school, I just didn't. After everything that happened between us, hearing this now pisses me off more than anything.

Feeling like I need to shed his weight from my life, I put my hands on Danny's, still holding my hips, and bring him closer. "Well, that's been a lie. I'm here, and no one can stop me from doing what I want to do."

His eyes twinkle as they look into mine. He brings me even closer, wrapping his arms around my waist and pushing his lower half into mine.

"Really now? Tonight may just be my lucky night then."

He leans down, kissing my lips lightly. Trevin's not the only guy I've ever kissed, but feeling Danny's lips against mine does nothing to calm my nerves; although, I don't stop him. This is what I need to get Trevin off my mind.

Backing away from me, I hear him hum his thoughts before saying, "Let's go get you a drink. Loosen you up a bit."

His hands intertwine with mine and pull me to the kitchen where we meet Morgan and a few other people.

"Here, girl. Just for you. Fruity, girly, and delicious. Just like the guy next to you."

"Hey, delicious I'll take, but fruity and girly needs to go." Danny laughs as he wraps his arms around me, pulling me into his front, and I go willingly. "Drink up, Lily. Let's have some fun tonight." His lips kiss below my ear before whispering, "I swear I'll show you a good time." Then he turns to talk to the group of guys standing behind him.

Morgan and I catch eyes and she smiles, bringing her cup up in the air to cheers my recent boy crush and me before we swallow most of its contents.

A low beat starts to rumble from the living room area, and before I know it, I feel fingers slip into mine and start to pull me away. With a drink in one hand and his warm hand in the other, Danny pulls me close to him and our bodies move in sync to the music.

Heat fills my veins as the alcohol sets in. My cheeks flush red and my mind cuts loose. My body feels free as song after song takes away the pain.

I'm flipped around so my back is against his front, and his hands start to travel down my waist, reaching my upper thigh. I quickly chug the rest of my drink, setting the cup aside so I can wrap my arms behind me, around his neck, and bring him even closer.

His lips meet my neck in soft kisses, running a line with his tongue up my throat to my ear. "How about we take this to my room," he whispers closely to my ear so I can hear him over the music.

Maybe it's the drink, or maybe it's just me desperate to get Trevin out of my mind, but I grab his hand, tugging him away from the makeshift dance floor as we start to head upstairs.

We don't make it far before I'm thrown against the wall and his lips are on mine in a feverish dance of desire. His hands reach to pull my leg up against his body, where I feel exactly what he wants thrusting into my center. The short skirt I have on is giving him especially easy access, and I feel his hands gripping my bare ass, tugging on my panties like he wants it now.

My hands shoot up, blocking his pursuit. "Not here. Where's your room?"

He steps back to give me his sexy, shit-eating grin before he pulls me toward the back of the hallway and into his bedroom. Once we enter, he turns to lock the door, and I'm hit with a strong dose of reality.

Reality that I'm in this guy's room, that I'm more than a little drunk off one drink, and that I'm about to have sex with him.

This isn't me.

This isn't what I want.

When he turns to walk toward me again, my phone dings with a text message. I reach for my small purse slung around my body to see who it is.

Three simple words are all it takes to completely stop everything that's happening. There, right in front of me, is a text message from Trevin:

I miss you...

I left the party last night after getting the text from Trevin. I've missed him more than anything I've ever felt, and seeing he missed me too was my complete undoing.

The look in Danny's eyes when I told him no was something I never want to see again. Saying I led him on, and even calling me a tease, made my stomach turn, but when he saw that it was Trevin's text that stopped our night together, he huffed off, saying, "Just friends my ass," as he slammed the door behind him, leaving me alone in his room.

I left pretty quickly after that, sending Morgan a text and heading straight back to my house. I laid in bed all night trying to figure out what to do. I didn't respond, because I wasn't sure what to say to him. He's going through a lot of changes, and I was unfortunate enough to witness it all unfolding in front of me. He can't believe three small words make up for what he did. He seems to think he can bring me in and out of his life on a whim, whenever it suits him. I miss him, I want him back in my life, but I'm not sure at what cost. I don't know if I could forgive him so easily.

I know exactly where I need to go today, so I hop out of bed, throwing on some clothes and head straight to the cemetery to visit Julie. When I arrive, the new headstone Trevin purchased for his mom shines like the special tribute he wanted it to be. He took his very first paycheck and had me pick out the best headstone I could find.

It was emotional for him to not be here to handle it himself, but he said he couldn't live another day with her having the small, insignificant one his father had purchased.

I sit down next to the engraved marble, running my hands over the grass in front, trying to fight the tears that are building up in my eyes. Julie and I had been close over the years before she died. She was such a loving mom to

Trevin and always treated me like the daughter she never had.

Wiping the tears that fall from my face, I talk to my old friend, hoping she'll guide me the way she used to.

"You must be so proud of what your son has become. I hope you're watching over him and guiding him right now. I know he needs it more than ever. He misses you like crazy. I went to see him in L.A. last month. The only things to remind him of home were pictures of you and me. I'm sad to say things weren't the same between us, either. I finally thought something was going to happen with us like you teased me about all those years ago. And, Julie, I wanted it to happen. Trevin's been such a big part of my life and I know no one will ever compare to him. But our lives are so different now. He's living his dream, but that dream doesn't seem to include me. I can't be mad at him for it, but it still hurts. God, it hurts so bad."

I look up, staring at the blue sky above me, and let out a long sigh. The grass feels cool on my skin when I lie down, thinking about Trevin—about us—and realizing, more than anything, I just want my friend back but not sure at what cost.

Chapter 12

She's not talking to me
And that has to change
I need her if I'm going to be
My life I will rearrange

- Trevin Allen

Lily - Age 18 November

"**W**hat are you looking at, sweetheart?"

My phone fumbles in my hand as my mother's words startle me. I brush a loose hair behind my ear and reply over my shoulder. "Nothing," I say and then turn around to face her, my cell phone in my hand. "Just…Trevin." My words falter.

My mom's brows lower in concern, her hand spooning mashed potatoes from the steel pot into a bowl. "You seem like something's wrong. Have you not spoken to him today?"

I shake my head, looking down at the last message he sent me.

Seeing his text sent me into a tailspin a few months back. I didn't respond but stared at my phone for a few days. I had no clue what to say. I miss him so much, but I honestly don't know if the Trevin I miss still exists.

"It's fine," I say, grabbing the bowl of potatoes. "I'll bring these to the table."

As much as I want to talk to my mom about what happened, I can't.

Never in my wildest dreams did I think he would be where he is now. I'm the one who got him the audition, so when I'm super lonely and missing him like crazy, I can't help but go into this self-loathing hole that I've created thinking this is all my fault. But it's not. This isn't about me and I need to stop feeling sorry for myself.

This is Trevin's dream, his everything, and I need to support him. No matter how much of a dick he was, I know I should forgive him. But not without him proving he deserves it first.

I place the bowl on the table and take a seat at the end near my dad who's at the head of the table. I'm placing my napkin on my lap when my mother walks into the dining room from the kitchen. My eyes widen when I see she's holding my phone up to her ear.

"Hold on honey, she's right here," Mom says into the receiver and hands me my cell phone. "Lily, Trevin's on the phone."

I raise my hand and take the phone from her. Holding the receiver to my chest, I whisper-yell, "Why did you pick up my phone?"

She startles back, her face twisted in confusion. "It was Trevin. Why wouldn't I answer the phone?"

I may not be speaking to him, but he's certainly communicating with me. Texts about what's going on with the band or poems like he used to write me come daily. He's called before, but I've never answered and he doesn't leave messages.

Knowing that he's waiting for me on the other end of the phone brings a mixture of joy and trepidation to my heart. And just like every other day, he's been on my mind. However, today more than normal. I know he doesn't have any family to spend Thanksgiving with—at least any family he actual wants to see—and I wonder if he's with anyone at all.

My heart starts to race and I finally put the phone up to my ear, but my voice leaves me when I try to say hello. Only a whisper comes out.

"Hi." Silence fills the line since I still can't seem to answer back. "Are you there?" he asks, full of anticipation. Hearing his voice just ripped a hole into my heart that I thought was almost mended.

This one is different, though. It isn't caused by hurt or distrust. It's from missing him—every part of him. His laugh, his silly nicknames, and most importantly, the way my insides feel at ease just by the way he said *hi*.

I get up from my seat to move to a more private area. "Yes, I'm here."

"It's so good to hear your voice. How are you?"

I take a deep breath, letting it out slowly and looking up at the ceiling before saying, "I'm good. What about you? I've been thinking about you today."

Happiness drips from his voice when he says, "You have? God, Lilies, I miss you so much."

"I miss you too, Trev," I reply because it's the God's honest truth. I just need to be careful not to fall right back to being us because we both aren't who we used to be.

For the first time in a while, I have a boyfriend who I actually like. He's nothing like Trevin, and I know he wouldn't approve, but I'd be lying to myself if that weren't one of the things I found appealing about him.

"Is anyone there besides your family?" he asks after a long pause.

"My grandparents are here, but that's it. Who are you spending today with?"

"Chad, one of my band members, invited me to his place, but I turned it down. I'd rather be home alone in this big house all by myself for a change. It doesn't happen very often." The way he says he's alone is so nonchalant, but I wonder if he really feels that way. Nobody likes to be by themselves on a holiday, and my heart aches a little knowing he is.

I'm not sure what to say without falling back into making sure he's taken care of, so I change the subject. That's not my job anymore. "How are things with the band?"

"Really good actually." His voice raises a few octaves, proving he's not just saying that and he's truly excited.

"Yeah, and how so?" I ask, just content to hear that happiness in his voice.

"The guys are cool. I'm starting to feel like one of them and not just the outsider I started off as. I wish you could have met them when—"

He stops and I hear the intake of his breath at the mention of my horrendous visit. I know he didn't mean to reference any part of it, and honestly, I hoped he wouldn't, so I ignore his slip up this time, hoping it was just that. "That's cool, Trev. I'm excited for you."

"We're planning a European tour that starts in January, so I'll be off seeing the world, one concert at a time. I still can't believe it."

"Me neither. I'm happy for your success, Trevin."

He pauses, his voice slightly lower. "That means a lot to me. You know I wouldn't be here without you."

I take a deep breath. "I know, Trev. Hey look, my family's at the dinner table, so I have to run." I feel bad cutting this short, but baby steps are all I can take right now. My heart is beginning to race and I'm not sure how I feel about it.

"Okay. Thank you for finally talking to me, even if you only did because of your mom. I miss you, Lily."

"I miss you, too," I barely whisper. "Happy Thanksgiving, Trevin."

"Happy Thanksgiving, Lily Pad."

Trevin New Year's Eve

It's 11:55 on New Year's Eve and the view from the very top of the Eiffel Tower sits before me like a painting. I feel like I should pinch myself for how crazy my life is now, but I know firsthand that this isn't a dream, I'm actually living out every single thing I ever wanted and more.

That is, except one thing. Lily has finally started to text me back and we've spoken a few times here and there, but that's it. I had to stop myself multiple times from begging her to come see me for Christmas. I knew it was too early. I'm still working on getting my best friend back, and I need to do that before I plead for her to visit me again.

So besides my late night phone call to her on Thanksgiving, I've pretended like the holidays didn't exist this year. Instead, I just focused on getting ready for our tour that we left for a few days ago.

Well, I guess that isn't exactly true. I did get her something for Christmas. After walking around every store I could think of, looking for that perfect gift, nothing said what I wanted it to say. Jewelry was so impersonal and other things gave her the wrong impression. So there I was, with more money than I've ever had and not a gift in sight that made sense. Who says money solves all problems? They obviously never had to earn someone's heart and trust back.

It needed to be something special; something that truly showed what she means to me. When the idea hit me, I called in a favor to my management at Sony Records, hoping they knew the right people and, of course, they were able to get me exactly what I needed. So, okay, maybe having money does help in these instances.

I was able to get her backstage passes and a meet and greet with the San Francisco cast of *The Nutcracker*. I wish I could have been there with her, but I didn't push that fact. When I sent the tickets, I also mailed a note saying I wanted her to bring her mom, Morgan or, God forbid, her boyfriend—but of course, I didn't say it that way.

Thank God she took her mom, and the pictures she emailed me were more than enough thanks. Seeing her face light up with the other dancers made every single thing worth it and proved to me why I'll work until the day I die to truly win her friendship back.

Now it's about to be 2000 and all I want to do is celebrate with her, even though she's across the entire world and it's only three in the afternoon there. I pull my phone out of my pocket, flip it open and make the international call.

"Hey, Trev," she answers with nothing but the happiness I've grown to love from her.

"Lily Pad, guess where I am?"

"Um…please don't tell me you're in the red light district with a hooker?" Even though she's joking, I can tell she's wary about talking to me. It's the way her voice comes up at the end. She does that when she's nervous.

"Come on, that was yesterday. Never two days in a row," I tease and she laughs in response. "No, seriously, I'm at the top of the Eiffel Tower and we're about to ring in the New Year here."

"Wow, Trev, that's so cool. I'm glad you called, too. This way, if everything crashes with this Y2K thing, I'll know firsthand and can go get my money out of the bank before the news hits," she teases, and I laugh knowing all that shit is crazy. "For real though, is it wild up there?"

"A little, but the band and a few other famous people—I have no clue who they are—were able to go up to a secluded spot, so it's not too bad."

I look around at the group I'm ringing in the new millennium with and shake my head. I turn back to the railing and look out at the view, knowing the only person important here is the girl on the other end of the phone.

"That's so amazing. I can't believe your life now."

"Right? I sure wish you were here, though. Are you hanging out with Conner tonight?"

She pauses before saying, "We broke up actually."

A rush of happiness pours through me but I keep it in. "Everything okay? Want to talk about it?"

"No, it's fine. He was starting to get on my nerves so—"

"Oh, hey!" I interrupt. "Sorry, but here we go. Start counting." We begin with ten and work our way down together. "Three, two, one, Happy New Year!" Fireworks start blasting over my head and the laughter I hear through the phone lights my insides as well. "You hear all that, Lily Pad?" I scream through the phone.

She laughs again. This time it seems real, like my Lily. "Yes, of course I do, Trevin."

"Happy New Year, Lilies."

"Happy New Year, Trevin. I'm not sure how your life could get any better in 2000, but I wish you the best."

"You too. I'll call you later, okay?"

"Okay, Trev. Have a safe night."

Lily *A few months later*

Sadness wraps around me as I make my way through the rows of flowers and headstones to where Julie's grave is situated. It's been three years since she passed, and I promised Trevin I would bring the flowers he picked out especially for her since he was still on the road.

Slowly, he's worked his way back into my world and we're becoming friends again, the way it was always meant to be. But that has nothing to do with me being here—I would come to visit today no matter what. Julie meant a lot to me too, and I can't help the tears that start to moisten my eyes as I approach.

When I hear someone rustling around ahead of me, I stop in my tracks, afraid to approach the commotion going on next to her grave.

My eyes meet with the unsettling yellow-tinted stare of Trevin's father. Since he's still my parents' neighbor, I see him on occasion, just in passing, but this is totally different. My pulse starts to race when he grunts his frustration, going back to attacking Julie's grave.

When I see him trying to deface the beautiful headstone Trevin purchased for his mom, rage sets in. I start yelling, "What in the world are you doing?"

"Get away from me, you little whore," he bites back.

I momentarily step back, completely shocked by his comment. I take a deep breath before continuing my strut toward him. I now know I will need reinforcements, quickly.

Dialing 9-1-1, I start to run toward him to stop his assault. "Stop! Don't do this!"

"This is all your fault. I know you had something to do with this. Trevin shouldn't have put this here. She didn't deserve this kind of monument. She was the worst thing that ever happened to me. I could've had so much more if she didn't tie me down with that asshole son of mine."

"9-1-1, what's your emergency?" the girl on the other end of the phone asks.

"I'm at McCallen Cemetery, and there's someone here trying to tear up a gravestone."

"Okay, I'll send a police officer out right away, stay on the phone with me until they get there. Are you near this person?"

She continues to ask me questions, but instead of answering, I'm more focused on stopping him.

He reaches back and between one moment and the next; he smacks me hard, the back of his knuckles making contact with my face. I fall to the ground just as a police car pulls up with sirens on.

The officer jumps out of the car, yelling for him to stop and put his hands in the air.

I whimper back, holding my palm against my cheek. A harsh pain rips through my face while I try to calm the frantic beating I feel taking over my chest.

"Fuck me," Dick grunts, holding his hands in the air and, thankfully, not putting up a fight. He knows there's nowhere for him to go.

The officer wraps Dick's hands around his back, securing them in cuffs while asking if I'm okay. Once he's in the back of the cruiser, the officer helps me to my feet, giving my face a once over and taking my statement for what just happened.

My nerves get the best of me and my shaking hands start to make it hard to function or think.

"Here, let's sit down on the bench," the officer says. We walk to the bench and he asks, "Is there anyone you can call? Do you have a car here?"

"I do, and yes, Officer, I can call someone. I know exactly who. I'll be fine. I promise. Thank you for coming when you did."

After asking me a few more questions and making sure I'm truly okay, he gives my shoulder a slight squeeze before getting up and leaving me to take Dick to the station.

I take a few deep breaths, working up the nerve to—for the first time— initiate talking to Trevin. I know because of what just happened, and who Dick is, he should be my first choice, but that's not why I'm calling him.

I'm calling him because I need him.

I need to hear his voice.

I need to hear him tell me it's going to be okay.

I need the reassurance that only my best friend can offer.

The second he answers, all the tension and pain of what just happened melts away, and I'm able to calmly tell him why I'm calling.

"Lilies, oh my God, that bastard. Are you okay? Please tell me he didn't hurt you? I'll kill him."

"No, Trevin, he didn't. I'm okay." And I am. After hearing his voice, I am okay.

Chapter 13

One chance is all I need.
To get what I want, to feel truly freed.
I'll do anything to make it right.
Only for you I'd join this fight.

- Trevin Allen

Trevin - Age 20

Shit is finally starting to slow down. For the last nine months, we've been on tour all over the fucking world, and I'm exhausted. While I was gone, I had my manager scout out a place of my own so I can finally have some peace from everything.

Living on the road, and then with the group of guys when I'm home, is getting to be too much. I need my space, I need my time alone, and more importantly, I need to figure out a way to get Lily to move down here.

She's in college at USF, and I'm trying to convince her to transfer to USC. She wants to get her teaching credentials. That's something that can be accomplished here just as easily as it could be done there. I know she doesn't trust me after the last time she came to visit, and I know I fucked up royally, but those days are behind us. I don't want her to move here to be with me—I just need my best friend back by my side.

I shouldn't have slept with her before I knew I was ready to commit. It was wrong to do it before I left, and even more so when she came to L.A. I had no business taking that from her at a time I couldn't offer her anything more. Toying with the relationship was wrong—I knew better, but I had to claim her anyway. It screwed up our friendship for a while, taking a lot of fucking work to bring us back, but I finally feel like we're there again, and I want to keep it that way.

She tells me about the guys she dates—all stuck-up pricks if you ask me—and teases me about pictures that end up in the tabloids about whoever I'm fucking this week. I don't know why anyone gives a shit who I stick my dick in. At twenty years old, I'm a rock star living the dream—it's all in fun. Surely, people don't expect anything different.

After parking my fully restored 1969 black Camaro in a driveway that I've never been in but am about to call home, I pick up my cell to call Lily.

"Honey, I'm home," I sing into the phone when she answers.

Laughing, she replies, "Yeah, what's it look like?"

"No fucking clue. Haven't gotten out of the car yet. I wanted to have you on the line the first time I enter our house."

"Trev, I'm not moving there," she protests.

"*Yet.* You're not moving here *yet*," I correct her.

"Whatever. Get your butt out of the car and go tell me all about *your* new place."

"Well, from the outside it looks like the photos they sent me—pretty secluded, tucked away with a long driveway leading up to it. I'll have to hire a gardener when I'm on tour—there's no fucking way I can keep up with this lawn."

"You've been a homeowner for all of five seconds and you're already bitching about up-keep. You rock stars, so lazy all the time." I love hearing her razz me—it reminds me of who we are.

I smile as I reach for the keys to my new place and unlock the door to my small slice of heaven. The place isn't outrageously huge, but it's exactly what I wanted. Something quiet, on a private beach where I can just be me.

My manager had the place decorated just enough that I would be comfortable, but not overdone making it look feminine. That will be Lily's job as soon as I convince her to move.

"So...how is it?" she asks.

"It's cool." I walk around, taking it all in, still in disbelief this is my life and I now own this thirty-three-hundred-square-foot house on the beach.

"Cool? Trev, my new nail polish is cool; your new album cover is cool. What you have is amazingly unbelievable. I can't wait to see it! I bet the pictures don't do it any justice."

Throughout the entire process, I've been sending Lily photos of places they had in mind for me, and she helped me choose this one. Who am I'm kidding—I only bought this one because it was her favorite.

"Only a few more days and you will. What time is your flight?" I ask as I flip on the light in my new bedroom. Just as I asked, the same three photos are tucked in the mirror of my new bedroom furniture. It's my little piece of home that keeps me grounded, and the only thing I said *had* to be done in terms of decor.

"My flight arrives at three. I've got to get going, though. Congrats on the house, Trev."

"Thanks, Lilies. See you then—oh, and don't forget my bracelets."

She laughs her goodbye as we hang up, and I throw my phone down on the bed. Walking closer to the mirror, I stare at the two women who will forever hold my heart in their hands.

Thursday takes forever to arrive, and finally, I'm at the airport to pick up Lily. I haven't seen her since I last left her at this same airport years ago, but I plan on making this experience a different one. This isn't us as torn lovers—this is us as best friends.

We've always had this silly relationship, so before I went to the airport, I stopped by the Disney store to pick up one of their stuffed turtles. Yes, I've seen *Finding Nemo*, and I loved that damn turtle. He was so much me and her combined into one character.

With my black cap pulled low so no one will recognize me, I make my way into the airport and over to a spot I can wait for her. A peace I haven't felt in months overwhelms me as my eyes meet hers from afar.

Her soft brown hair is pulled back just in front, showing an innocence I never see from the girls down here. It's refreshing to see a woman in her natural state of beauty, instead of being painted up with unnatural colors that cover their eyelids. Not Lily—she's never worn much makeup, and I'm glad the older she gets, the more I can tell she's not trying to keep up with what society thinks she should look like. She's the only true-to-herself person I know.

The look on her face proves she's just as apprehensive of this hello as I am, but I don't give a shit anymore. She's my best friend, and I will do whatever it takes to make this right. When she's close enough, I run up to her, pick her up and swing her around. Not caring who sees as her feet leave the floor and we twirl in circles. I have my best friend here, and all is right in the world again.

"Trevin, put me down!" she laughs as her bags fall to the floor.

I squeeze her tighter. "God, I'm so glad you're here."

We pull apart to look at each other as she whispers, "Me too."

"I got you something." I hold out the turtle with a big shit-eating grin on my face.

She laughs as she pulls it into her, giving it a big hug. "Thanks, Trev. Here, help me with my bags."

I pick them up and we make our way out to where my car is parked. Nothing can ruin today. If she weren't my gravity, I'd be floating away on cloud nine right now.

Our car ride home is just like old times. Thankfully, everything about my best friend is exactly as I remembered, and we're acting like we're twelve again.

I roll up my sleeves as I drive down the road and hear Lily gasp when she catches sight of my newest tattoo, which covers my right inner forearm.

"What's that?" she asks, grabbing for it before I can say anything.

Proud of what I've done to my body, I turn my arm over to reveal the ink that covers every bit of skin from my wrist to my elbow. It's all done in black and shaded ink. The sun's rays peek out of the clouds down onto a pond of lily pads with blooming flowers and my mom's name inscribed in the clouds.

I wasn't sure how she would take the tattoo I got to honor the two most important women in my life. The smile that covers her face and the tear forming in the corner of her eye tells me she knows the thought behind it, and nothing needs to be said.

At home, we walk to her room where her face lights up at the sight of what I've done. I had an interior decorator help me with this, just for her. Of course, I had to throw in my own touch—a candle resembling a lily pad sitting on her dresser. But she was able to find amazing photos of all different types of dancers and a bedspread with the perfect woman's touch. I wanted her to know this would always be her room—no one would ever step foot in it, much less sleep in it.

"Trevin, you're too much. I love it, though. Will I ever live down this damn nickname from you?"

I kiss her forehead. "Never. When we're ninety years old and my teeth are falling out, you'll still be my Lily Pad. Go ahead, get settled and I'll show you the rest of the place."

After giving her a tour of the house, we walk into the kitchen. I go to offer her a drink but realize I have nothing but beer in my fridge. "Shit, sorry. I guess I failed on that part. Want to go out somewhere?"

"No, not really. Let's just order a pizza and hang out like we used to."

I shut the fridge. "Sounds perfect."

And it is. Everything about having her here is perfect. We ordered a pizza and I sat on the floor with her lying on the couch, talking, laughing, and listening to music all night long—just like we used to.

At two am, I see her yawn out of the corner of my eye, making me realize the thought of sleep sounds good to me, too. "You ready to hit the sack?" I ask, standing up from the floor.

She yawns again, stretching out her arms before sitting up and gathering her cup from the table.

I take it from her. "Here, I got that. You head on to bed. I'll clean up."

She leans in to give me a quick hug goodnight and goes her separate way, to the opposite side of the house to the room I hope one day will truly be hers.

Lily

I wake up to a view of the beach to die for. I knew I'd love this house, but I wasn't sure how it would be with Trevin. My emotions were all over the place yesterday, and I'm relieved to be back to our old selves.

He's been asking me to move here, and I kept telling him there was no way I could. The truth is, I didn't know if I could handle it. But if me living here is anything like it was last night, I'm totally in. Not only is this house amazing, but I truly have my best friend back.

My parents couldn't afford for me to live off campus, and staying in the dorms as a senior is getting old. If I move down here, he said I wouldn't have to pay rent, and I could get a job to cover my food expenses.

I'm ready to take the plunge.

Jumping off the bed, I run out of my room, excited to share the news with him. I throw open his bedroom door only to find him passed out, lying flat on his stomach with his arms tucked around his pillow.

It's amazing how much he's changed. The slight beard, that he keeps trimmed so it's more of a stubble, covers his jawline, making the boy I once knew look more like a man. His body is still lean, but I can see a definition of muscle that is pulled taut with his arms gripping his pillow.

Once I'm finished ogling over the new him, I run straight to his bed, jumping on him to wake him up. "Get up, Trev!" I say, running my hand through his messy hair.

He growls in response before grabbing the pillow to cover his head. "Are you kidding me right now? Why are you waking me up so early? Maybe it's a good thing I can't convince you to move down here."

"Well sorry, too late for that. Come on, I have an appointment at USC to register for fall semester in a few hours, and I don't want to be late."

I wait for what I said to sink in, and only a few seconds later, he sits up, throwing the pillow off him. "Wait. What?"

"You heard me. If I'm going to move here, I need to make sure I get the classes I need to graduate in time," I say with a big smile on my face.

"Are you shitting me?" He throws his pillow directly at my face. "This whole time you planned on moving here and just weren't telling me?"

I laugh as I catch the pillow before it smacks me completely. "Sorry, I had to mess with you a little. So get up. Let's get going so we can check out the campus."

I hop off his bed and get ready for the day. Embarking on my new normal with Trevin, as friends, the way we're meant to be.

Registration goes smoothly, and I'm able to transfer all my classes so I can still graduate next year. Our weekend is better than I expect, and I'm ready to move here full time. I just need to head home to get my things. I'll have about a month before school starts, and the thought of lying on the beach, wasting my time away, sounds amazing.

I'm flying back today to get my things before driving back down. I couldn't convince Trev to come with me, even though he has the week off. He still wants nothing to do with his father or anything about our hometown. I hope to change that one day, but we have a while to go so I don't fight him on the subject.

My friend, Morgan, is planning on making the drive and staying with me for a few days, so I'm excited about our road trip.

When Trevin drops me off at the airport, I'm reminded of the last time I left him standing outside this very door and am so thankful that we've been able to move on. I lean over to give him a big hug. "Thanks again for everything this weekend. I'll see you in about a week."

"Yeah, call me to let me know you got home safely, and keep in touch. I'll make sure I have more food in the fridge when you get back."

I hit his chest. "Don't lie. No you won't. But don't stress about that. Food and groceries are on me from now on. It's the least I can do for letting me crash at your place."

"Lilies, I told you. It's your place, too. I'd have none of this if it weren't for you; don't forget that."

I smirk as all the memories of me teaching him guitar flood my brain and I smile, giving him another big hug. "I'm so proud of you, Trev." So much of our life is coming full circle. Everything about us, our childhood, our relationship—it's all coming into focus. My role in his life then and now. I've always loved him, and I always will, but maybe my purpose was to be his gravity, and not his lover.

"I know." He smirks. "Now get going so you can pack and get your ass back here."

I laugh, getting out of the car, and head to check in for my flight. As I wait, I decide to go to the newsstand to grab the new *Cosmopolitan* to read on the plane, but everything stops when I see the latest tabloid. Pictures of Trevin walking through an airport carrying the Crush turtle he gave me are splattered on the front page. There are three photos in all. One by himself, one with his arms wrapped around me, and one with us walking out together with the words: *Stone Cold's Playboy Guitarist Smitten Over Mystery Girl*. And there, in a small circle is an up-close picture of me smiling at him.

I never even saw a camera or anyone taking our picture. I can't help but wonder if this is my new normal—and whether or not I'm equipped to handle it.

Chapter 14

Living my dream
One day at a time
But to my heart it may seem
I've still got many hills to climb

- Trevin Allen

Lily – A few months later

The tabloids haven't stopped and I've officially made the cover four different times, everybody wondering who I am and where I came from. Once I started school, we noticed photographers following me around. His manager decided we should do an interview to stop the rumors and set the record straight—Trevin is still very much on the market and he and I are just friends.

I'm not going to lie, the *just friends* part hurts. It always will. The look the writers gave me during the interview made me feel inferior. I know they thought it was because I didn't fit the look of a rock star's girlfriend. The pity in their eyes made me want to tell them we've been there, done that, and at one time, he did want me, but really, none of it matters. It's not who we are now, and the interviews weren't about me, so I just sat back, answering any questions they asked me directly, but otherwise just going along with the flow.

The dance team at USC was already established, but I had my coach at USF contact the coach here, and thankfully, she gave me a private tryout. Making the team was the icing on the cake—after, of course, being here with Trevin. I've also been able to find a job as a dance instructor to advanced girls, ages nine to eighteen, and I love every minute of it, but lately, my focus has been entirely on school, one class in particular. I've always struggled with math, and now, it's about to push me over the edge.

No matter what my teacher says, it doesn't click in my head and frustration fills me to the brim. Now I'm sitting at our kitchen table on the verge of tears when I see I got yet another question wrong on my study guide. I've been working on the same problem for over an hour, trying to figure out where I made my mistake and getting nowhere.

The feeling of Trevin pulling my chin up to look at him breaks me from my depression. I didn't hear him come home, and when I look at the clock, I realize it's two thirty in the morning.

"What's wrong, Lilies?" His hazel eyes are hurting for me.

"Math. That's what. I don't get it. I do the right steps, but I keep getting the wrong answer. If I do this, I get to this point, then it goes with this but divides into this and—"

He stops me. "Breathe. It's okay. I think you need to take a break. You're going to make yourself crazy."

A quick burst of laughter escapes from my mouth. "It's too late for that…"

"Come on. Time for bed. You can work on it again tomorrow."

He tries to close my books and pull my chair out, but I stop him. "No, I can't. I have to study, because my test is in a couple of days and I have your concert tomorrow night and—"

"Lily Pad." He leans down to look me in the eye. "Don't make me carry you out of here. It's late. You need sleep." He tilts his head, daring me to question his threat.

"Fine!" I throw my hands on the table, push my chair away, and then I stomp off like an errant four-year-old, mad at their parents for making them go to bed.

I hear Trevin chuckle under his breath, and I can't help but turn to give him the dirty look I know is painted all over my face.

When the sight of my bed comes into view, I realize just how tired I am and I crawl in my overstuffed, pillow-top bed. Like a balloon slowly deflating and falling from the sky, my eyes close and I drift off to sleep in a matter of minutes.

When the sun shines through the blinds, filling my room with the morning rays, all I can think about is math. I need this class to graduate, and it would kill me if I had to retake it. When I roll over, the sight of my book sitting on my nightstand catches my attention. I sit up to see a stack of papers on top of it and a note written from Trevin:

Gravity

Here, try this. I looked over your notes and this book to work up a study guide that will teach you in a different way that you can understand. I hope it helps!

Trevin

I sit up in bed to wipe the sleep from my eyes and make sure I'm seeing this correctly. Sitting there are four pages of explanations to problems, all broken down to show each step. It's a crazy amount of work, but the best part is, I actually understand what he's done with each problem. I see where I was going wrong and how I was dividing where I should have been multiplying inside the parentheses before I divided.

Trevin was always good in school, especially math, which I'm sure helped in his ability to pick up music the way he did. His brain just works that way, and I'm amazed he was able to figure out my homework without ever taking a single class. The thought makes me wonder what his life would've been like if his mom hadn't died, but I remind myself everything happens for a reason. He's living his dream.

I can only imagine how late he stayed up working on this for me, so I don't wake him when I leave for class. Instead, I write him a note simply stating, *You're the best!* and secure it to the fridge so he doesn't miss it.

As I exit my class, I notice him sitting in the parking lot, leaning against his car with his hat pulled low so no one easily recognizes him, holding a coffee cup that I know is meant for me. Warmth fills my soul as I see my best friend standing before me, someone who has done so much for me, sitting here doing what he always does. With everything going on in his life, and getting ready for his tour along with a big show tonight, it warms me to see him here, making sure I'm all right.

His smile grows when he sees me walking toward him, and I can't help my arms as I throw them around his shoulders, hugging him tightly, almost knocking the coffee out of his hands but not caring one bit.

"You're amazing. I can't believe you did that for me!"

"Did it help?" he asks, squeezing me tightly.

"Yes, it totally did." I pull back to look at him directly, not releasing my grip, though.

Our faces are less than an inch apart, and my eyes fall from his hazel rounds to his pale pink lips. For a brief moment, my chest tightens and butterflies I haven't felt in years flutter around, but I quickly let go and grab my coffee instead.

"This is for me, right?" I taunt. He's been bringing me coffee almost daily for weeks now.

He laughs, shaking his head in disbelief at our momentary pull before stating, "You know it is. Now let's go. You can come help me pack and get everything ready for tonight."

Tonight is the first time I'm going to see Stone Cold live—not only live, but I get to have the entire experience as they perform to a sold-out show at the Staples Center. Their four-month tour starts this evening, so I'm going to be living alone for the next few months while he goes on the road.

We both hop in his car, and before he pulls out of the spot, I put my hand over his resting on the shifter and lean in to kiss his cheek. "Really though, thank you very much. I can't tell you how much I appreciate your help."

He nods. "It was nothing. Glad I could help." Then, he backs up and heads toward our house to get ready.

When we arrive at the stadium, he shows me their lavish bus. He talks about where they'll be and how things will go down. I followed his stops online for their last tour, so I get the gist. I know he truly leads his *real* rock-star life when he's away. A different girl greets his bed every night, while alcohol and drugs flood his body. He's kept me sheltered from this aspect of his life—never bringing girls to the house and keeping his friends away.

It all makes me a nervous wreck, but I have to remind myself I'm not his mother, or his girlfriend. I just smile and beg him to be careful. He assures me he always is, but the thought doesn't calm my nerves.

Sitting backstage, waiting for the show to start, females flood the area in droves, giving each band member their pick for the night. At this rate, they can have five women to each one of them. I'm forced to tamp down the jealousy threatening to consume me. My only place in his life is as his best friend—that role means I swallow the envy, walk up to him, kiss him on the cheek and wish him luck. "I'm going to go grab my seat so I'm all set when you go on."

He snakes his arm around my waist, pulling me to him. "You sure? You can hang out if you want."

I look around the room, at all the women who I definitely don't fit in with, then back to him. Regretfully, I acknowledge to myself I don't belong in this part of his world. "It's okay. You need time to focus and get ready. Break a leg out there." I smile, playfully backhanding his chest.

"Thanks. Here." He grabs one of the security guards. "Sean will take you to your seat. Enjoy the show."

I smile as I shyly walk away from the entire scene. When I turn to wave my final goodbye, I see one of the women has already staked her claim on Trevin. Her body's pressed firmly against his. I'm disappointed to see his hands moving up her tight, leather miniskirt. When she reaches up to kiss him, he turns his head quickly, denying her what she wants as his eyes look directly into mine.

Without thinking, my hand instantly goes to my mouth. The feeling of his lips flashes through my mind, only to remind me of the intense moment that lingered in the air this afternoon when I wanted them pressed against mine again. On my first visit to his house, Melissa had told me that Trevin didn't kiss anyone. I remember reading an article about him once that mentioned it as well, but I dismissed it, having kissed him more than a few times. I completely disregarded it as false information.

I can't be the only girl he's ever kissed.

Our eyes lock for a second too long before Brad, the lead singer, blocks our view. I turn to walk out of the room, heading to my seat to enjoy the show.

The band knocks it out of the park. Even though I'm not big on rock music, I've become big fans of theirs and I love watching Trevin in his element. The only time I see him truly smile is when it's just the two of us sitting doing nothing, and when he's on stage. He enjoys every minute, and it comes through in his performance. And I'm not going to lie—he looks damn sexy out there, playing his guitar with ease and singing back-up.

After the show, I'm escorted backstage to meet the band, and as I turn the corner, I see a woman wrapped around Trevin as he sits on the couch, downing a beer. When he sees me enter the room, he pats the girl's ass, telling her to get off him to make room for me to sit down. The girl glares at me as she moves on to the drummer who already has another woman on his lap.

His arm wraps around me, and when I feel sweat drip down my back, I swat him away. "Ew, Trev, you're all sweaty."

He laughs. "Why yes, I am. Most girls don't mind that."

"Well, it's a good thing I'm not like most girls," I spit back.

He leans in, wiping his sweaty face and hair all over my neck, teasing me. "Yes, it is a good thing you aren't like them." He pushes me against the couch so I'm lying flat on my back and he's covering me, wiping his sweat on me, cackling at his disgusting behavior.

"God, you're so gross," I yell as I push him away.

His lips quickly brush mine, not romantically, but a quick, friendly kiss as he gets up to grab a towel and throws it my way.

When I sit up to wipe myself, I notice women watching me, and no doubt questioning the fact that they just saw Trevin kiss me. They're probably wondering who the hell I am, and I'm not going to lie...I love the feeling it gives me, even if it was just a friendly kiss.

Surprisingly, within ten minutes, Trevin is grabbing my hand and escorting me out of the venue to a waiting limo in the back.

"Are we leaving so soon?" I ask.

"Yeah, this is my last night with you and my own bed for a long time. I want to take advantage. A bus with four guys for four months gets pretty nasty, pretty quick," he says with a laugh.

Even though I know the next few months will be filled with multiple women, the thought of him wanting to spend his last night at home with me makes me beam.

Once we're home, we pop some popcorn, put on a movie—that we don't watch five minutes of—and talk the night away until the sun starts to come up. When the bus stops by at five in the morning to pick him up, we say our goodbyes and go on about our lives. Apart for the next few months—he'll be on the road, and I'm going to bed to get some sleep before our big show tonight at the dance studio.

Chapter 15

No matter how far away I am
I'll always give a damn
I'd be there by car, plane, or tram
No matter how far away I am

- Trevin Allen

Lily – 21st Birthday

I woke up this morning with something only a rock star—or someone who has people who will do *anything* for him—could pull off. The crazy man had someone build a pond on our front porch using a child's blue plastic pool full of…you guessed it, lily pads. I'm lucky I didn't have my hands full as I opened the door, or I would have fallen right into it.

I wasn't sure if I wanted to call him and yell because of the silly nickname and how I almost broke my face on his birthday present, or just sit and smile at how thoughtful his surprise is. I have no idea how he was able to pull something like this off while he's on the road, but deep down, it genuinely made my day.

It's my twenty-first birthday, and I have plans to go out with my friend Jordan, who's on the USC dance team with me. Finding friends has been a little harder than I anticipated, primarily because of who Trevin is. Some people recognized me from the tabloids, making it difficult to figure out if they wanted to be my friend or just get close to him. My rule of thumb is if they mention Trevin within the first few minutes, I know they have ulterior motives.

Even though I'm not a big drinker, she's convinced me to go out with her to a bar tonight to celebrate. I just wish Trevin was here. He still has about a month left on the road and is God knows where right now. I've tried to keep up with the different cities, but he's traveling a long stretch of highway today between shows.

The intercom on the front gate buzzes and I know it's Jordan here to pick me up. The sound makes my stomach turn, and I hope I made a good decision giving her our address. This is the first time I've had anyone over. Even though Trevin says it's okay, I don't want to ruin his home life by blabbing where he lives to the wrong people.

She's heard of Trevin and Stone Cold, but thankfully, I'm the one who told her I live with him and she doesn't follow the band enough to know about our *friendship*.

I open the garage door since our front porch is still covered by my makeshift pond. "Hey, come on in. Let me grab my purse and we'll head out," I say, motioning for her to follow me.

We walk inside and she stops instantly. "Wow. Okay, I know you said you live with Trevin, and I know he's supposed to be some kind of rock god, but holy shit. You actually live here with him?" She looks around with her mouth open, staring at the open room lined with windows from floor to ceiling.

I sigh, shaking my head. "Yes, I live here with him. Did you think I was lying?"

"Okay, I'll admit, I looked him up, but I don't know…I guess I didn't fully believe you. I mean, look at you. You're not exactly a rock star kind of girl," she says, looking around the place and motioning to me.

I know she wasn't intentionally insulting me, but it still hurts since it's exactly what everyone else thinks of me.

"I know I'm not, but I told you, we've been best friends since we were eight. We grew up right next door to each other."

"I'm not gonna lie, I saw a ton of pictures of him and he's a hottie. You've really never hooked up with him?"

I give her a look, hoping she'll drop the subject. "It's not like that. Come on, let's go."

Thankfully, she lets it go and we head out to the bar. The place is crowded and we have to squeeze our way through the college boys trying to get at all the girls dancing around half dressed.

I look down at my normal jean shorts with a cute tank top and my flip-flops. I don't fit in with the girls here, yet somehow that makes me happy. The more I stare at them, the more I see how silly they look, putting themselves on display. I don't want to ever be like them, and if that's all guys want, then I'm content being single.

We make our way to the bar and Jordan waves down the bartender, who spots her flowing blond hair and walks straight up to her with a smirk covering his face. He's cute, so I sit back to watch Jordan and take notes on how she flirts. I've never been much of a flirt, but if I'm ever going to get a boyfriend, I'm going to have to learn.

"Excuse me," I hear someone whisper into my ear. "Can I buy you a drink?"

I turn to see a tall guy, clean shaven with dark hair that's styled so it's messy but cute.

"Thank you, but my friend here is already ordering for us." I smile sweetly, motioning to Jordan. She's still wrapped up in conversation with the bartender who doesn't look like he's going to be making our drinks anytime soon.

He laughs. "Yeah, I wouldn't count on that if you want it quickly. Here…" He grabs my hand, pulling me to another part of the bar and getting the attention of one of the other bartenders.

"So what can I get you?" he asks in my ear again.

"I'll take a cosmopolitan," I reply.

I'm totally lame. I have no clue what to order, so I went with the stereotypical female drink from *Sex and the City*. Inside, I shake my own head at my decision.

He orders our drinks and turns to hand it to me. "Here you go."

"Thank you," I respond before bringing the drink to my lips to take a sip.

"Do I get to know your name?" he asks, placing his hand on my hip to bring me in closer to him.

"I'm Lily." I speak into his ear so he can hear me over the crowd, which might not have been a good idea. His grip held me even closer to him instead of moving back to where I was before.

The lack of personal space makes me uneasy initially, but I take a deep breath and decide to enjoy this guy. He seems nice and he's certainly cute.

I've dated here and there, but I always end it before it goes anywhere past a month or two. None of them have felt right, or gave me that feeling deep inside that girls talk about. I need to get out of my head and try to date someone. I know I'm not getting any younger and I'd like to get married and have kids one day.

"What brings you here tonight?" he asks. Our bodies mere inches apart, and the way his warm breath dances against my neck sends chills of excitement down my spine.

"Actually—" I stop when I feel my phone vibrate in my pocket. I take it out and he releases me a little to give me room to look at it.

An instant smile fills my face when I see it's a message from Trevin:

Happy bday Lily Pad. Wish I could be there. Did you guys go to that Fire Falls place?

I type back a quick response:

Yea, we just got here.

Then I put my phone in my pocket and look back to the man who's still waiting for my reply. "Sorry, but yes, it's my birthday," I say with a shy smile on my face.

"Well, happy birthday, pretty girl." He pulls me back into him. "I'm Joe."

My lips tilt into a small smile. "Hi, Joe. What about you? What brings you out tonight?"

"Same thing. My boy over there"—he points to a crowd of guys hollering while doing rounds of shots—"it's his birthday as well and we're here to celebrate."

"Hmm, small world, with birthdays and all." I bring my drink to my mouth to avoid any awkward silence since I have no clue what else to say.

My phone vibrates again and I grab it, knowing it's Trevin:

Be safe. Don't get ice cream with anyone unless he looks a lot like me, then please, go right ahead.

I reply:

Oh, don't worry about that. You know I don't live the crazy promiscuous lifestyle you do.

Before I can put my phone back in my pocket, he replies:

Ouch, that hurt, a little ;-)

I smirk and I put my phone back in my pocket when I hear Joe ask, "Do you have anyone special you're talking to?"

I look up, surprised. "I'm sorry. No. I mean, yes. But no. He just wanted to say happy birthday."

"So is he your boyfriend?"

"No, just a friend."

He pulls me closer to him again. "Good. Can I be your friend, too?"

I gaze at him shyly, tempting a sexy smile. "Maybe. Tell me about yourself?" I ask as I bring my drink up for another sip.

Before he can reply, I feel an arm wrap around my shoulder, pulling me away from Joe.

I turn quickly to stop whoever thinks they can touch me until I see Trevin pulling me into him. Before I can say anything, his lips are on mine. I'm shocked to see him, but his soft, warm lips feel so amazing that we both stand there, pressed against each other. I feel a moan release from him and his mouth opens, slipping his tongue into mine, and I welcome him with my own sigh of relief.

Nothing feels as good as him pressed against me. It's been months since I've seen him, and the fact that he's here, with me on my birthday, brings tears to my eyes.

We kiss for probably a minute too long, running our tongues softly against each other's. When he nibbles on my lower lip, I feel his reluctance to pull back, but finally, he does. His forehead drops to mine, and he lets out a long, steady breath as he holds me tightly.

"Sorry, I got carried away there," he says with trepidation.

I look up at him. "I guess I did, too."

I start to move my hands up to my mouth to wipe my lips, but he stops me short. "No, don't wipe it off," he says before he pulls farther away from my front but tucks me into his side. He turns to Joe and says, "Sorry dude, but she's with me tonight."

Joe stands up. "Fuck you, *dude*," he spits back at Trevin as he gets up from his seat to go back to his friends.

"Were you seriously talking to that asshole?"

"I was, what's wrong with that?"

"So many things. Come on." He grabs my hand to pull me out of the bar.

"Wait, my friend's here." I pull him back to where Jordan is still talking to the bartender. I walk up to whisper in her ear, "Hey, look who just showed up?"

She turns to see Trevin standing there, sticking out like a sore thumb with his black spiky hair and worn out black cut-off vest in a bar with a bunch of preppy co-eds. I'm even thrown off a little more when I notice a huge guy covered in tattoos eying anyone around Trevin, giving them a look that says *Don't even try*, and believe me, they all back down and look away instantly.

His arm catches my attention and I can tell he's gotten a new tattoo he seems to have left out of our conversations over the last few months.

It takes Jordan a second to put two and two together, but when she does, she jumps up from her seat. "Holy shit, is that Trevin?"

The bartender looks up and gives Trevin the biggest smile I've ever seen. He's star-struck, and I can tell he knows exactly who he's looking at. "Shit, man. Trevin. You're my fucking idol. Can I make you a drink?"

Trevin smirks. "Thanks, man, but I'm cool. Just came to pick up my birthday girl."

I lean in to give Jordan a hug goodbye. "You okay if I take off with him?"

"Are you kidding me?" She looks at Trevin, who's looking directly at me like there's no one else in this entire bar. "How is he here? Isn't he supposed to be somewhere on the east coast right now?"

I look at him, the reality of him being here finally sinking in. "Yeah, he is. I guess he wanted to surprise me for my birthday."

She smirks. "Just friends my ass."

I tilt my head. "I told you, it's not like that." I hoped she was wrapped up with her bartender and didn't just see us kiss.

"Uh-huh. Okay. Have fun with your hottie rock-star *friend*."

We leave the bar hand in hand and he walks me to a running car that's waiting at the front door and the scary guy with Trevin hops in as our driver, giving the bouncers a nod as he walks by. I slide in back, staying on my side of the car but grab his knee as he reaches his arm out so he's touching my shoulder.

"How are you here?" I ask.

"Come on, I wasn't going to let you celebrate your birthday without me." The hand lingering on my shoulder rubs small circles nonchalantly as we talk.

"But don't you have a show?"

"Yeah, tomorrow in Chicago. I have to fly out at four am."

I look at my watch to see it's just past ten. "That's in six hours. Why would you come all this way for only a few hours?"

"To be with you." He shrugs as he moves his hand off my shoulder and leans forward to tell the driver to take us home.

I sit back, amazed at the man Trevin has become. I can't get over how sweet he is to fly all this way, just to surprise me, and spend a few hours with me on my birthday.

We're dropped off at our house and Trevin almost falls to the floor, laughing at the sight of our front porch covered with the makeshift pond. "That turned out awesome!" he says, full of pride from his surprise.

I hit his arm. "You're lucky I didn't fall face first into it. They put it right on our front door."

"I know, I told him to. But I knew I'd be here to clean it up."

"And that's a good thing because it would have stayed there until you got back."

He starts to push the sides down to let some water out so he can pull it off the porch. I grab my phone to take pictures, and of course, he looks up, giving me his crazy, one-eye-lifted rocker face and holds up devil horns with his other hand while sticking his tongue out. I shake my head, laughing at him and his crazy ways.

Once we make it into the house, he stops, taking a deep breath before walking to the couch and plopping down with his right arm and leg resting on the back.

He sighs. "It's so good to be home."

I throw a pillow at him. "I know you just used my birthday as an excuse to come back. You just missed that couch."

It's true. It has become his favorite place, and whenever he's home, he lays right there, in that same position, either watching TV or lazily playing his guitar.

He throws the pillow back at me, sitting up to give me room to sit. "So tell me about school."

"No, my turn first. Tell me about this new tattoo I saw." I reach for him and pull his body closer. It covers his entire right arm, from his shoulder to right above his wrist so his bracelet still stands out on its own, but blending perfectly with his original one. The design is intricate—a snake wraps around from top to bottom and a Salvador Dali looking clock fades down an old-school looking hourglass. Directly in the middle of it all is one single lily. The snake sinks his fangs into an apple resembling the forbidden fruit.

I run my fingers over the flower before looking up at him. He's looking right at me like he wants to say something but can't open his mouth. We stare at each other, neither of us saying a word, before he gets up to change the subject.

"Yeah, it's no big deal. Some guy on tour with us is a tattoo artist. He did it for me about a month ago. So what's there to eat in this place? I'm starving."

He walks to the fridge while I'm left contemplating the meaning of his latest ink. This is the third tattoo he's gotten, and every one of them points to me somehow, but he's never mentioned their meanings. I'm almost afraid to ask. I don't mention us, or what we mean to each other. We're in such a good place right now and my heart would break if I lost him again. Every piece of me wants him to be mine, but not at the expense of losing him altogether.

We spend the rest of the night just like we have so many times before, with him on the floor, me laying on the couch behind him and talking the night away. At two thirty in the morning, a car comes to take him back to the airport. It's the best birthday I've ever had, yet it was the same night I've experienced hundreds of times before.

Chapter 16

You may say you have a boyfriend.
But I know that won't be the end.
Your future will forever be mine.
To get there, I'll cross every line.

- Trevin Allen

Lily – Age 22

I've been seeing Nathan for a few months now after we met at a frat party that Jordan dragged me to. I felt like a fish out of water until he came over, sitting with me all night and talking about school, dance and life in general. He never once bothered me about not having a drink in my hand so I knew he was someone I could feel comfortable around and even wanted to get to know better.

Tonight's the first time he's coming to my place to hang out for more than just a few minutes. He hasn't wanted to before, and I can only imagine it's because of Trevin. I think Trevin intimidates him, even though I keep telling him he's just a normal guy.

He doesn't get the relationship Trevin and I have. Of course I lied about our brief past together, but he says us living together makes him uncomfortable. It's been the only fight we've had, but it seems to be coming up more and more frequently, and I'm beyond annoyed by it.

Thus my reasoning for having him come here tonight. I figure if he hung out at our place more then maybe he would start to believe me. He'll see that

Trevin and I have different lives and it's not that big of a deal we live together. Honestly, it's my last ditch effort to see if he's someone I still want to be with, because whoever I date has to be okay with my friendship with Trevin.

When I walk in from school, Trevin is sitting on the back porch, playing his guitar, so I head out to remind him to be on his best behavior. He seems to get enjoyment out of making Nathan uncomfortable and it has to stop.

"Okay, Trev, you're on your best behavior tonight," I say as I walk up beside him.

"I still don't know what you're talking about. I'm always nice to Dathan."

"His name is Nathan. Come on. For me? I like this guy and he's going to be hanging out a lot more since you're heading out on tour. I need someone to keep me company in this big house while you're gone."

"Really? Like that douche, *Nathan*, could do anything to protect you. What kind of badass goes by *Nathan*? At least shorten it to Nate."

"Trevin!" I yell, putting my hands on my hips in anger.

"Fine, I'll be nice. I promise…" He sings *promise* while strumming his guitar and giving me his puppy dog eyes.

I can't help but smirk, even though I attempt to keep my lips shut and show him I mean business.

"Come here, Lily Pad." He tries to change the subject. "Sit right here." He points to the front of the lounge chair he's sitting on. "Let's teach you how to play, finally."

I laugh. "Are you kidding me? Don't you remember how horrible I was?"

He smirks. "Yeah, how can I forget." He winks. "But that was years ago. Come on, let's try again."

When I sit down in front of him, he reaches up, grabbing me and pulling me back to him. He wraps his legs on either side of me so I'm tucked into his chest and the guitar is sitting on my lap.

I feel the warmth of his arms as they move around my waist before placing his hands on me and showing me where to hold the guitar.

"Now bend your fingers around the neck so you can reach the sixth string just as easily as the first string." I do as he tells me to. "Now, with your other hand, hold this pick." He places a pick in between my fingers. When we touch, I swear a shock of electricity flies from my fingertips to my toes and I have to close my eyes and take a breath to calm everything inside me down. "Now start by just strumming down, trying to hit every string as you move down."

"Okay, like this?" I say as I move down the strings. I feel his laugh more than I hear it. I turn to face him over my shoulder. "Stop laughing," I say, even though I can't keep a straight face and break out in a small giggle.

"I never thought just moving down the strings could sound bad."

I turn to hit him with my hand that's holding the pick, but he stops me short by grabbing it with his own. His fingers intertwine with mine, bringing them to his lips and holding them there for a brief moment in an apology.

"I'm sorry, am I interrupting something?" Nathan asks, storming out onto the back porch.

I jump, pulling my hand from Trevin and putting the guitar on the end of the lounge chair. Smiling my biggest smile for Nathan, I pretend nothing's going on.

Because nothing was going on. Right?

I shake my head, focusing on Nathan's anger and already feeling like this might be the end. "Hey, babe. I didn't know you were here." I try to fake a smile.

"Yeah, how could you hear me knock when you're out here with him, all cuddled up?"

"Sorry, man." Trevin gets up. Holding his guitar by the neck, he walks by us without making eye contact. Just as he passes by Nathan, he whispers, "How could I resist, though?"

Nathan's eyes get big, and I have to admit, mine do too, but I try my hardest to hide it, blowing the entire situation off and grabbing Nathan's hands. "Come on. Let's make dinner. I went shopping for everything we need."

Thankfully, Trevin grabs his keys, heading out for the night and lets Nathan and I hang out alone. After he leaves, Nathan calms down, and admittedly, so do I.

I start to open the chicken just as Nathan slides in around me, putting his arm around my waist and kissing my cheek. He's always so sweet in his hellos, and I love that he's making up for his missed opportunity from outside.

Our conversation flows freely as he tells me about his day and we move in sync around the kitchen. He reaches into his bag for a bottle of wine, holding it up and saying, "I thought a nice dinner called for a nice bottle of wine."

I let out a quick laugh before I bring it back in, seeing he's totally serious so I turn around to hide my face and start opening up cupboards. "That's nice of you, but I honestly don't know if we have any wine glasses."

"You're not serious are you?" he chastises.

"Well, you know I'm not much of a drinker, and I don't think I've ever seen Trevin with a glass of wine." I laugh.

"Well, then I guess he doesn't have as good of taste as I thought. Let me look."

He looks high on the shelves from behind me and reaches in, pulling two wine glasses from the way back with a smile on his face. "Jackpot," he says with pride.

I look at the dark red wine he's pouring, wondering if it's something I'll enjoy. People talk about wine like it's this prestigious thing and it's not normally something college guys drink, at least I didn't think so.

He holds up his glass, motioning for me to do the same and taps his with mine. "To us."

I smile sweetly, clinking them together and bringing it to my mouth. I slowly let the dark liquid fill my mouth and choke as it burns and causes a strange bite low in my throat.

He laughs at my inexperience, which slightly annoys me. He knows I'm not a drinker and the frown on my face must be evident when he stops and tries to show me the ins and outs of drinking wine. I go along with it, just to appease him and try to focus on making our dinner.

Once we've eaten and have the kitchen all cleaned up, we head to my room to watch TV.

We're not twenty minutes into the movie and it's already forgotten. He moved quickly, making sure all our clothes are off instead. This isn't the first time we've been together, but it's the first time in my room, and it adds a whole new dimension—a completely different element.

This is technically Trevin's home, and that thought makes me almost feel guilty for being intimate with my boyfriend here. It's silly, but I can't shake the notion.

I need to push Trevin out of my mind and focus on Nathan. But every thought I have turns from Nathan to Trevin. As I consciously breathe in, I think of Nathan's eyes and his soft lips, but my mind drifts off to Trevin's, and the mental comparison of the two smacks me upside the head. Refocusing, I reach down, wrapping my hand around his dick and note it's not as big as Trevin's from what I remember.

No matter what I do, every thought comes back to my best friend.

I shake my head to clear my mind, not thinking that my lips were linked to his.

"What? I'm sorry," Nathan states, pulling away from me.

"Huh? Why are you sorry?" I reach up for him.

"Because you were just shaking your head like you were saying no."

"What? No, nothing like that. Come here." I place my hands on either side of his face, pulling him down to me.

He reaches over to grab a condom from his wallet just as my door swings open.

"Honey, I'm home! Can I cuddle in here tonight?" Trevin says as he steps into the room.

We both jump to cover ourselves. "Trevin, what the hell?" I yell, grabbing the comforter.

"Fuck, he's still here?" Trevin says with overly animated disappointment.

"Yes, he's still here. How could you have missed his car in the driveway?"

I'm irritated. "Why did you just barge in here without knocking?"

"Yeah, man, can you please give us some privacy here?" Nathan says as he makes sure I'm fully covered.

"No worries, I've seen it all before," Trevin admits, not making any move to leave.

"Trevin, get out!" I yell.

"Whatever," he says as he turns to leave. "I'll be out here when he leaves. Come hang out, okay, Lilies?"

He shuts the door and Nathan looks at me, clearly pissed off about the entire situation. "What does he mean he's seen it all before?"

"Don't worry about him. Here…where were we." I reach for him, hoping we can continue what we started just so I don't have to explain, but he pulls back farther.

"Have you slept with him?"

I look down, not wanting to answer because I'm not willing to lie, and he won't like the truth.

"I'm sorry, Lily, but I can't do this. I told you I didn't like your relationship as it was, but knowing you guys have slept together is too much. I'm out."

He gets up, putting his clothes back on as I reach for my robe. I'm not sure what I can say or even if I want to make the situation better, so I just sit quietly. Really, I'm done having the same fight. I'm not ending my friendship with Trevin, so I guess it's best that Nathan leaves.

He stops at the door before opening it. "Wish this could have been different, Lily."

"Me too," I say, not trying to stop him.

He opens the door, only to see Trevin standing right outside with a smirk he's trying to hide.

"Aw, are you leaving so soon?" Trevin taunts.

"Fuck off," Nathan surprises me by saying and walks past him and out of our house.

Trevin comes in and jumps on my bed so he's sitting beside me. "Sorry, was that because of me?" he says with his puppy dog look again, I seem to be getting that a lot today.

I grab my pillow, throwing it at his face. "Yes, that was because of you. You knew exactly what you were doing. Don't deny it!"

"Me?" he questions, bringing his hands up to his chest acting surprised.

"Trevin! That was messed up, even for you. Why did you barge in here?"

"Come on, you can't actually be into that guy?"

"Well, I was," I try to say in a demanding tone but fail and look down, playing with the strings of my robe. I don't even believe what's coming out of my own mouth. Why is finding a true boyfriend so hard for me? I shake my head and stand up, turning my back to him and walking to my dresser to pull out a pair of underwear from my drawer with that thought fueling my anger again.

"Are you seriously upset with me?"

"Yes, Trevin, I am," I say, thrusting my body back to face him and slapping the pair of panties down on my leg in frustration.

"Over that guy? Come on, you weren't that into him. I could even tell that."

"That's not the point, Trevin, it's just the fact that I want *someone*. You get to go off and do whatever you want"—I put my panties on and pull them up under my robe as I go off on my rant—"with whoever you want and I try to date a sweet honest guy and you step in, trying to ruin it." I walk past him to my closet.

"Okay, I'm sorry. But that guy's a douche. You can do better."

"How would you know? You never even got to know him," I bite back while I pull on a pair of jeans.

"I just know you, and I could tell. Call it man instinct. That guy wasn't the one for you."

"Ugh!" I drop my robe so my bare back is to him as I slip on my bra. "Trevin, you are so frustrating. I want a boyfriend. I want that someone in my life. You're leaving again on tour and I'm all alone in this house."

He's quiet, so after I slip my shirt over my head I turn to him, standing like I'm ready for more of a battle. But the look on his face pulls on my heart strings, and when his shoulders slump slightly forward, I take a deep breath and sit next to him.

"Can you just for once let *me* decide if they're good for me or not? At this rate, I'll be the lonely cat woman who tells everyone how she once was best friends with a major rock star, but no one will believe me because I'm batshit crazy from being alone all the time." I laugh at my own joke.

"Come on, Lily Pad, you know it won't be like that. You'll create a new kind of crazy old lady with all the ponds you take care of." He jokes, hitting my shoulder.

I laugh, grabbing the pillow next to me and hitting him with it before he easily rips it out of my hands.

"Seriously though, I'm sorry. I'll try to stay out of your life, at least a little bit more." He winks. "I promise. Now come on." He puts the pillow down beside him and starts to get up. "Let's go get some ice cream, just like old times…" He wiggles his eyebrows, never letting go of the sexual innuendo. I roll my eyes thinking about my mom every time it comes up.

I go to throw the pillow at him again and he stops me.

"I was trying to *get ice cream* and you interrupted," I respond, shaking my head at him with my eyes wide open, trying to prove my point.

"That's because you only get ice cream with me," he states with a smirk on his face and a wink to his eye.

He reaches his hand out to help me up and I take it. I should be mad at him, but I guess I know deep down Nathan wasn't the one. Trevin probably just saved me from wasting a lot of time, but a sadness I can't seem to shake still rattles around inside me.

Shaking off the feeling, we head out of my room, going to get ice cream for real this time.

We pull up to Baskin Robbins in his Camaro, and instantly, people look our direction, but not because of who he is, rather because of his car. He's so proud of it and loves the low rumble it makes when it's idling.

The smaller beach community we live in doesn't pay much attention to who Trevin is, so once we step out of the car, all eyes go back to their business as we walk into the building, and we're hit instantly with the strong smell of sugar overload.

He orders his favorite—cookies and cream in a sugar cone—but not me. I'm a fan of the plain cone. There's nothing like that last bite that finishes the experience with the perfect mixture of cone and ice cream that leaves a smile on my face.

Afterward, we walk back out front to sit at the tables to enjoy the early summer night. With his back to the front door, I notice a younger teenage boy walk in, eyeing Trevin and turning to his mom when he figures out who he's truly looking at. I love watching the amazement in people's eyes when they look at him in absolute awe—it's the same feeling I have when I see him, but I know it's in a different way.

Even though Trevin is talking about his upcoming tour, I can't take my eyes off the kid. I can tell he's struggling—wanting to approach Trevin but too scared to do so. I can't hide the smile on my face anymore, and finally, Trevin turns around to see what I've been staring at this entire time.

When he sees the young boy staring, he smiles and waves him over. The excitement and surprise that flashes on the kid's face makes me let out a loud laugh. He freezes, pointing to himself and saying, "Are you talking to me?"

Trevin laughs and says, "Yeah, come here. What's your name?"

The boy jumps and walks toward Trevin, taking a deep breath and obviously trying to hide his nerves. "I'm…I'm Thomas. You're Trevin, aren't you?"

"Sure am. Here"—he pulls a chair from the table next to us over to our table—"have a seat with us."

Again, the look on his face is priceless. I love when Trevin does this. Any chance he gets to talk to kids who are obvious fans, he does. He says he does it because he remembers when he was in their shoes and what he would have given to meet some of his favorite band members. Honestly, I think he loves it just as much as the fans.

"Oh, man. Wow…I mean, thanks, man." The poor kid fumbles around, grabbing his seat and stumbling on what he should say.

"This is my best friend, Lily Pad," Trevin says with a wink.

"I'm Lily, nice to meet you, Thomas," I respond but he's not interested in me, so I lean back in my chair, letting Trevin and his fan have their moment. They discuss the band's new album and how this kid plays the guitar, hoping to be as good as Trevin someday.

This right here is what I love about Trevin.

He has such a big heart, just like his mom did. Take away his silly, crazy antics and this is what you get. A man who remembers what it was like to be a fan and always wanting to do the right thing, only because he knows it's right. Not because he's trying to prove a point or make some cover of a magazine. No matter how famous he gets, he's still himself deep down, and I know Julie would be so proud of him now.

How will any guy I date ever compare to him? How could they? He's truly one of a kind.

My kind.

"Okay, Thomas." His mom walks over, putting her hand on his shoulder. "Let's leave this gentleman alone so he can get back to his night with his girlfriend."

Trevin winks in my direction before looking up to the woman. "Really, it's no trouble at all. I was him a few years ago."

"Can I get a picture with you, Trevin?" Thomas asks.

"Of course!" Trevin happily gets up as the boy's mom pulls out her phone to take a photo. The smile stretching far across Thomas's face is contagious, and I can't help but grin at our new friend. Trevin's face is what gets me the most—he has the same smile spreading wide, from ear to ear. And my heart melts even more.

Thomas leaves and Trevin turns his attention back to me. "What's that smile for?"

"I just love watching you with fans."

"What? That kid was cool," he says in defense.

I laugh as I pop my favorite bite in my mouth and savor the flavor, letting out a subtle moan of satisfaction in the process.

When I come back from my trance I notice Trevin laughing at my little show. "Now that's getting some *ice cream*."

"Stop." I hit his arm. "Besides, I tried that earlier and you stopped me, remember? I have to get pleasure elsewhere now."

"Hey, I can fix that very easily," he teases.

"Just get in the car." I laugh.

Instead of heading straight home, Trevin turns the opposite direction, heading for Highway 1 to drive around and enjoy the coast with the music blaring through the speakers. The radio station's having an old-school night, so when *Paul Revere* by the Beastie Boys comes on, we jump at the chance to turn it up, singing, "Now here's a little story…"

Both of us spit the lyrics without missing a beat, and I can't help but laugh when Trevin raps about a wiffle ball bat with spirited motions right before an overly animated, "Sooooo."

By the end of the song, my cheeks hurt from smiling and my voice cracks from singing so loud. It's been years since we sang like that, and he's the only person I would ever dare show that side of me. It feels good and I wish I could be free like this more often.

I look up to see the light of the moon illuminating the break in the waves against large rocks on the shore. When Trevin spots a turnout in the road, he pulls over, turning off his lights but leaving the radio loud so we can hear it as we get out of the car to enjoy the view.

Thoughts of how different my night turned out than when it started cross my mind, but knowing there is nowhere else I'd rather be puts nothing but a smile in my heart.

When I reach the front of Trevin's car where he's already sitting, I can't hide the happiness seeping out of me, and the look on his face makes it better.

We lean against his car, sitting in silence that's more comfortable than it would be if I were here by myself. When his hand reaches for mine, entangling our fingers together, it just makes my night even more perfect.

No crazy ideas run through my mind from his motion, though. This is us. We'll sit like this on the couch, watching TV or him listening to music while I study. The night is no different than any other until the radio starts to play Bush's *Glycerine*.

Thoughts of our first kiss run through my mind. When his fingers start to stroke the back of my hand, holding it slightly tighter, I know the same memories are entering his, too. For the first time in a long while, I allow myself to remember what his lips felt like that night. The moment he got up to move onto my bed and I stopped him, kicking myself for years afterward for doing so.

I wanted him so badly that night. The first time his lips met with mine, I felt everything in my body light up in a way I've never thought possible. I said his name in desire, a deep need that overwhelmed my senses, but he took it the wrong way, instantly getting up and leaving my house without looking back.

I tried to tell him to come back, that I wanted more, but he apologized first, acting like it was a mistake, so I pushed my thoughts aside, trying to ignore the growing feelings I had for my best friend for years to come.

But now here we are. Back to the same feelings with the same damn song. Suddenly, I feel like I'm fourteen again, and my heart is beating so strong I'm surprised he doesn't feel the beat running through my veins.

When his thumb grazes mine, I glance down before looking up at him. Through the moonlit night, I see the same young boy I met so many years ago, only now I see the man I always knew he'd be. His light stubble covers his hard jawline and his eyes darken as they take me in with the same look of confusion, fear, and desire I know I have written all over my face.

An urge I've never felt threatens to deprive me of the air I need. When my tongue nervously slips out to lick my suddenly dry lips, I watch as his eyes follow every centimeter I cover, parting his in response. My head fights with my heart when I feel his body get closer to mine, pulling me into him with a force I can't deny. Our eyes meet once again, both silently asking if this is smart, if we want the same thing, if it's worth the risk, if it's the right time. Neither of us willing to move forward but not willing to stop this force pushing us together.

I feel his breath on me, mere centimeters away, so I lick my lips one more time right when an obnoxious tone fills the silence around us. We both jump when we realize the phone in his pocket broke the trance the moon had put on us.

Like nothing ever happened, we both part, moving to our separate spaces. He answers the phone and I take a deep breath, trying to fill every raging nerve in my body with calming air.

"Yeah, Arnie, I'm here with Lily, what's up?" Trevin says into the phone, looking down and kicking the dirt and rocks slightly.

There's silence for a while, so I look up to Trevin now staring at me. The blankness overtaking every part of him worries me to my core.

Instantly I rush to him. "What's wrong?"

He blinks away his thoughts. "Okay. Thanks for the call," he says and hangs up.

"Trevin, what is it?"

He moves away from me and walks to the edge of the cliff. Opening his arms wide, he lets out a deep yell that comes from his toes. The sound reverberates off the shoreline and bounces back through the hills around us, replaying his anguish. I can tell it cleanses his soul, but a fear rips through me and I need to know what just happened.

Reaching down to his feet, he picks up a handful of rocks and starts to throw them one at a time with every ounce of energy he has into the ocean, cursing under his breath with every thrust of his arm. He bends down for more rocks but instead falls to his knees.

With trepidation, I walk toward him, keeping silent until he's ready for me.

His hands run from the back of his head to his front, grabbing at his hair over and over again as he grunts his frustration more to himself than to me or the ocean.

I dare to approach a little closer and wait until he sits back in a normal position with his arms resting on his legs and his head down. Cautiously, I wrap my arms around his, putting my head on his shoulder, waiting silently for him to fill me in.

Fighting his inner battle, he calms his breathing, letting out a *fuck* under his breath before resting his head against mine.

"What happened, Trev?" I whisper, rubbing my hand against his.

"It's my dad. He…" He takes a deep breath before continuing. "He died of liver failure." His voice cracks when he admits the truth, and I know telling me what happened has ripped his heart back open.

"When?" I ask.

"This morning. He's been in the hospital for a few days, though."

I knew his dad had reached out a few times, but Trevin didn't want anything to do with him. Now I wonder if he knew how serious it really was. The way he's reacting to the news proves he's struggling with that decision.

"Are you okay?" I ask, leaning down, trying to look into his eyes.

He blinks away a tear. "Yes… No… Fuck, I don't know."

"It's okay, Trev. I get it. He was still your dad."

"But was he? I remember him as the asshole who caused my mother's death, who made my life a living hell…who bought me a hooker for my sixteenth birthday." I can't help but flinch in surprise, causing him to laugh. "Yeah, never told you that one. Don't worry." His lips show a hint of a smile, as he nudges my body with his. "I didn't do what you think. I promise you were my first."

My body goes from sad to nervous in a matter of seconds. After the moment we shared just before his phone rang, hearing his dad died, then talking about our past together, I feel like things have been thrown out like a game of fifty-two card pickup and I'm frantically searching for the ace of hearts.

Trying to bring things back to what's important, I ask, "So what now? Do you know if he wants to be buried or cremated? Did he have a will?"

He laughs in irritation. "I have no clue. I know I should care, but I'm not sure if I do. I told Arnie to just deal with it, do the bare minimum and move on."

I hold his arm tighter. "Are you sure?"

"Right now…yeah. That's all he deserves, and he's lucky he's getting that. Arnie said he'd get back to me when he hears anything about the will. Then there's the house and his stuff." He shakes his head. "I leave on tour in just a few days. I can't deal with all this now."

"It's okay. I'm here. I'll help. My mom's been bugging me to come visit. Now that I'm boyfriend-less…" I jab him in the side, teasing him. "…and you're leaving, I guess I can head home to sort things out for you."

He looks my way, nothing but seriousness showing in his eyes. "I'd like that a lot, Lily."

I give him a small smile and rest my head on his shoulder, doing the same thing I've always done. I hold on to him tighter, praying he knows I'm here. I'll always be here for him.

The familiar sound of Trevin's ringtone sings through my room. "You miss me already?" I answer. He's only been on the road for three hours, so I'm surprised to see him calling already.

"You know it." I can only imagine the smirk covering his face right now. "But I just heard about the will. Turns out he left me everything."

"Okay, so what now?"

"I sell it all. I don't want any of it."

"But Trev, it's your family—"

"Hear me out." He cuts me off. "I have an idea. An idea that I know would make my mom happy. What should have been done with her life insurance money years ago."

He pauses for dramatic effect and I laugh. "So…tell me!" I yell.

"I've hired a company to sell it all and I'm forming a foundation in her name to pay for dance classes and music lessons for any child back home who can't afford it."

The excitement in his voice melts my heart and my eyes fill with tears, waiting to spill over. "Trevin. Your mom would have loved that."

He doesn't say anything but I know he's looking up to the sky, mouthing his words to his mom like I've seen him do many times before.

"So do you think you can still help? I'll book you a flight so you can meet the realtor and get things situated."

"Of course, you know I'd love to."

"Okay, good. Before you sell it though, will you look through and just make sure nothing of mine or my mom's is sold? Just box it up and put it in storage. I'll get to it eventually." He laughs, knowing he'll probably never get to it, but I get it.

"No problem. And hey, I'm really loving this idea."

He pauses for a moment. "Me too," he says quietly. "I've got to go, though. I'll call you later?"

"I'll be here. Be good, Trev."

He laughs. "Bye, Lilies."

A few days later, I'm walking off the escalator from the passenger only area of the airport when I see my mom bouncing up and down.

"Ahhhh, my baby's home!" she squeals.

Being the only child can be exhausting sometimes. I saw her a few months ago, but my mom acts like it's been years.

"Is it bad that I'm happy you're here, even though it's under such bad circumstances?" she teases, whispering under her breath like she doesn't want someone to hear that Trevin's dad passing away has brought her some sort of happiness.

They've lived with him as their neighbor for years now, so there's no having to explain Trevin's feelings or even their thoughts about the situation. We all know the truth, even though none of us are saying it. We can't deny that we're somewhat happy he's finally gone from our lives.

After spending some time with my mom and dad, I decide to walk over to Trevin's childhood home. I opted to go by myself, even though my mom offered over and over again to go with me. This was something I wanted to do on my own.

So many memories fly through my head as I walk up to the front door. Visions of Julie smiling brightly every time she would greet me fill my heart with happiness, knowing her memory will forever be ingrained in this community with this foundation.

A time warp enters my vision and I'm brought back to being fifteen years old. Not much has changed to the place except the cleanliness of it. Grime covers what used to be cherrywood coffee tables, and the kitchen Julie once took pride in looks like it hasn't been cleaned in years. Quickly noticing that nothing in this portion of the house will be salvageable, I turn to go upstairs and head for Trevin's room.

Upon opening the door, I can tell this is the first time in years anyone has done so. The room still is everything Trevin. From the posters on the wall to his school notebook open wide with a pencil on top of it.

When I glance at the notebook, my heart skips a beat. I see the beginnings of a poem that was never finished with the title, *When I Was Eight* written big across the top and underlined twice.

I pick it up to read it closer:

When I was eight she walked into my life
The little shy girl who didn't know how to ride
One day I'll make her my wife
My love for her I'll never have to hide

She holds my heart,
The only reason I'm still here
From her I could never be apart
As my life would be nothing but fear

So until then I'll wait
Until then I'll love from the inside
I know what's in our fate
When our worlds will finally collide

Memories of the night he left swarm my head, hitting me so hard I have to sit back on his bed, remembering every touch, every kiss, every emotion. When I look to the left, I see a box sitting under his bed that's slightly exposed. I reach underneath to grab it and pull it up to the bed.

There's nothing that could have prepared me for this, and tears start to fall instantly when I see the box that's dedicated to me. To us. To everything we have been to each other. In the box is every note I wrote him, pictures of us through the years, the matching walkie-talkie to mine that's still across the yard in my room. Fliers from my dance recitals, and pictures of my name along with Lilies hand drawn in a million different ways on scratch pieces of paper to entire sheets filling every inch.

If I ever questioned Trevin's true feelings for me, I have no doubt now, and I know I feel the same way. I always have. One day, I hope we'll find the right time where we can be together. Till then, I'll keep his secret close to my heart.

Chapter 17

One more hit, One more drink
Taking me to the brink
One more hit, One more drink
Please help me before I sink

- Trevin Allen

Trevin - Age 22

The most god-awful noise stings the air and I hear the voice of a female mumble something, but I just roll over, ignoring her and the pounding in my head.

When it goes off again, I grab my pillow, covering my face and my ears. "Trev..." I hear her say as her hand reaches over to hit my back. "Trev, your phone won't shut up. Answer it already."

I sit up, looking to see if I recognize the girl sleeping in my bed. But then I remember I'm not in my bed. I'm in some hotel in God knows where and I think the girl's name is Summer, or Sunny—shit, I don't know.

The noise finally stops and I take a deep breath, drinking in the calmness of silence until it starts up again. "What the fuck?" I whisper as I hold my head.

Last night was crazy, even for me. I search for my phone just to make sure it's not Lily—anyone else can wait until I'm awake. This calling at five in the morning is bullshit.

I see it's Chad, the other guitarist in the band. Knowing him, he's gotten himself messed up with some chick and needs me to bail him out. *Not this time, bro.*

I silence the call, but before I can turn it off, he calls again.

"Chad, fuck man, can't you call someone else to bail you out this time?" I force out as I rub my eyes in pain.

"Trev, it's Brad... There's been an accident. You need to get down here dude."

"*What the fuck*? What happened?" I stand up too fast and almost fall back down before I get my bearings.

"Man…" He pauses. "We were all pretty fucked up. Some people started fucking around on motorcycles." He stops again. "Fuck, man, just get your ass down here. We're at Houston Methodist Hospital. It's not looking good, bro."

"Fuck…I'm on my way."

I start to get dressed and nudge the girl passed out in my bed. "Summer…" I take a guess, hoping it's right. "I've got to get out of here. You have to get up."

"It's Sunny and whatever, leave," she says nonchalantly as she turns her head to the other side, not giving a shit that I'm heading out.

I look around, noticing this isn't my hotel room so I have nothing here. This must be her room, so I guess it doesn't matter if she gets up or not.

"Thanks for last night." I kiss the top of her head. I'm not a total dick.

"Yeah, yeah, yeah." She waves her hand without turning around. "See you next time. You have my number."

I do? I shake my head, looking more closely at her when I realize who she is. Fuck, my life is so messed up, but I do remember Sunny now. She and I hook up every time I'm in Houston. For a minute there, I didn't even know what state I was in.

Whoever thought having a different girl every night was an awesome way to live was wrong. It blows something fierce sometimes. Trying to erase my own lame idea of a love life out of my brain, I push my way through the mounds of people sleeping in the living room area of the suite and out the door to the elevator.

The front desk calls me a cab and I head straight to the hospital. When I arrive, there are news cameras everywhere, and security has to move everyone bombarding the cab so I can get to the front door.

"Is he alive, Trevin?" one reporter shouts.

"Where were you last night? How come you weren't with the rest of the band?" I hear another yell.

I tuck my head and push my way through the doors, thankful the hospital is blocking anyone from entering the facility. I walk to the desk, but before I can say anything, Chad comes around the corner, calling my name. "Hey, Trev, he's this way."

I turn and walk toward Chad, who looks like hell. "What the fuck happened last night? Where were you? Where's Kyle?" I question without greeting him.

"We were all together. Kyle and Brad started fucking around on these guys' bikes. They wanted to race and things got out of hand. Kyle's in surgery with a broken leg and cracked ribs, but Brad…man…Brad's not looking too good. He flew off the bike and Kyle hit him dead on, ran over him entirely. I watched the entire thing like it was happening in slow motion."

I watch in shock as Chad trembles, remembering the details. I can't believe this is happening. We sit helplessly in the waiting room for hours before Brad's parents race through the doors. His mom looks a wreck, like she's been crying for hours, and his dad is as white as a ghost.

I stand up to greet them. "Pam… Rick…"

"Trevin. What's going on? Is he all right? Oh my God!" his mom cries out as she wraps her arms around me in a tight hug. His dad pulls her off my body so she's crying on his shoulder again. "I'm sorry. Just seeing you made everything too real," she says through her tears.

I push my hands into my pockets, not quite sure how to act. It's been years since I've been around any caring parent, let alone a mom. My heart breaks at the thought, but I try to push it aside to focus on Brad. "It's okay. No word yet on his condition. I keep asking, but they won't tell us anything."

An eerie silence wipes over us as we sit down, trying to comfort each other while we wait for any news.

After another hour, a doctor finally comes to the waiting room. The look on his face is somber and my stomach starts to turn the closer he gets.

"I take it you guys are here for Brad Foster?"

"Yes," his dad says, standing up as fast as he can. "How is he?"

He looks down, and I know instantly what he's about to say. I've been told this before, and that's a look you never forget. A look of lost hope, of sorrow and of pity.

"We did the best we could," he says. Pam screams and almost falls to the floor before Rick catches her. "Brad had too much internal damage and there was nothing we could do. I'm so sorry for your loss," the doctor says with sadness in his eyes before he takes a deep breath, leaving us to deal with the loss of our best friend, their son, and the leader of our band.

Chapter 18

Partying, drinking, girl after girl
All looking for my lips to give me a whirl
Spiraling down to the bottom I see.
Only you and I know, it's not even me.

- Trevin Allen

Lily – Age 23

Trevin is spiraling out of control and I'm not sure what to do. He feels like he's lost everything and has admitted more than once, I'm the only reason he stays around at all. That's a lot of pressure for anyone, let alone me. I want to be there for him, but at the same time, I'm trying to finish my master's degree along with still teaching dance—my plate is overflowing. Worrying about Trevin's mental stability is more than I can undertake.

He, on the other hand, sits around all day, getting drunk. I'm still trying to get used to the random people camped out in our house and the parties going on at all hours of the day and night. I try not to focus on the details of what their parties entail, knowing it will only make me mad. There's no doubt that Trevin's doing drugs, but every time I ask him about it, he shies away, but not before he tells me to stay away from his drama. Each time he walks away, I wonder how he expects me to do that in our current living situation. He's my best friend—I can't help but worry.

What's worse is he hasn't touched his guitar in months. I can see the light in his soul dimming, slowly fading away. This isn't who he wants to be, but I have no clue how to bring him out of this funk. The band, the music…they were his life, and now he's a shell of what he was with it gone.

A huge fight broke out between the other two band members, Chad and Kyle, over their involvement in Brad's death. Poor Trevin was stuck in the middle. He was the outsider, brought into the fold late in the game, and they'd all grown up together. He wasn't there, he wasn't involved, and somehow, his absence on the night of Brad's death left him sidelined and on the fringe.

Within the few years he was in the band, he made more money than any normal person would in a lifetime, but now I sit back, watching him blow it on partying, countless people using him, and everything he shouldn't be doing.

My class got out late tonight and I have no clue what I'm going to be walking into at home. When I left for school, there were a few people over, none of which I recognized, and that always freaks me out. He doesn't need to be hanging out with new people; they're using him for who he is and what he can get his hands on—all at no cost to them, of course.

To my surprise, when I get home, Trevin is sitting on the couch with his head in his hands and his arms resting on his knees. He doesn't budge—not even flinch—as I come in, so I sit next to him and nudge him with my knee.

"Hey, you," I say as playfully as I can.

He chances a look in my direction, giving me a meager smile. "What's up, Pad?" He tips his chin the way guys do in acknowledgment before putting his head back down in his hands.

I only caught his sorrow-filled hazel eyes for a brief second, but I can tell whatever he's on, he's lit. And him only calling me *Pad* sends up huge red flags. He may have multiple nicknames for me, but he's never called me just Pad.

"You all right?" I put my left arm around his back in an effort to comfort him and my right arm on his knee to try to ground him.

He pulls his head up and searches my eyes for a few breaths before he cocks his head to the side and opens his mouth. "Why are you still my friend?"

I laugh, thinking he's playing around. "Um, because you need someone to keep you tied to reality, duh."

He smirks, that sexy smirk that always gets me somewhere deep in my chest, before he says, "No, really? I mean. Look at me. I'm a total loser with no family, now no job, and nothing to do with my life. You're going to college. Trying to make something of your life, and I'm sitting here, floating away into the oblivion."

"Come on, Trev...don't talk like that. Where did all your friends go? I thought I would come home to a full house." This is not the Trevin I've ever known—this Trevin scares me. Us being friends isn't a choice, it's not an option, it's who we are. The world doesn't make sense without him in it, and that goes both ways. He is just as important in my existence as I am in his. The gravity we joke about, the undeniable pull, the reason people don't understand it—they've never experienced it.

He stares at me, remorse cloaking his features. "I kicked them out. I'm sorry I always have randoms over. People you should never be around. You're this amazing person and I hang out with some pretty fucked-up losers." He hasn't said it, but I know exactly where his mind is right now. This is exactly how his dad was when he was growing up. Trevin hated living with it then and knows I do now. But he forgets: he couldn't stand his dad, and I adore him—problems and all.

"It's okay, it's your house. You can have whoever you want over."

"No, no, no. Don't say that." He shakes his head much harder than necessary as his words start to slur. "This is your house. All of this is for you." He tries to stand, opening his arms wide to make his point, but falls back on the couch with a thud.

I wrap my arms around him. "Hey, Trev, are you okay?" I ask, running my hand on the side of his face and forcing him to look at me.

"No, I'm not. Everything I've ever had is gone. Except you. You're the only thing that keeps me here. But even you're going to be gone soon. You're graduating and you'll move on." He stops, hesitating for a moment. Or possibly analyzing where he'd be with me gone. "And I'll still be here. Doing nothing."

"Why would you say that? I'm not going anywhere." Whatever definition our relationship takes on, I won't leave him. Without him, Lily Pad doesn't exist.

"Yes, you will. You'll leave me. You *need* to. I'll never be good enough for you. God, I've tried my whole life to be what you needed. But no matter what, I'll always be just me and you deserve more than just *me*."

"Trev, what are you talking about?" I'm not a stranger to his ramblings. When he's intoxicated, he talks about some random stuff, but this is different—this is life altering.

"Lily, I've always loved you. You'll always be the one. These lips…" He tries to point to his beautiful mouth, but his arms aren't moving that well. He's losing motor function as his words flow together. "These lips have never touched anyone else's…they've only touched yours. I'll never let anyone else taste them—they're reserved solely for you. Always. But I won't let you degrade yourself by being with me." The pain in his eyes is almost tangible. I ache for him, wishing I could change pieces of his past, desperate for him to see his worth.

"Trev, come on, you're scaring me. Here, get up, let's get you some water." I try to pick him up, but I'm no match for his large frame. He outweighs me by close to a hundred pounds and has twelve inches of height on me. His body is dead weight I simply can't control.

"I love you, Lily. Forever. I always will."

I watch as his eyes roll back in his head and his lids close. Unable to maintain any control over his body, he falls back against the couch. Frantically, I sit him up, slapping him in the face. The more scared I get, the harder I hit. "Trevin! Wake up! Trev!" I'm screaming in his ear, hoping for some type of reaction. But I don't get a response, nothing. He's passed out, but it's more than that—he's drenched in sweat and his skin is cool to the touch. Holding his head in my hands, his pulse beats wildly against my fingers on his neck... unnaturally fast.

Delirious, I scream, "No!" as I run to call 9-1-1. I'm almost positive he's overdosed, but with nothing around to indicate what he's taken, I'm clueless and unable to help the operator.

Everything is a blur, moving at the speed of light, yet it feels like it's going in slow motion as I talk to the 9-1-1 operator. The paramedics show up within minutes, not the hours it seems to be. With Trevin strapped to a gurney in the back of an ambulance, I jump in with them, helplessly watching as they hook him up to machines and force a tube down his throat.

The monitor shows his heart rate at 150, so they inject something into his arm. Readying the electric shock paddles, they wait to see if the medicine counteracts the attack the drugs are causing on his body. Thankfully, the frantic beeping coming through the machine starts to slow and they put the paddles away just as we pull up to the hospital.

As they race him through the emergency room, I'm escorted to the waiting area, alone, left to wait in complete despair.

It's late, but I call my parents anyway because I don't know what else to do. They listen to me cry as I tell them everything that's been going on over the last few months. I've kept most of it to myself so their opinion of Trevin wouldn't be altered, but I can't do it anymore.

"Okay, honey, calm down. Are you alone?" my mom asks in her soothing mom voice that I so desperately needed to hear.

"Yes, I am. I'm freaking out, Mom. What if something happens to him? What if they can't help him?"

"Don't think like that. Think positively. That's what Trevin needs right now."

"Mom... God...I'm just...I'm scared. He's..." I start bawling as I hold the phone to my ear and cover my face with my other hand. I'm all alone, standing in the middle of the emergency room fearing the worst and knowing without Trevin, my life would be over.

"I know, sweetheart. I know. Is there anyone you can call? Jordan maybe?

I can hop in the car right now, or check the flights down there."

"No, Mom." I take a deep breath. "It's okay. I can call Jordan, I'm sure—oh, wait, here comes a nurse that rushed back with him." I stand up and my stomach threatens to defect from my body as she approaches. "Can you please tell me what's going on?" I beg.

She grabs my arm and leads me to a chair. "Dear, he's going to be okay," she says in the sweetest southern accent I've ever heard as she pets my hand. "The doctors pumped his stomach, and gave him more medications to counteract whatever he riddled his body with, but thankfully, he's doing all right now."

When she tells me I can come back to see him, tears pour out of my eyes. Just when I thought there was nothing left to shed, they came on in full force.

"Mom, did you hear that?" I say into the phone, relief flooding over me.

"Yes, I did. That's so amazing to hear." Her voice cracks slightly. "I knew he'd be okay. Now go give him a big hug from us and call me later."

"I will. Love you, Mom."

"Oh, honey, I love you more than you will ever know. Trevin too."

I smile, knowing they do love him just as much as I do. He'll forever be a part of our family.

The feeling of relief that flows through me is stronger than any words I could ever articulate. Trevin's been my world since I was eight years old. I don't care what it takes, I will help him fix his life. Together, we'll find the Trevin I know...and bring him back to me.

Seeing him lying in the hospital bed, he looks frail, a fragment of the man I love. I can't help but take his hand, the way I've done so many times before, and pray that my comfort will bring him back.

I feel his hand slowly return my grip, as he turns his head slightly and opens his eyes. Regret evident in his stare, he whispers, "I'm so sorry."

"No, Trevin. Stop."

"No, Lily, I didn't mean to—I swear. I just wanted to numb the pain. They said this new herbal drug, Spice, was just like weed. I wasn't trying to kill myself. I don't want to die. Please believe me."

I lean down, placing my lips directly over his. I leave them there longer than necessary to ensure he knows that it's okay—*we're* okay. After a few seconds, I pull back. "I know, Trevin. You can't anyway; I won't let you leave me. Not yet."

He smirks, my favorite cocky grin, while he grips my hand with more intensity. I wonder how much he remembers of what he told me. I've heard countless stories over the years, but tonight was the first time he's confirmed he's never kissed anyone but me. Knowing he's kept that piece of us sacred fills me with pride, hope and love for the boy, the man, who needs me now more than ever.

Trevin spent a few nights in the hospital and had to undergo a psychiatric evaluation, but he comes home tonight. We've been talking a lot, like we used to, which I've missed. I've seen glimpses of my Trevin coming back to me, and I need to ensure we stay on this path once he's home.

As we walk through the door, he sets his bag down and turns, wrapping his arms around me. "Thank you, Lilies. You're always there for me." We hold each other tight, not saying anything and just enjoying the moment of having him home.

"Okay." I break up the reunion, patting his back. "So, what's the plan now?"

He pulls back, looking around our place. "Fuck if I know." He shrugs.

"Have you thought about looking into therapy? Or why don't you play your guitar? I haven't heard you play in months." Trevin needs to get back to his roots and the things he loves—the ones that bring him peace, not heartache.

He lets out a loud sigh. "I guess you're right. Don't think I haven't noticed the subtle hints you've been dropping." He winks. "I guess my guitar was always a form of therapy for me."

I moved his guitar out to the living room a few weeks ago, hoping if it were in front of him he would pick it up. I've moved it around multiple times in a silent game of do-you-see-me, hoping to entice him to play. At least I know he was paying attention.

He sits on the couch and finally lifts the instrument to his lap. This is probably the longest time he's gone without playing since the day I taught him how to strum all those years ago. I watch as his fingers feel around the neck of the guitar, moving up and down the strings until he holds his hands in place and starts to play.

It's a song I've heard him strum a hundred times, but this time has so much more meaning than in the past. He actually hums the lyrics and sings a few of them as he plays through the chords. I've only heard him sing once, many years ago, at his mom's grave. Sitting here now, the tears fall freely, running down my cheeks, and dripping from my jaw to my lap, listening to the lyrics his mother had hoped would define him.

I've never been able to hear the song *Simple Man* without being overcome with emotion. But today, instead of my eyes being consumed by sadness, they fill with hope. I have my Trevin back. And it dawns on me what his next step needs to be.

I patiently wait for him to finish the song—to reconnect with his soul and that special place with his mom—before I ask, "Why didn't you ever sing in the band?"

He looks up, keeping the guitar in place with his hand pressing it against his chest. "That wasn't my role. Brad was our singer."

"But, Trev, you're good. Why don't you try vocals?"

"You're the only person who's ever heard me sing. No one's ever asked. They needed a guitarist, I filled the role, and on we went."

"Well, what's stopping you now?"

"Me? Sing?"

"Yeah. Why don't you start your own band? You could be the lead singer and guitarist. You already have the following. I'm sure the record label would give you a shot."

He sighs and I see the desire in his eyes. "I do miss it…" he admits as he strums the guitar again, playing a few slower chords from one of his old songs.

"Come on, I know you could do this. And you'd be amazing at it. You belong on stage, Trev."

I sit back and watch as his lips slowly tilt up to a smile that he's trying to hide. He's considering it, I just need to encourage him, but for now, I've sparked the flame. I stay silent, waiting for him to work through his thoughts, and I can feel the tiny bit of fire growing into a blazing inferno. He's taking the idea and fueling it with passion.

"You know," he says without looking up, continuing to slowly pick away at his guitar. "While we were on tour, I started writing some lyrics. I was going to pitch them to the guys but never got the chance."

"Are you serious?" I jump on him, excited.

He laughs as he shields his guitar from my frontal attack.

"Can I hear them?" I'm worse than a kid on Christmas morning.

He focuses on the strings, strumming a few more chords, before answering, "Fuck it, why not." Getting up, he walks to his room and heads back with a notebook in his hand. Setting it down on the coffee table, he goes over a song and a few chords before finally performing it.

I look down at his notepad to see he's written *Those Nights* in large letters across the top. I listen to the words as I read along. Finding all of it very familiar—he sings about our childhood, the nights we stayed up talking, listening to music because he didn't want to go home to his parents fighting.

I'm instantly in love with the calmer vibe this song has over the harder stuff Stone Cold always played. It's still rock but more new age, more true to who Trevin is. Every section is another piece of our past, an admission of his wish to have had those times last. When he finishes, he hesitates to look in my direction, opting to sit silently. He continues going over chords, pretending to be working on the song. But I know him better. He's a nervous wreck as he waits for my reaction, so I let him sweat it for a few seconds.

When I finally wrap my arms around him and his guitar, I announce, "I love it."

He glances at me without moving his head; instead, he peeks through his long lashes and gives me his sexy smirk while raising his eyebrows slightly. "Really?"

I hit him. "Yes, really! I'm telling you, Trevin. This is it. You need to do this, and that song is just the beginning."

"But what about the other guys? I'm not sure if I should call them or if they'll even get back together."

"No, Trev, I'm sorry to say but that ship has sailed. This song, this is you. Not them."

"But those guys made me. They brought me in, showed me this world."

"Yes, they did but they also left you here, alone when shit hit the fan. Those guys aren't going to make up anytime soon. And it will never be the same without Brad."

He looks down, strumming over some chords before sighing. "You're right. It won't."

"Don't look at it as leaving them. Look at it as starting anew. Only this band will be you. All you. Trevin, look at me."

His head slowly turns to meet my eyes and I grab his hand from the guitar to hold it in mine.

"It's about time you did something for you. You deserve this."

He smiles and I watch as the corners of his eyes crinkle with the slightest pool of moisture forming before he blinks them away. "I don't know what I'd do without you, Lilies. I hope you know that."

"I know, Trevin. I'd be lost without you too so don't you dare ever pull that shit on me again," I tease, hitting his shoulder, causing him to reveal a small smile.

"I promise." He leans in, kissing my forehead before turning back to his guitar and showing me the next song.

We sit the rest of the night, going over all the pieces he's written, and I'm shocked by how much he already has done. There's a healthy mix of fast songs and ballads, but all of them have a unique sound that fits Trevin more than anything I've ever heard him play.

I see so much of him, of us, in his songs, and I know this was his escape while on tour. His way to stay grounded and true to himself while he was away.

Chapter 19

Like the North Star she'll show me the way.
For me I'll know she'll always stay.
Even when I don't deserve her love,
Her life, I'd never make a mess of.

- Trevin Allen

Trevin - Age 23

Yet again, Lily has saved me in more ways than one. After Brad passed, I had no clue what to do with my life or myself. With Chad and Kyle not talking to each other, I was left—as the outsider I always was—to fend for myself and deal with the loss of him and our band alone.

It never occurred to me to start my own, but Lily seemed to think I could do it. Now, here I sit in a big fancy office, waiting to hear my fate. When I called my old manager, Arnie, he was excited by the thought of doing something new. He got me into the studio immediately, and we started laying down some tracks.

Yeah, I had the name Stone Cold behind me, but everyone knew I wasn't an original member, so I didn't get a free pass. I had to work my ass off to prove myself—and my lyrics—on my own dime to make this happen.

It cost me a small fortune to do it the right way, but I couldn't think of a better way to spend my money. I auditioned a ton of different people, and ended up with a group of guys who form the band I'm calling Escape Velocity. Together, we've worked on creating our own sound, each member adding their unique style to the overall blend. The only piece of the equation I wouldn't budge on was the name—it wasn't open for discussion.

Escape Velocity was something personal to me. I wanted a tribute to Lily without being blatantly obvious. My entire life she's been what kept me grounded. I played around with names, but kept coming back to synonyms for gravity. Then I came across Escape Velocity—the speed an object needs to attain a gravitational pull of another body. For years, it seemed like the music industry has tried to pull me away from Lily, and I know I need to work harder to keep her there—to not escape her velocity.

I never thought I'd enjoy being the front man, but honestly, I more than like it—I fucking love it. Playing guitar was always my passion, but now I can fully pour my soul into the music, leaving me to feel more complete than ever before.

The door opens and I turn to see a man in a suit enter the office. He walks to his desk and shakes my hand before sitting down. "Well, Trevin, I must say, we played your demo for some focus groups and the ratings came back off the charts. Higher than anything we've done in quite some time. They love the new sound you've got going here, and we do too."

He slides a piece of paper over to me and I lift it up, pretending I know what I'm looking at, but in reality, I don't. My manager and the lawyers handle this piece. I'll let them hash out the details. I'm just excited to be getting the chance.

"It's an offer for one album with the option to renew if sales hit the numbers laid out here."

I stand to shake the man's hand. "Thank you, sir. I won't let you down." I hold up the paper. "I'll get this back to you right away."

Once I leave his office, I immediately take out my phone to call Lily. She answers on the second ring, greedy for information. "Tell me, tell me, tell me," she demands without saying hello.

"They loved it. We got a deal. Escape Velocity is officially a signed band."

Her screams fill the receiver, making me laugh as I pull the phone away from my ear to keep from losing my hearing. Her happiness is contagious, and I can't wait to shout to the world—I'm back.

But, first things first. After years of college and then grad school, Lily finishes her master's program tomorrow and will be walking in the ceremony. I'm throwing her a party she'll never forget.

Her parents and best friend from high school, Morgan, flew in today to help me set everything up. I've invited Jordan and her sorority sisters along with all the friends I've ever heard her talk about. Even though we've lived together all these years, she rarely brings anyone to the house. She doesn't want to invade my privacy by allowing people to know where I live, but I've always wondered if it's more because of how different I am than the people she associates with.

They're all college-going, preppy, Abercrombie, flip-flop wearing douches, but that doesn't mean we all can't hang out. Yes, anytime she's tried to go on a date, I've scared them away, but that's because none of those guys were good enough for her. A few of them lasted past the first couple of dates, but that was only because I was on tour. Once I got home, I ensured things ended pretty quickly for them. They complained to her that I was possessive, but so what, maybe I am. Really, I just want what's best for her.

When I pull into my long driveway, I see the tent set up between the house and the ocean. I'm not sure how many people would actually show, but I wanted to make sure we had enough room. Thank God her mom is helping with the catering, because I truly know nothing about setting up this kind of event. My only responsibility at the parties I've thrown was to make sure there were enough alcohol and drugs to last the night. But not this party—this is all about class and sophistication. Nothing is too much for my Lily, and I want this party to show exactly that.

After all the preparations for tomorrow are done and we all have dinner, her parents head off to their hotel I set them up in, but Morgan stays behind to spend the night with Lily. We sit down in the living room, me in my normal spot on the floor, and Lily right behind me on the couch. Her hand drapes over my shoulder. Instinctively, I reach up to lace my fingers with hers—it's second nature; we do it every time we're hanging out like this.

Morgan sits across the room on the couch, eyeing us suspiciously before calling us out. "Okay, you two. Give up the goods. What's really going on here?" Her eyes go back and forth between us.

Lily slowly moves her hand back to the couch. "What do you mean?"

"Oh, come on. You guys have been like this for years. And now you've lived together for how long? You can't tell me *nothing* is going on."

I reply honestly, "No, nothing's going on."

"Yeah right. You guys both sat down, instantly connecting, like it was one hundred percent normal to sit like that. You seriously want me to believe that nothing's ever happened between you two."

"Well, yeah, but that was a while ago." I try to blow it off and make light of the past interaction.

She sits up straighter, grabbing the chair. "Are you serious?" She looks at Lily. "And you never told me!"

I squint my eyes, turning to look at Lily for confirmation. "You never told her?"

Morgan has been her best friend, besides me, for years. I thought girls told each other everything. I couldn't imagine why she would keep this a secret.

"How many times have I asked you and you swore up and down that nothing has ever happened?" Morgan's in utter disbelief.

That hurt. She actually lied to her best friend about me.

"Wait, so what happened? How far did you go?" She points her fingers back and forth between Lily and me.

Lily sighs. "Okay fine, we kissed a few years back."

The way she says it cuts even deeper, like it was a small peck—something insignificant. We've done way more than kiss, and I don't understand why she's lying about it, especially with me sitting right here.

Morgan jumps up. "You kissed him?" she yells in disbelief. "But it's a well-known fact he doesn't kiss *anyone*." She stops and points her finger at me. "It's kind of weird I know that, by the way, but the damn tabloids had a field day with that piece of information a few years back," she says all cynically to me.

I'm kind of shocked and not sure what else to say. Obviously, she doesn't want anyone to know she's been with me, especially Morgan, but I don't know why.

Lily sits up so she's directly behind me. "Yes…we've kissed a few times and…" Lily's voice starts to trail off.

"And…wait, holy shit, you had sex with him and you never told me?" The look on Morgan's face is shock and disbelief.

I turn to look at Lily, questioning what she's thinking.

She covers her face with the blanket next to her. "It was a mistake a long time ago. I just wanted to forget it ever happened, okay?"

What the fuck?

She wants to forget it ever happened. I can't imagine why. I mean, I know I fucked up when she came to visit, but I cherish the memories of the two times we've had together. I can't believe she's saying this shit.

"Mistake or not, I'll get you to spill the details soon enough," Morgan proclaims.

Lily takes the pillow next to her and throws it at her friend's head. "Can we please change the subject?"

I turn so Lily and I catch eyes. She stares at me for a brief second before I look away, saddened by what just went down, and even more confused than I've ever been.

With the subject officially changed, we spend the next few hours chatting in the living room. Morgan gets up to go to bed and I look at Lily, whispering to her to stay out with me. Thankfully, she does and says goodnight to Morgan, telling her she'll be in shortly.

Once we're alone, I turn to look at her, getting right to the point. It took all I had in me to avoid having this conversation in front of Morgan, but I need answers. "What was all that about?"

She refuses to meet my stare. "I don't know."

"Lily…" I place my hand under her chin, watching her eyes naturally gravitate to mine. She's shocked to hear just her name with no silly attachment. "Why didn't you tell her about us?"

She lets out a frustrated sigh. "I never knew what to tell her."

"The truth works."

"The truth…really, Trevin? What, that you came to my room, we had sex, then you left? She would've had questions and I didn't have answers."

"Okay, but why continue to deny it?"

She sits up, putting her head in her hands and running her fingers through her dark brown hair. "I don't know. I just didn't want anyone to know."

"Why? Are you ashamed of me?"

"No, Trev! God, no!"

"Then what?"

"I just…it's just…" she stares straight through my eyes and into my soul, but she's speechless.

I'm not going to sit here and listen to her say she's ashamed of our past or maybe even regrets what we did. I get up to walk to my room before I hear something that will crush me, something I won't be able to come back from.

"Trevin, wait," she calls after me, but I keep moving. It's not until we get to my room that I turn around to shut the door and find her directly behind me. "Please wait."

"Wait for what? To hear you say you regret our past? You regret pieces of us we shared?"

"I don't regret it." Her voice is meek and she refuses to take her eyes off the floor.

"Then look at me. Look at me and say that."

She looks up, staring directly into my eyes, opening her windows and allows me to connect with her soul again. A piece of her I never thought she'd give me back. "I don't regret it. I'll never regret it."

We stare at each other, both daring the other to look away first, but instead, we stand completely still. Unsure of where to go from here.

She reaches out to grab my hand. "I'll never regret being with you, Trev."

I lace my fingers with hers, pulling her closer, inches from me.

Her eyes travel down to my lips then back up. "Have you still never kissed any girl but me?"

"No, I haven't. My lips are only yours. Forever." With that, I pull her into me, pressing my mouth to hers, feeling her part, welcoming me in.

My tongue moves in to sweep across hers, making my cock instantly hard as my hands grip her body, bringing her impossibly close to me, desperate to feel her warmth against me.

Goddamn she feels good. So real. So mine.

Her hands loosen their grip and when I feel them slide between us, my heart starts to tear in two when I figure out exactly what she's doing. Her lips pull away from me slightly as her hands inch up farther to push me back. My body moves but my lips remain glued to hers, needing to hold on to this for just a few seconds longer.

She pulls back even more, forcing me to stop, knowing I've gone too far. She looks directly into my eyes without hesitation and takes me by surprise. Instead of stopping me, or leaving my room, she closes the door and wraps her arms around her body. Taking the hem of her shirt in her hands, she lifts the fabric completely off, dropping it to the floor at our feet.

Joy overcomes my soul when I realize she's not rejecting me, she's inviting me, and I finally have my Lily once again. I rush to her, pulling her roughly against my chest, wanting every inch of her body forged to my own. Her fingers start to move under my shirt, lifting it up, causing an animalistic growl to form in my lungs and escape from my mouth before I have any control to stop it. I don't want to stop it. I want this. I've always wanted this and, fuck me, I'm not going to stop any reaction my body gives when it finally gets what it's been craving for years.

We pull apart only to take my shirt off, and for me to start to unbutton her short shorts. Instantly, I fall to my knees, needing to worship at the feet of the woman in front of me—praising what she's offering.

My lips brush across her soft stomach as I inch her shorts down her waist, trailing my fingers behind them. The fabric moves with my touch, down the length of her and the sides of her feet as I help her step out of them.

Looking up at her from my position, she offers me a shy smile and nods her head, reassuring me this is actually happening—she's not going to stop me—she wants it, too.

I smirk in response and her head falls back in laughter before she wraps her hands around the base of my neck. Her fingers pull me up to her, and she almost moans the words into my ear. "I love that sexy smirk of yours." Nipping at my ear with her teeth, enticing me further.

I turn to walk us to my bed, picking her up to place her on the mattress and then crawl on top of her. Her legs spread like the wings of a butterfly, welcoming me, before she wraps them tightly around my waist.

Holding myself up by my arms, I start to rock into her, pushing my hips against hers then pulling away. The small moans escaping her mouth are fucking sexy as hell. I try to swallow each and every one of them.

Her hands reach for my belt so I lift my hips to give her better access.

Instead of trying to remove them completely, she reaches in, wrapping her hand around my cock and starts stroking my length.

Sensation rips through my body like I've never felt before. I've had women touch me countless times, but it's never felt the way it feels now. Lily and I have been together twice, and both times were still very new to us. But not now.

This is real.

This is us.

We've waited years for this and fuck, I don't ever want to lose this again. My lips reclaim hers, wanting every taste, every lick, every touch to last forever. I need her. Unable to wait any longer, I lift my hips, using one hand to push my pants and boxers down. She assists, pushing them down my legs with her feet until they're finally off.

Starting at her neck, I kiss my way down her body, cupping her breast before removing her bra completely. I've never gotten to study her body the way I am now. I swear it's the most beautiful thing I've ever seen in my life. Her skin is so soft, her breasts so full and natural as I move them around in my hand. Licking at her taut nipple before I suck it into my mouth. The sound of her sweet moans drives me further while her hands grip my back, drawing me nearer.

Making my way farther south, I run my fingers under the edge of her panties, spinning them around my finger so I can pull them down...teasingly slow. I want to memorize every inch of the beautiful angel before me.

At her feet, I pull them completely off, kissing the tops of her toes, running back up her thigh, her stomach, her breasts and finally to reunite with her lips. I lay between her legs, poised at her entrance but waiting for approval.

Our lips part and she whispers, "Trevin…"

"I love you, Lily." I interrupt her. "I always have. I always will."

When her eyes tear up, I ease my way inside, connecting with her, sealing our lips, cherishing the sensation of her body moving against mine. Everything feels so good, so right. I never want this night to end. I need it to last forever—this time it has to.

I move slowly in and out, leaving my lips melded with hers, enjoying every moan, clinging to every gasp, adoring every sigh separately as they escape from her. Everything about this moment is perfection, and for the first time in my life, I truly make love to the woman I can't get enough of. My pace is slow, constant, methodical, and oh so fucking good. My hands run down her arms, interlacing our fingers, and I pull them above her head, keeping them there for me to hold.

"I love you, Lily." I continue to pepper her with kisses.

"I love you, too, Trevin." I hear her say it just as much as I feel it, and I completely lose control. No one has told me they loved me since my mom died. The emotional and physical overload is too much to handle. My grip tightens and I hold her as close as humanly possible, but it's not enough.

My body starts to shatter from the inside and I can't hold on any longer. I speed up my tempo, rubbing my body against her, making her pulse race as I feel her body slicken more, allowing me to move faster, smoother, hotter.

My lips reach hers just in time to swallow her moan as I feel her insides clench my cock in pulsating grips as she rides out her orgasm.

I push hard against her, taking her wave, gripping my hands on either side of her face. With more intensity than I've ever shared, I kiss her, pouring all my feelings into this single release. When I find my own, I let loose everything I have inside her.

We both stay gripped around each other, neither of us wanting to ever let go. Our lips remain connected as we enjoy each other's taste and cherish the desires we've kept at bay for so long.

I feel myself start to go limp and my cum begins to ooze from her body. Releasing her mouth, I whisper, "Don't go anywhere." I get up to get her a towel. Warming it quickly, I walk to her, wipe her clean of my release and throw the towel to my dirty clothes pile before crawling back into bed and pulling her close to me.

"Please stay with me," I whisper into her hair as I wrap my arm around her stomach, pulling her back directly into my front.

She folds her arms over mine, holding me tightly, saying, "I will." She brings my hand to her mouth and kisses it.

"I meant it, Lily…I've always loved you."

"Me too, Trev, me too."

Chapter 20

Finally the girl is mine.
I'll show her the world
And everything that's fine
Because finally the girl is mine.

- Trevin Allen

Lily — The next day

I wake up in Trevin's arms, just like I should have been for the last few years. Everything about last night felt right. It was perfect. He was perfect. I've wanted this for so long, but the thought of losing my friendship with him again always held me back. Last time we tried this was a disaster, but we were younger, things were different. I'm praying this time we can make us work.

His lips press against my shoulder and a smile covers my face.

"Good morning, Lilies," he whispers in my ear.

"Good morning, Trevin." I hold my arms tighter against his before running my fingers over his friendship bracelet.

"You know I only have one left; you're going to have to make me a new batch here soon."

I smirk, letting out a small laugh. I never thought I'd be making friendship bracelets for a grown man.

"But first, are you ready for the first day of the rest of your life?" he asks.

"Does it include this every morning?"

"Hell yes." He flips me over so he's lying on top of me, kissing down my neck while rubbing his hands over my breasts. His fingers graze my side, making me squeal from my ticklish spot. The warmth of his breath and the way his laughter dances on my skin have me on cloud nine.

My trance is broken by a voice coming through the door. "Yeah, just friends my ass. That better be Lily in there, Trevin, or we have a missing girl on our hands."

Trev looks up with his sexy grin, waiting for me to respond.

"Yeah, I'm in here," I respond, cupping his face in my hands. "And yeah, I guess we're more than just friends."

His lips find mine faster than I can say anything else, and I begin to laugh through his attack.

"It's about time, you two. But seriously, get out here. We have to get you ready and I'm starving," Morgan declares from behind the door.

I give Trevin a peck on the lips and start to get up.

"Wait." He stops me before I can walk away. "So, we're actually doing this?" He grabs my hand. "Me and you? You're going to tell people and finally make this thing work? Publicly?"

"Yes, Trevin. I want this. I've always wanted this. Maybe now we both are at a place where we can make this happen."

I watch as his face lights up and he drags me back down to the bed. He matches his lips with mine and positions our bodies perfectly together until we hear the rattle of a hollow door being beaten on.

"Hello! Get up! We've got to go!"

We both laugh and succumb to the fact that we really do have to get out of bed. I kiss his lips to reassure him. "Don't worry, I'm not going anywhere. Remember, I live here, too."

We both grab our clothes before opening the door to Morgan standing out front with her arms crossed, giving us both an I-told-you-so look. Trevin wraps his arm around my back, pulling me to him to kiss the top of my head.

"Uh huh, so you've been lying to me all this time?" she asks.

I look at Trevin before turning back to Morgan. "Well, not entirely. Come on, I'll fill you in." I grab her hand, pulling her to my room to give her the *Readers Digest* version of my relationship with Trevin.

I was nervous to tell my parents and my friends about Trevin, but surprisingly, everyone had the same reaction Morgan did, declaring it's about time. And they're right. It is about time we pursue what we've both wanted for so long.

Today's a new day. I've officially graduated from college, Trevin and I are finally where we both want to be, and Trevin's new band just got signed. Life couldn't get any better.

He never leaves my side at the party he's thrown for me. Any chance he gets, he's got his arm around me, kissing my cheek, or pulling me aside to sneak in affectionate touches better shared privately.

Everyone from school is here, along with my sorority sisters and the girls from my dance team. I've never been so free or so happy in my life, but when Trevin says he has a surprise for me, my heart beats through my chest in anticipation.

Nothing could have prepared me for the sight of all my students walking out to a makeshift stage to perform a special dance they choreographed, only for me, to one of Trevin's new songs.

Pride seeps through my soul as I watch girls I've worked with for the last few years, proving to me what I've helped them achieve. I have to fight back tears when I think of how far some of them have come.

Once they're done, I run up, hugging them tightly and praising them for how amazing both the choreography and their technique were.

Trevin walks up, putting his hand on my shoulder, and I turn instantly to give him a big hug. Thanking him for the amazing surprise.

Satisfaction shows through his smile before he says, "Anything for my Lilies. I'm going to go grab a beer, can I get you water or some ice tea?"

"You know what?" I say, looking at him. "Make me a drink. Something you'll think I'll like."

He laughs. "Seriously?"

I'm not a drinker, never have been. I've had a few drinks here and there, but it was always at a bar or some college party. Never during the day just hanging out.

I laugh. "Yes, just hush and get me a drink." I swat playfully at his chest.

"Hey, if the woman wants a drink…" He holds up his hands in surrender and kisses my cheek before walking away.

One drink turns into two, which becomes three pretty quickly. The day falls into night, and the DJ Trevin hired turns the sophisticated party into a dance club.

Trevin and I dance, wrapped around each other all night as the drinks flow endlessly. My love for him, in this moment grows more and more as the night progresses, and I never want this to end. I want to freeze this moment, putting it inside a snow globe so I can shake it to relive the magic all over.

The people surrounding us slowly fade away, leaving only a few remaining, but it doesn't matter. Only he does. My perfect day is about to be my perfect night when Trevin picks me up and carries me to the house. We ask the staff he hired to make sure everyone leaves and then lock the house up behind us.

"And where do you think you're taking me?" I ask jokingly as the alcohol starts to make my head spin along with the fact I'm being carried.

"To our room."

"Our room?"

"Yes, didn't you know?" He looks down to smirk at me. "You no longer live in the room down the hall. You live in mine. Ours."

He kicks open the door and throws me on his mattress. I squeal in response before gaining my bearings and climbing to my knees. After shutting the door, he slowly stalks toward the bed, removing his shirt and throwing it on the floor.

"Do you know how many nights I dreamed of having you in my bed?" he asks as he yanks my shirt up and over my head. "Do you know how many times I practically had to handcuff myself to this headboard just to stop me from walking down to your room and taking you any way I wanted?" He unhooks my bra and throws it across the room. "Fuck, Lily. I've loved you for so fucking long."

I stand up, looking him straight in the eye, and slide my skirt and panties down my legs until I'm completely naked, offering myself to him. With his face at my stomach, I lean in, running my fingers through his crazy hair, making him look up into my eyes. "Then take me already," I whisper.

Before I can blink an eye, he tosses me back to the bed, and his pants are ripped off. Everything about both of us is so primal, lust filled, such a desperate need that we don't take our time. He enters me with a powerful thrust, leaving me screaming my response. It's intense, so different, but I only want it more and harder. Our movements are passionate, not rational, but fucking amazing. We're running a marathon together and never want to reach the finish line.

My fingers yank on his hair as he sucks my neck like he's dying of thirst and he's trying to save his life with one last drop.

"Ah, fuck," he growls as he pulls out, flipping me over and slamming into me again.

Holding onto my hips, he thrusts hard against me. His fingers dig into my skin as he completely loses his mind and I love every second. I want it; I need it, harder, faster, stronger. I feel like I can't breathe but air is still the last thing I need.

Right now, in this moment, all I need is him. Inside me, connected to me, making me feel this way. I can't hold back and unfamiliar sounds start flying out of me. I have no idea what's happening inside me, but I know I never want it to stop.

Trevin falls back against his heels, lifting me so we're sitting with my back to his front and I'm almost on his lap. One arm wraps around my chest as the other starts to explore areas of my body while he keeps the same pace sliding in and out of me.

"I fucking love you so much. This is so unreal. I never want this to end," he growls more than says into my ear.

His voice alone is my undoing. I lose all control, my insides spasm around his cock, my eyes roll back in my head, my breath hitches, and my head falls back on his chest.

"Fuck yes, Lily, give it to me, let me feel you squeeze my cock." His words continue as I ride my high, frozen in ecstasy, feeling him slam inside me with his own release.

This is truly the first day of the rest of my life, and I want every day to end just like this.

Chapter 21

A good luck bracelet at the age of nine
Now a tattoo to show you my love
Knowing our hearts will forever intertwine
For in you, I have the best of.

- Trevin Allen

Lily – Trevin's 24th Birthday

Escape Velocity is gaining traction, but it's taking a lot of work. Ever since I graduated school, I've made Trevin's band my main focus. We've been on the road for the better part of a year, playing any gig the band can get. They've opened for some big names and played smaller venues as the headliner.

I had to quit being a dance instructor due to our travel schedule, and when I look down at the body that used to be tone with lean muscle, I now see curves and bulges I never had before. Trevin says I'm crazy, but he doesn't see what I see, so I just went and purchased some new clothes, which were needed to fit my role as his girlfriend anyway, and try not to think about it. I'll get back to my right size when everything slows down since there are more important things to worry about right now.

Especially on a night like this, a special night for us. Tonight, Escape Velocity is headlining a show at the Fillmore in San Francisco. The venue is smaller, only holding around two thousand people, and we're hoping for a sold-out show.

But that's not what makes tonight special.

The Fillmore is where everything started for Trevin. Where I took him on his eighteenth birthday to try out for Sony Records. Now, six years later, we're here, together, and he's going to be on the stage once more. Stone Cold was too big of a band to play here, so this is his first time back since he auditioned that day.

Even though we've been living on a small tour bus with three other guys, life has been great. Alex, the bassist, Dylan, the drummer, and Trent, the other guitarist, are pretty decent guys for being rock stars. Most of the time, they hang out, playing video games or watching movies while Trevin and I cuddle, talk or fool around in the back of the bus as we travel from show to show.

They haven't bitched much that I tag along, but really, with Trevin as the front man, they know not to say much. He's made it known that I'm his and I go wherever he goes.

I thought after seeing him perform so many times, I'd get sick of his show, but I know I never will. His voice does things to me that should be illegal. I can't believe he never wanted anyone to hear him sing. I swear, his voice tears into my soul, putting a hold on my heart that makes it hard to breathe. I have to close my eyes, allowing his voice to rush through me like it's feeding my need to live.

He has a unique sound that's soothing one minute then deep, rough, and sexy as hell when he fluctuates his tone to make a point in the lyrics. He doesn't scream his lyrics but almost growls them like when we're making love. That's why it hits me so deep. I know his music is just as important as I am, and I thank God every day we finally took the step to be together. How I lived for so long without him inside me, I'll never know.

I take my spot on the side of the stage, wrap my arms around myself, and wait to fall into the trance his voice sets me in as I watch him do what he loves. Pure happiness is the only way I can explain what I feel when I see him up there.

Just like every show, Trevin bounces around, playing his guitar, and sings as though his life depends on it. He's amazing to watch and the crowd eats up every second—they all move with the music, singing the lyrics they know.

Not me, if I'm not one hundred percent transfixed on the man I love, I'm closing my eyes, letting his voice take me away to a place in my heart that will forever be his. At the end of every show, he sings *Simple Man*, and points to the sky, saying, "I love you, Mom." And when the song's over, I melt. It's by far my favorite part of their show.

After the performance, Trevin is more hyped than normal, and since it's his birthday, he wants to celebrate.

"I have an idea," he says, rubbing his sweaty face all over me.

"Ew, come on." I push him back, reaching for a towel. "What?" I ask as I wipe off my forehead.

"Let's get tattoos." He gives me that sexy smirk that gets me every time.

"You're kidding, right?" I laugh back.

"Come on, we can get matching ones. Something only for us. To remember tonight, six years to the day that you changed my life forever."

He's impossible to turn down. "Okay, a small one. Maybe. What did you have in mind?"

"You'll see." He grins and pulls me toward the door where a car sits outside waiting for us. It's supposed to take us to the hotel so we can have a normal night off the bus for his birthday, but I guess he's got other plans first.

"Haight Street, my man," he directs the driver.

"Really, you want me to get a tattoo on Haight Street?"

"Hell yeah, I do. Come on, I just played at the Fillmore, of course we're going to hang out on Haight Street now." He has a point. I still have to pinch myself that this is my life now. My life with Trevin.

The driver pulls up to Haight Ashbury Tattoo and Piercing, and the nerves in my stomach start to turn uncontrollably. I'll admit, in the past year and a half, I've changed a little. I dress a bit more the part but still try to maintain who I am inside. I don't have any piercings or tattoos, which is very different than the other girls I see with the rest of the band. They all have the quintessential "tramp stamp" along with short leather skirts and high heels I would break my ankle in.

We enter the tattoo parlor, and the person standing behind the counter instantly recognizes Trevin. Turns out, he was a huge fan of Stone Cold and has been following Escape Velocity ever since they started.

"Dude, anything you want. This tattoo's on the house," the guy says after he has Trevin sign his autograph.

Trevin looks at me, winking, before looking back to the guy. "Well, this is my girl, Lily Pad." He smirks when I hit his arm. "It's my birthday, and you see here"—he holds up his wrist to show him the bracelet he continues to wear—"she made this for me when we were nine years old and has had to make me a new one every time it breaks. So I was thinking, maybe I'll just have it tattooed on me so it's there forever."

I wrap my arms around him, leaning up to kiss his cheek. "And I'll get the same," I say.

He turns and our lips meet in a sweet kiss before he looks back at the guy. "You think you can do that?"

"Hell yeah, we can," he responds.

"Then…" He shows him his wrist. "Where the string hangs down here, I want it to say 'Lily.'"

My eyes go wide when he says he wants it to say my name.

He starts laughing at my surprise. "Yes, just Lily, no nicknames for something that means this much."

"And I want mine to say Trevin," I say, intertwining his hand with mine.

"You got it." The tattoo artist leads us back to a room where he proceeds to draw the bracelet around my wrist, giving it a thin braided look and Trevin written on the inside of my wrist.

Trevin holds my hand and kisses my lips as the guy starts on the inside of my wrist since that will be the most painful spot. It can only get better from there. I'd like to say it hurt like hell, but having Trevin's lips pressed against mine made the pain disappear and washed the fear away.

Before I know it, the tattoo is finished and it's Trevin's turn. He's gotten so many tattoos he's used to the pain and tries to show off a little for me as well. I decide to mess with him, straddling his waist, wrapping my arms around his neck, kissing him with everything I've got and grinding into his crotch ever so slightly.

The tattoo artist had to stop a few times when we got carried away and Trevin couldn't keep his arm still, which made it all that much more fun.

"Happy birthday, baby." I place my forehead against his and move to sweep my lips against his softly.

"I love you, Lily," he whispers so only I can hear, keeping this moment ours alone.

Chapter 22

Join me, take my hand.
Enter my world so you can understand.
Fly with me, so high away.
I'll show you there's no other way.

- Trevin Allen

Lily – Age 25

"Lilies, come on, time to get up," I hear Trevin whisper in my ear as I lay in bed.

"My head." I pull my hand up to see if it will stop the pounding caused by last night's festivities. "What time is it?"

He laughs. "It's one thirty in the afternoon."

Ugh! Really? That's just wrong.

This has become my life. We party the night away, then sleep till noon, only to start the process over again. It's mornings like this that I sometimes wish I was the good girl who never drank like I used to.

Escape Velocity is getting more publicity but still looking to make their big break. They're on the road constantly, playing any gig they can get, and it's paying off—for every aspect except my head.

I've gone from someone who never drank or partied to someone who gets wasted almost every night. I'm embarrassed to admit that Trevin has become the more responsible one between the two of us.

"Come on, I made breakfast—or lunch I guess it should be now." He jokes as he hops in bed, wrapping his arm around me, pulling me into him when I pull the sheet over my head.

I peek out of the sheet only to kiss his lips and curl back in bed to sleep a little longer. When I finally emerge from the room, Trevin is in his normal spot, laid out on the couch playing with some new songs on his guitar. They've only got a couple more songs needed to finish their new album.

"There she is." He sits up, allowing me to lay on the couch as he moves to the floor in our everyday spot in the living room.

"Stop it. Don't make fun." I try to keep my voice low so I'm not talking too loud.

He gets up to get me a plate of food and a glass of water. "Here you go. This will make you feel better."

I sit up to put the plate on my lap and pour the syrup on the pancakes and sausage he warmed for me. The thought of him standing in the kitchen with no shirt, humming songs, makes me sad I missed my favorite part of him cooking.

"So where are you playing tonight?" I ask before I place a bite in my mouth.

"Nowhere. We have the night off, remember? It's Trent's birthday so everyone's coming over here."

"Oh, yeah…okay…" I hold my head with my free hand and use my other to bring food to my mouth. "I might have to take a night off from drinking."

He gives me a heartwarming smile. "Yeah, I think that's a good idea for you. It's okay. We can still have fun." He kisses my forehead before sitting back down on the floor to work on his song again.

Trevin

"How are you doing?" I whisper in Lily's ear and wrap my arms around her from behind.

"I'm good. Now I know why I hardly ever went to parties in high school or even college. They aren't anywhere near as fun when you're sober," she laughs.

It's getting late and poor Lily has been sitting here just hanging out all night. It's obvious she's been bored, but I don't want to push her to drink since she already said she wanted to take the night off, so I have another idea.

"Here, open your mouth." I hold the little pill up in front of her.

I feel her tense, questioning, "What's that?"

"It's X. Trust me, I'll be right here keeping you safe."

She opens her mouth, fully trusting me to take her to a different high she's never felt. Flipping her around, our lips meet as I kiss her, excited for what's to come. X has been my favorite drug for years, though I've never offered it to her.

We're in such a perfect place right now and the effects ecstasy offers only brings loved ones closer—it's the most intense joy, love, and overflowing emotions for the people you're with—sensation overload.

And she'll be with me.

Not even an hour later, the party starts to wind down and only a few of us are left hanging in the living room. With everyone either drunk off their ass or rolling, the vibe in the room slowly changes when Trent and some girl start kissing on the couch next to us. Normally, that's not a big thing, but the effects of X bring a longing for human touch. Any other time, you can ignore it, but when you notice their soft, exploring hunger to be with one another, a part of your brain starts to take over and you feel that same need deep down in your soul. It's euphoric…spiritual.

A groupie named Shannon gets up to turn off the light, leaving us basking in the blue glow of the moon, then starts to walk toward Lily. I sit up straighter in my seat, surprised to see the attention being shown to my girl.

Lily's tucked in my lap in the corner of the couch, sucking on a lollipop. I watch, mesmerized by the clenching of her jaw and the intense pleasure she's getting from my fingers running up and down her arms and through her hair, proving to me she's rolling hard.

I watch as Shannon sits on the floor next to Lily. She reaches out to grab her hand, interlacing their fingers and rubbing her thumb softly over Lily's, sending what I'm sure is pure ecstasy through Lily's body. Her skin rises with goosebumps in response.

I'm riding my own wave, so once I'm comfortable that Lily is okay, I sit back, enjoying the high and the intense joy I get watching my girl.

She seems to be enjoying Shannon's advances, so when Shannon looks at me for approval, I nod with a smile on my face and watch as she reaches up to kiss Lily. It's just a tiny peck, and Lily smiles when Shannon pulls away. She leans in again, kissing her longer, softer, intertwining their lips and tongues.

Blood flows directly to my cock at the sight of the woman I love with another girl, but I sit back, waiting to make sure Lily's down with what's happening. When Lily's hand runs through Shannon's hair, pulling her closer, kissing her stronger, excitement rushes through me. I'd never push—or even ask—Lily to do anything like this, but she appears into it and I'm more than ready to play.

Lily sits up straighter and I move more behind her, caressing her body with my hands and kissing her neck.

Shannon slowly reaches down and starts to remove Lily's shirt. I pause, anticipating Lily's reaction, but to my surprise, she lifts her hands, allowing Shannon to completely remove her top. I continue my intimate assault on her neck, cupping her breasts from behind before Shannon leans in. She unhooks Lily's bra from behind and removes it completely. Lily's lips stay locked with Shannon's and a sight I'd never thought I see flashes in front of me when Lily reaches down, removing Shannon's shirt as well. Once it's off, Lily's hands reach behind to grip my knees, pulling me closer into her.

"I'm right here, baby." She wants the reassurance I'm with her—that I'm close.

She breaks the kiss with Shannon, only to turn and match her lips with mine. The taste of Shannon's cherry lip balm peeks through, but I still taste my Lily, my forever.

Shannon tries to break our kiss and reach for my lips but I turn away. No matter how drunk I get, or how high I am, that's a promise that won't be broken—my lips are for Lily only. She smirks when she realizes even like this she won't get a taste of me and opts for Lily by standing her up, unhooking her short jean shorts and pulling them down her legs until she's stepped out of them completely.

Beautifully naked, Lily stands in our living room with everyone around, yet no one seems to notice. I look up to see Trent, Alex, and some other guy mixed up with a handful of girls themselves, so I'm not concerned if they see her like this.

Shannon's eyes reach mine as we share a quiet moment of approval again before she drops to her knees, running her fingers around Lily's pussy before leaning in to lick her ruthlessly. I stand up, only for Lily to fall back against my chest, letting out the sexiest moans as one hand reaches up to pull my hair and the other grips Shannon's head in front of her.

I hold her tightly as her body starts to roll with the waves of ecstasy running through her veins. Her sounds are loud and primal, making me wish I was buried deep inside her. Her hands move lower, grabbing my cock, gripping hard, and I know she has the same thoughts I do.

I rub my hand over Shannon's head to get her attention. With my eyes, I nudge her to join the other guys so I can have Lily to myself. She smiles in acknowledgment and stands up, walking away toward the rest of the group so I can make love to the woman I'm crazy about. Turning her in my arms, I wrap my lips around hers, claiming what will be mine forever.

I feel as she tugs on my pants, undoing my zipper before pulling them down along with my boxers and pushing me back against the couch. She climbs on top of me. As she holds my cock in place, she lowers herself down, slow and steady.

I watch as every centimeter of my dick enters her and causes more fire to rip through her body. She's losing control of her mind, her heart, her soul. This is exactly what she's done to me since the first day I laid eyes on her behind that fence. The fact that we're here, together like this now, makes me believe there is a God in heaven looking down on me.

Her forehead leans down, touching mine, and we stare at each other, loving one another as she rides my cock slowly.

It's by far the most intense time we've ever had together, and I know it's the X poking through, but it only shows what's truly there, what I already knew in the bottom of my heart.

Lily will always be my forever, and I intend to make that final here real soon.

Chapter 23

You say I let you down?
I protected you
Loved you
All I could do.
But you left me with a broken crown.

- Trevin Allen

Lily – The next day

My mouth is dryer than I've ever felt in my life. Trevin's lying underneath me, but it's not our bed I'm in. I open my eyes to see I'm in our living room and we're sleeping wrapped up in each other on the couch. Even though there's a light blanket covering me, I'm laying here naked.

I'm more shocked by the fact that Trevin's bandmates and several random women I met last night are all asleep on the floor or on the other couch. I can only assume they, too, are naked beneath the blankets covering them. My head begins to spin as I try to remember what happened last night. It all comes rushing back in a flash. I remember kissing a girl…*holy shit, I kissed a girl!* Then she went down on me…*oh my God.* Then it was just Trevin and me. But it wasn't just the two of us. *But was it? Did I really have sex with him with all of these people around?*

My stomach churns and I quickly go to get up, grabbing the blanket to wrap around me. Leaving Trevin naked on the couch, I rush to the bathroom, barely making it before I throw up—except nothing comes out but dry heaves.

"Hey, Lilies, you okay in there?" I hear Trevin as he knocks on the door.

Thank God I locked it so he can't come in. I'm not ready to see him yet. I'm not sure what to say. What to think. I need to sit here longer to let the shock of what happened last night sink in a little more.

The only thing I know with any certainty is this is not me. None of it.

"Yeah, I'm fine. Can you get me some toast or something?" I manage the words in a barely audible whisper.

"Yeah, of course." I wait to make sure I hear him walk down the hall.

Once I know it's safe, I open the door and run to our room to put on some clothes before opening the sliding glass door to sit on the deck and clear my head. This has always been my favorite place in the house. I love listening to the waves crash against the shore, calming everything around me as I just sit and breathe.

I think back to what my life used to be. I worked my tail off to get my master's degree but haven't done anything with it. And I miss dancing; I miss it so much. Since I graduated, all I've done is travel with Trevin, living in a tour bus, and drinking more than I ever have. But last night was just too much. I've never done drugs, of any kind. I've always been against it, and this is exactly why.

Never in my right mind would I have kissed another woman, much less had sex in front of people we know. If this is just the beginning of my life, I'm scared to think of what I'll be doing when I'm thirty. Every party, every drink, every tour just gets worse and worse. All it does is bring out more parts I know aren't me.

All I see now is I'm losing sight of who I am. There has to be a way to get my identity back without losing him. How can I find some kind of balance? A way that he can be a rock star and I can maybe go back to teaching dance, or finally look for a student teaching position.

I war with the notion before deciding there can't be a happy medium—I either lose him or myself.

But he's my everything. Always has been.

"Here you go." After putting down my toast, he pushes me forward so he can sit behind me like we do every time we're out here.

Only this time, I stop him. "I'm sorry, babe, but can I please sit out here alone? Just for a bit?"

It's the first time I've ever turned down a chance to be with him, and the confusion on his face is all too real. He's just as aware of my rejection as I am.

"Everything okay?" He leans down to make eye contact with me, completely clueless that I'm slowly dying inside. I nod, fighting back tears, afraid if I open my mouth I'll lose it completely.

"Hey, Trev, do you know where my keys are?" Trent calls from the sliding glass door.

Trevin leans down to kiss my forehead. "I'll be right back." And then he heads into the house.

We took the keys from the people we love and hid them at the beginning of the night to make sure everyone was safe. Right now, I'm selfishly praising that decision more than I should. I just need a second to gather my thoughts, my feelings, my fears of what I know I have to do. I've never been one to make rash decisions, but last night was my wake up call. I need to remember who I am before I'm lost forever.

Not even a few minutes later, Trevin is back by my side, kneeling beside me, rubbing his hand across my knee. "Here, I brought you some water. Are you feeling okay? Can I get you anything?"

Our eyes meet and tears run down my face that I can't hold in anymore. Trevin's the most amazing man I've ever met, and I know I'll never find someone who loves me as much as he does, but the cost of that might be too high a price for me to pay.

His hand reaches up to wipe my tears away. "Lily, what's wrong?" he asks in the most loving voice, which kills me even more.

I take a deep breath, letting more tears fall as I lean my face into his hand, allowing him to fully support me before I completely crumble at his feet.

"I can't do this, Trev." I choke out the words through more tears.

Confusion mars his face. "Do what, Lilies?"

"This." I point back to the living room where I woke up.

"What are you talking about?"

"Trevin, this isn't me. I woke up naked in a room full of people."

"But it was okay; I was there. I protected you," he pleads as I see the fear reach his eyes.

"But this isn't me, Trev. None of it. I made out with a girl last night. I had sex with you in front of other people. That's not what I want. Sex is something special, just between us, but we were in the middle of a group orgy, in our living room at that." My sobs have turned to irritation over him allowing this to happen.

"But I was right there. I made sure no one touched you but her. And I didn't touch her at all. You're all I want, Lily."

"But you let it happen!" I push his hands off me. "I trusted you!"

"And you can trust me. I was right there the entire time making sure you were into it. You were safe. How should I have known to stop it?"

"That's the point, Trev. You gave me ecstasy; you should have known that this isn't me. This whole lifestyle isn't me. I've never been this person. I never drank or partied all night. Now that's all I ever do. I worked my ass off for my degree and it just sits in my old bedroom. It's not even hanging on the wall."

He sits, speechless, staring at me with fear written all over his face.

Both of us sit in silence, not sure what to say and scared to death of what the other is thinking.

After a few long minutes, I grab his hand, finally finding the courage to stand up for who I am, who I want to be. "I love you, Trev." I look up as tears roll down his face. "I just can't do this anymore. I need to find me."

"Okay, then we'll change. We'll cancel the upcoming shows. We'll stay home every night. Just you and me."

I place my other hand over his. "No, Trevin. I can't let you cancel your shows. You've worked too hard and the new album is almost finished, which means you'll just be touring more."

"I don't care about any of that." He throws my hands off his and stands in frustration.

"Don't say that. Music is your life."

"No! No, Lily, *you* are my life."

"And you're mine. I just need a break."

"From me?"

"Not from you. From this!" I hold up my hands. "From all of it. I need to remember who *I* am."

He rushes to hold my hands again. "You're Lily Pad. The girl I've loved since I was eight years old, and the woman who helped me find my way when I was lost."

Tears fall freely down my face. "I know, Trev, but that girl is fading away and now *I'm* lost."

"You can't do this. You can't leave me."

"I'm not leaving you. I just need to go back home for a while."

"Please, Lily, I can't do this without you."

"You can. You need to. And I need to. I'm so proud of everything you've accomplished. And I'll be here." I place my hand on his heart. "This will forever be mine."

I take my hand and hold up his wrist to show our matching tattoos. "Nothing changes between us in here." I place my other hand over my heart. "We've been apart before. We can do it again."

"No, Lily…please don't do this," he pleads as tears fill his hazel eyes.

"I have to, Trev," I say through falling tears. "I love you. Remember that. I just need to love me again, too."

His lips meet mine in a desperate plea to change my mind. I have to fight every urge inside me to not fall into him, stay and live this life forever. But that fuels my drive even more. I can't live this way forever. One day, Trevin won't be there to protect me, and then I'll truly hate myself—and him.

I have to do this for me.

I break away from him, whispering, "I love you, Trevin." Then run into our room, grabbing just the necessities before I change my mind.

When I leave, I see him standing at the closed glass door. We stare at each other, tears falling down both of our faces before I turn, leaving him there and doing the hardest thing I've ever done in my life.

Walk away.

Chapter 24

How did she leave me?
How did she walk away?
She said she needed to be free
I just need her to stay.

- Trevin Allen

Lily – 3 months later

I can still barely breathe without Trevin by my side. I wonder daily if this is the right move, but when I'm reminded of waking up naked on the couch, I know it is. I don't want that for my life. Now I just have to figure out what I *do* want.

Trevin still calls every day, but we haven't seen each other since I walked out of our place. The phone calls hurt like crazy, but every time it rings, I can't help but answer. I won't let him come here, though; he's begged on more than one occasion but that would be too much right now. Things are at a standstill with us, which is okay with me—I'm not ready to let go of him. Not yet, anyway.

I was able to find a job student teaching at the junior high school Trevin and I went to, and had lived with my parents until a few weeks ago when I was able to get my own place. Trevin offered over and over again to help pay for it, but I couldn't take his money. I was doing this for me and I needed to do it alone.

I have enough savings from when I was a dance instructor to cover my expenses through my student teaching term, and thankfully, I was able to sign a month-to-month lease. Anything more than that felt too permanent, and I'm definitely not ready to make that kind of commitment.

I went back to the dance studio I once was a member of, and the owner offered me a job instructing their advanced class on the spot. She said she'd had a hard time finding the right fit and I came at the perfect time. At least this situation is perfect for someone. I haven't danced since I graduated, and I have to admit, I'm finally starting to find little pieces of me tucked into the everyday feel of my life.

By far the only highlight of this entire situation is I've been able to help with Trevin's foundation he built for his mom and get even more kids involved in both music and dance.

I try not to think too much about the future, just day to day to get me by until I figure out what I truly want. My dream was to become a teacher, so as long as I'm working toward my goal, I feel like there's a reason I'm putting myself through this torture of being without him. At least I keep telling myself that.

It's late, but there's a knock at the door. When I open it, I see it's my neighbor with a delivery for me. "Hey, Lily, the UPS man asked that I sign for this when you weren't home earlier."

He hands it to me and I see it's from Trevin. I thank him, and after shutting the door, I rip open the envelope to find the completed CD for Escape Velocity. A few of the songs were released before the album was complete, and I'm so proud to see they're doing so well on the charts.

A smile warms my soul when I see his picture, along with the rest of the guys. It's a new photo, and even though Trevin is trying to look hard, I see the pain in his eyes and it breaks me in two.

A note card falls on the floor. After picking it up, I flip it open to read:

I miss you every day. Please come home.
I love you,
Trevin

I hold the note to my heart as tears fall freely down my face. I wonder if any of this will ever get easier. I want to go back but crave a normal life. My fear is he will end up changing for me the way I did for him.

I walk to my computer to pop in the disk, hitting play and lying on my couch, listening to the songs I've heard him practice over and over until they got them right. His voice still affects me just like it always has, making my heart hurt even more.

A new song starts with a heavy drumbeat that's slow and steady, intense. He talks about trusting him, becoming one of them, only for him to let you down. The entire song only has a few lyrics, but those lyrics are us—our whole relationship; the differences between him and me. Repeating the agony of letting me down when I trusted him implicitly.

Then the next song, *Without You,* plays through the speakers and my heart bleeds when he sings about everything he could do without me, but he wouldn't want to and now, he's nothing at all.

I can't fight the hard sobs that rip through me. Here I am, doing this for me, and he thinks it's all his fault. I know he's hurting, but I don't want him to believe he let me down. I'm the one who made the decisions to drink, to become someone I didn't like. He never forced me. He never told me to quit my job instructing, he actually asked me over and over again if I was sure quitting was the best thing for *me*.

Every step of the way, he asked about me, if I was okay, if I was taken care of—even that night. He was there and I'm the one who allowed that girl to kiss me. Not him.

Me.

With another knock on my door, I wipe my tears before answering it. The sight of Trevin standing on the other side with nothing but apprehension on his face answers every question I've had these past three months. I've asked him repeatedly not to come here, but right now, in this instant, the mere sight of him fills every question that has plagued my heart for months.

I reach out, pulling him to me. I kiss him like I'm dying for air and he's my lifeline to oxygen. I can't get enough. I need him, and before I can think, he's picking me up, slamming the door with his foot and walking me straight to my bedroom.

"Trevin." His name rolls off my tongue in desperation as he lays me down on the bed. "I was wrong. I'm so glad you're here." My confession seals my overflowing heart.

"Thank God, Lily, I need you more than you could ever know."

"You didn't let me down, Trev."

"You listened to the song?"

"I did. This wasn't your fault."

He sits up. "It was, Lily. I corrupted you. You never even drank before we were together."

I put my hand on his arm. "But, Trev…they were my choices."

"And I shouldn't have given you that X. I told you to trust me and I let you down."

"Hey." I pull his chin up to me. "Let's not worry about this right now. You're here, and I've missed you. That's all that matters."

"God I've missed you." The look in his eyes tells me more than the words from his mouth. Lightly, he presses me to the mattress, meeting my lips with his. He proceeds to express his love through a kiss in a way he never has before.

There's not an inch of my body he neglects, kissing every exposed bit of skin. He takes his time and slowly removes one piece of clothing before moving on to another.

I've never felt so loved, so treasured, and I know he's trying his hardest to show me exactly how much he's missed me.

And it's working.

When his lips work their way up my thigh, around my navel and back down my waist, I can't help but push my hands through his hair, trying to put him exactly where I need him, to fulfill an ache only his tongue can cure. His laugh tickles my stomach right before I feel warm moisture lick its way through my slit and wrap around my clit.

Sensations fly through my body and my head drops, missing the way he's always made me feel, no matter what he's doing. When his fingers start to work their way inside me, a hunger I haven't felt in months screams from inside and I reach down, pulling him up. Done with this slow game, I remove his clothes in a hurry.

Once he's naked, his hands reach for mine, pulling them up above my head with his. He slowly positions himself, pushing inside me with the most delicate of touches. Our lips meet as he holds me tightly with his arms, making slow, sweet love to me while he whispers his undying love in my ear. He reiterates how much he missed me and how grateful he is to be here with me.

The first time we were together, he came to my house, just like this, with a desperate need to connect with me. Everything we've been through, and here we are, right back where we started. My mind is a mess, but all I can focus on is him being here. For me. And I want him. I'm ready to make this work. We can make this work. Somehow, we'll find a normal life together without either of us losing the other.

He continues to slide in and out of me at a slow, steady pace, bringing me to an orgasm quickly, and when I fall over, he holds me tightly. "I've missed you so much."

He tumbles over quickly after and we lie, holding each other, until I go clean myself up and grab some water. Once I'm back in my room, I lie on his chest, listening to the beat of his heart in the silence around us.

"Lily," he says.

"Shhh…don't talk. Not right now. I just want to be here with you. We'll figure everything out. Okay?"

"Okay."

He kisses my head and we drift off to sleep, wrapped in each other's arms, the way we're supposed to be.

Trevin

I can't believe I'm here, with Lily. I wondered if I'd ever get the chance to see her again. She kept telling me to give her time, but I couldn't stay away any longer. The need to see her got too intense. I hopped on the first flight I could get to head straight to her.

I've been lying here, with her asleep on my chest for what seems like hours, and I finally feel grounded again. Without her in my life, the fear of floating away into oblivion wears on me.

I hear my phone vibrate, but I ignore it. It's not until the third call that I slide out from under Lily, trying not to wake her up and reaching down to see who's calling.

Seeing Arnie's name, I glance at the clock to find it's two in the morning. I step outside to keep from waking Lily, and after taking a deep breath, I hit the answer button thinking this can't be good.

"Arnie, what's up? Everything okay?"

"Trevin! Yes! Everything is more than okay! I just got the call of a lifetime. This is it, man. This is your shot! Not only will the album be listed as number one on the charts tomorrow morning, but Oz Fest just called! They're touring Australia and the lead singer of Cut Throat just went into rehab. They want Escape Velocity to join the tour, immediately!"

I sit silent, not sure what to say. This is huge news. *Huge.* This is the break we've wanted, the one we've worked for. Being on the Oz Fest tour would get us the notoriety we need, and with the album being number one, this is it. We've finally made it.

"*Hello*? Are you there, Trev?"

"Yeah, sorry…*fuck*, are you kidding me?"

"No, I'm not, kid. Here we go. Are you ready to be back in the spotlight?"

I sigh, running my hand down my face, not sure how I feel about this. This is everything I've ever wanted, and I've worked so fucking hard for it, but that leaves Lily dangling in the air. I know she won't go on tour with me. And we haven't even discussed anything about us yet.

I hear Arnie speaking, but I don't fully comprehend any of it until he screams my name, "Trevin!"

"Yeah, fuck, sorry. What?"

"Were you listening? We need to leave in a few hours. Where are you?"

"A few hours? I, um…I can't. I'm up visiting Lily in our hometown."

"Fuck you, you can't. Get your ass to the airport, now. You're not passing this up. I'll set up a private plane to come get you. We don't have time for anything else. You have to leave now. We need to be on the flight to Australia in three hours or we miss the next show."

I do the math in my head, an hour to the airport from here, an hour flight, then I still have to get all my things. I don't have time to talk to Lily. I try to stall. "But my stuff…"

"I'll get it. The guys are packing all your gear, and I'll go to your house to get the other things. We don't have time. Whatever you don't have, you can buy. It's Oz Fest, man. Get your head on right and get your ass to the airport, now!" he screams into my ear before hanging up.

I hit end on the phone call and look into Lily's room. She's still fast asleep and I've never been so torn in my life.

I know she'll understand. She's been there with me every step of the way, and this is the opportunity of a lifetime. I just wish it wasn't happening right now. I can only pray she'll understand why I had to leave with everything unsettled between us.

I don't even have time to think about it, though. I have to go. Now. I'm the leader of this band. I've brought these guys together and I can't let them down. I know I won't leave if I wake her, so I decide to write her a note, praying to God she'll understand.

Lily,

Please know I love you more than anything in the entire world. I got a call at 2am with an offer to join Oz Fest in Australia. The only catch was we had to leave right away. You know this is a huge deal for us, for the band, for you and me. Please forgive me for not waking you up, but I knew I wouldn't leave you if I did. Know that I want to be here with you and I'll be here again the second I get back.

I love you forever,

Trevin

Lily

Confusion of waking up in a cold, empty bed rattles my brain when I open my eyes. For a second, I think it was all a dream, but the ache between my legs reminds me it was all too real and Trevin really did come here for me.

The first genuine smile wraps around my face in a while and I get up out of bed to go hunt down my man. Praying that it will be just like old times and I'll be greeted by my shirtless god making me breakfast in the kitchen.

When I sit up and see a note sitting on my nightstand a feeling of despair tightens around my stomach, clenching my insides and stealing my breath as I reach down to pick it up.

I feel like every ounce of happiness I have ever felt was just ripped from me and I crumple the note, throwing it across the room before I turn back to my pillow and cry like I never have before. Absolutely astounded that he would leave like that, in the drop of a hat when his other world beckoned. Showing me where I truly stand.

Chapter 25

Another life is made
Another life is craved
Another life is going to fade
Because another life is made.

- Trevin Allen

Lily — One month later

"**M**organ, you have to look, I can't." I walk out of the bathroom. I don't need a stick to tell me I'm pregnant. I already know.

"You're pregnant." The pain is visible in her eyes.

I sit down, letting out a big sigh, covering my eyes with my arms crossed over my face.

"Can I ask who the father is?"

I look at her and she shrugs, giving me an apologetic look, but she's right. I never told anyone Trevin showed up that night, or more importantly, that he left without saying a word.

Just a fucking note.

"It's Trevin's."

"Wait, what? How? You told me you guys were over."

"We are. I wasn't sure what we were but he showed up about a month ago saying all the right things, and I was so desperate to have him back we had sex, not even thinking of the fact that I missed my appointment to get my shot. The dates got messed up with me moving here and switching doctors. I had so much on my mind I just forgot. I called this morning to make an appointment, and they said I was well over a month past due. When they said I needed to take a pregnancy test, I just hung up. Knowing exactly what the sickness I've been feeling lately was. I just called you over here for support—for confirmation of what I already knew was true."

"Okay…so what happened after he was here?"

"He left, just like that. In the middle of the night he got a phone call to join Oz Fest and left without even trying to wake me up."

"Ouch…"

"Yeah, ouch… The pain of waking up alone was enough to finally cut ties with him completely. It just proved my point that we're two different people with different priorities who aren't meant to be together."

She sits down, holding my hand and looking directly into my eyes. "But maybe you're not that different, and this baby is showing you that you *are* meant to be together."

"No." I sit up straight. "He's a rock star for God's sake. I'm a junior high student teacher living in the same small town we grew up in. I tried to live his lifestyle, and I was just becoming someone I didn't want to be. It will never work."

"Will you keep the baby?"

I look at her, shocked she would even ask. "Of course I'll keep the baby."

"Then you have to tell him."

"No. I told him not to contact me. He needs to live his life, touring the world. God knows where he even is right now."

I leave out the part that he's called me every day, sometimes two to three times a day. I was able to avoid them for the first few weeks but he finally caught on and called my parents on a night I happened to be there. They convinced me to talk to him, but it just made everything worse. He begged me to forgive him, saying he was coming home, quitting the band and leaving it all behind.

My anger over him ruining everything we fought so hard to get fueled my fire and I told him if he did, he would have no chance of ever seeing me again. That's exactly what I didn't want. I would never ask him to sacrifice music for me. I couldn't live with myself if he did. But that hasn't stopped him from trying. Every time my phone rings, my heart sinks. It's getting harder and harder to hit the ignore button, but I think he's finally starting to get the message.

"You know this baby changes everything though, right?" Morgan states very matter-of-factly.

"Does it?" I get up, turning on my computer to show her the latest video I found about Escape Velocity. The video was taken by a concertgoer at a recent show, so it's grainy, but you can't miss the message. "Come watch this."

She gets up, sitting in the chair closer to the computer as we both watch Trevin alone on stage with a microphone stand in front of him. He begins with, "I'm going to play something brand new for you all. Everyone has loved and lost, and sometimes, after a while, you begin to realize that you have to say goodbye, even though you'll be theirs forever. This song is called *Forever*, I hope you like it."

Tears start to fall down my face as the low beats of the drum start off in the darkness behind him. Trevin doesn't have his guitar for this song, so he grabs the microphone, holding it like it's the only thing keeping him from drifting away as he leads into the song. He sings about what is wrong with him and how he can't get over me. The chorus of the song repeats over and over about how his feelings are forever, but what gets me the most is him talking about having one last kiss before letting me go.

When the song is over, he mumbles into the microphone, "I'll love you forever, Lily," before walking away and off the stage.

"Are you kidding me right now?" Morgan asks. "That was a love song. For you. Only you. Why are you saying that? You need to call his ass right now."

"Did you miss the part where he said it was time to let me go?"

"Oh stop, that's because *you* are cutting *him* off."

"And he's moving on. This is what's best."

"No, it's not. And if you don't tell him then I will. I'm not going to stand by and watch you ruin this just because you're being stupid."

Morgan's always had a give-it-to-me-straight attitude, but right now, I'm not in the mood. I know she doesn't buy the line I'm telling her but she needs to back off. I can't handle any more stress. I keep telling myself that what I'm saying is true and it's getting me through the day. So far none of this feels real and if I keep my emotions in, maybe all this pain will finally go away.

Instead of spilling my heart to her, I bite back, protecting my damaged soul for just a little longer. "This is not your decision!" I pause, taking a deep breath. She doesn't deserve me being mean to her. "Besides, he's on tour for a few more months anyway. Let me get used to the fact that I'm pregnant first. Then I'll decide what I'm going to do."

The next day, I'm sitting at my desk waiting for the students to change classes. My mind has been anywhere but on my classes today so I don't notice Mason, one of my more outgoing students, until he walks up, placing a magazine cover on my desk.

"Hey, Ms. Pace…are the rumors true? Did you used to date Trevin Allen from Escape Velocity?"

I look up, shocked a student would know anything about my personal life. "Um," I say, not quite sure I want to confirm any information for my students.

"Well, I know he's from here and you guys are about the same age, but when I saw this cover, I knew it had something to do with that tattoo you have on your wrist."

I instinctively cover my wrist with my other hand. I've tried to keep it hidden by bracelets or watches while I'm teaching, but I know they've all seen it.

I glance at the magazine cover to see a picture of Trevin leaning in toward the camera with his signature one eye raised, mouth open, rock star pose, but this time, he's holding up his wrist pointing directly at my name that's written on his tattoo.

Mason looks down, seeing the inside of my wrist and the name Trevin sticking out from my hand.

"It is you! You're the girl he wrote *Forever* about. Man, Ms. Pace. That's awesome. How come you broke up with him? God, I'm such a big fan. Do you think I could meet him? Will you get back together with him?"

He continues to shout out everything he can think of as I close my eyes with every emotion flooding through me, but I try to keep my cool. "Come on, Mason, that's enough about my private life. Now go sit at your desk so we can get class started."

He walks to his seat, whispering to every person he walks by and showing them the cover of the magazine. Just what I want—my entire class knowing my rock star past. I can't imagine what they must think of me. I'm sure they all think I've partied and done drugs—they'll never take me seriously now.

Chapter 26

Two souls bound together to form one.
No matter what you say, we'll never be done.
I'll fight for you, for us I'll pray.
In my heart there's no other way.

- Trevin Allen

Trevin — 6 months later

I am so glad to be home. My life has been one concert after the next, traveling from city to city, country to country, and even though I'm ready to crawl into my own bed, I have something more important on my to-do list—I've got to get Lily to talk to me.

There wasn't much I could do from the road. She's consistently ignored my phone calls, saying the way I left her was the straw that ended it all, but she won't be able to ignore me at her doorstep. She told me if I left the tour, she'd never speak to me again, so I finished it out, I fulfilled my obligation—now she has no choice.

All I want is her. Even after that fucking song. Man, that song blew up after I played it live. I thought it would help me heal, help me through the pain of not having her with me, but it didn't. Every time I sing it, I just want her more. She's my forever, but the only thing I was wrong about with that song was that it was time to let her go. I can never let her go.

I had a private plane waiting on the tarmac the second I landed to take me straight to the small commuter airport in our hometown that's full of more hobby pilots and Cessna planes than private jets, but I didn't care. I was not going to wait one second longer than I had to before I could see my girl.

I ring her doorbell and am overwhelmed with questions that flood my mind when the sight of my sweet Lilies appears with a belly three times her normal size.

"Trevin…" She trails off, looking down at her stomach and back at me with surprise written all over her face.

"Lily, what the fuck?" I can't even think straight. So many questions come up like bile ready to fly out of my mouth.

How is this possible?

Am I seeing things?

Who's the father? Oh fuck. Who. Is. The. Father?

She goes to shut the door, but I stop it faster than she can slam it and step inside. "You're pregnant?"

"Go away, Trev. It's time to let me go, remember?"

Me? Go away? Is she kidding me right now? How in the world does she think I would just walk away after seeing her like this? I need answers and I need them now.

"Stop it!" I hold her face between my hands. "No, it was *never* time to let you go."

My brain starts to mentally do some math, trying to figure out how long I was gone, and guessing—even though I have no clue about pregnant woman—how far along she is. I'm just praying my intuition is right.

When my eyes bounce from her belly to her face in rapid succession, I choke on my words. My voice cracks when I say, "Please…tell me it's mine."

She doesn't say anything, just looks away. Excitement and fear intertwine with every breath I take as I wait in anticipation.

"Please!" I beg. "Tell me it's my baby you're carrying."

She looks up and our eyes meet. When they fill with tears, my heart overflows with happiness, but she remains quiet.

"It is, isn't it?" I smile bigger than I've smiled in the past year knowing that my girl, my best friend, is carrying my child.

She places her hands on my wrists, pulling them away from her face, stating, "Yes, it's yours." And then she walks away.

I grab her, pulling her into me. "We're having a baby?" I lean in to kiss her, but she stops me.

"No, I'm having a baby. You have a rock band to tend to."

"Fuck that. No I don't. Everything has changed now. You're moving back to LA with me. We're doing this together. I want to be with you, Lily. I want us to have a family."

"No, Trevin. You can't just barge in here, thinking just because I'm pregnant I'll come running back to your life. I'm not going back there. What, just so you can leave me in the middle of the night again? That doesn't work, Trev."

"I thought you would understand. I couldn't wake you because I would have never left, and I couldn't miss out on that opportunity. Come on, that was the big break *we*"—my hands move back and forth between her and I—"were waiting for."

"I know, Trev. I get it. But it just proved why I left in the first place. We are two completely different people. I like my life now—the slower pace. I'm me again. I'm dancing again. I can't do that and travel with you on tour all the time."

"But, Lily."

"No *but Lily*. Do you know how devastated I was to wake up with you gone?"

I look away, ashamed. I knew it wasn't right, but I didn't have another option. I never could have left if I had to look her in the eyes.

"Yeah, you know how I felt and you know what you did. You love me one minute and leave the next. How can you lift me up like that only to drop me back down without a second thought? Leaving the way you did only proved that you'll drop everything when an opportunity calls. I can't join you again because all I was doing was losing myself. But if you leave your music then in the end you'll lose yourself. I would never want that to happen. We just aren't meant to be, Trev."

She starts to walk away but I stop her again. "Lily, don't do this. I love you."

"Stop. You promised me. You looked me straight in the eyes then vanished before we could even talk. Trevin, I'll always love you. I'd do anything for you, but it's time we accept our fate and move on."

"You're wrong."

"Just leave, Trev. I can't handle you being here," she says through tears falling down her face.

"You can't handle it because you know what you're saying is wrong."

"Please, Trev, just leave me alone."

"I'll prove you wrong, Lily. I'm going to be here for you. We'll be together," I say as I pull her into me, holding her tightly before letting her go.

It's the hardest thing I've ever done, but I know I have to prove to her we're meant to be, and I will be a father to our baby.

Chapter 27

To be with her I'll crawl to the end
My love for her will never bend
I'll fight my way through to have her again
Because I've loved her since we were ten.

- *Trevin Allen*

Trevin - The next day

When I walk through the doors of the house I called home for the last few years, sadness hits me like a punch to the gut. This place is not my home. My home is where Lily is and I'm only wasting time if I stay here.

Without a second thought, I head back out the door for boxes, ready to leave this place and make a home with Lily, once and for all, with her as my wife, and with us as parents.

I'm sweating profusely as I pack everything like the mad man I've become. More focused on what I need to do than I've ever been before and not caring about anything else around me.

When my phone rings and Trent's goofy face appears on the screen, I pause, ready to tell him the good news. "I got news bro." I don't even bother saying hello.

"Well, good morning to you, too. What's up? You miss my ugly ass already?" he taunts into the phone.

"I'm moving. Up to Nor Cal, back to my fucking hometown if you can believe that."

"Shut the fuck up. You hate that place. Why in the world would you do that?"

"Lily." I don't have to say anything else. I don't have to explain, I don't have to go on and on, giving them a reason to stop me. They already know. They've been there every painstakingly horrible day I was away from her.

What I love about these guys, they get it. They're just like me. They're all tough and act hard on stage, but all of them would give up their world for a girl, just like I'm about to.

"Okay then. Here we go. I always liked San Francisco. When are we moving?"

Pride of the band I created ignites in my chest. I've grown to love these guys, and his willingness to move, to support me, to keep our band together gives me more drive than I've ever felt before. I can have both my band and Lily.

There's no other choice.

"Now. I'm already packing. We have a month or two we can rest but we need to get back in the studio right away if we're going to ride the wave of Oz Fest and not let anything die down."

"Fuck yeah we will. I'll call the guys—you focus on you and I'll handle the rest."

There's a pause on the line before I stop and get real for a second. "Hey, Trent?"

"Yeah, man?"

"Thank you…"

"Anytime, bro. We're family. We're here for you. You'll get her back."

A small smile forms on my face as I hit the end call button and drop the phone on the couch before I collapse on it as well.

Family. Lily's always been the only family I've ever had. Now I have my band mates and a baby on the way. For the first time in my life, I feel like things are starting to happen the way they should.

I just need Lily to see it that way, too.

I can't help but shake my head as I see the sign welcoming me into my hometown. A place I wanted so far away from years ago is now a place I just signed paperwork on a new house for. Funny how things come full circle.

It took me a week to settle all my affairs, pack and find my new place, but things are happening pretty fast and I'm riding this crazy train until I have my Lilies back—forever.

It's amazing what you can do if you have money. I found the perfect place, perched high on a hill, secluded and exactly the place to call home with my family. I was able to offer them cash with a five-day close and they jumped on it, allowing me to move in six days later.

The moving trucks pull in only a few minutes after I do, and once I let them in, I bail to head straight to Lily.

I've called her every day, sometimes multiple times a day—even though she never answers. That doesn't stop me.

She answers the door dressed in her tight leotard that shows her belly even more than the last time I saw it. My heart swells as I hold out keys by the ring, offering them to her and saying nothing else.

What I didn't expect was her response or the hatred she spits out. "What now? Why are you handing me those?"

"I'm making this right." I drop my hand, deflated by her lack of enthusiasm.

"By handing me keys?"

"I sold the Redondo Beach house and bought a place here. A place for us. A home. These are for you. So you can come and live with me here."

"No, Trevin." She looks down, hiding her eyes from me. "You can't just walk in here, handing me keys like that makes everything okay and I'm going to move right back in with you like nothing else has happened."

"But why not? You said you wouldn't move back down to LA so I moved here. You can't do this Lily. I need you."

When she looks up, her eyes are glossed over, but she runs her hands over them, removing the emotion I saw poking through. "Trevin, just stop. You *think* you need me, but you don't. I'm just the only thing you've ever known."

"I love you, Lilies. I've always loved you, and I always will."

"I love you too, Trev, but we've already proven love isn't enough."

"No...what we proved is that we belong together. I won't let you forget. I'll be here every day to show you how much you mean to me. You're right, though. You are the only thing I've ever known, but you forget I've been around the world. I've had the chance to know something else and I know I don't want to. I chose not to. Because I chose you. I *choose* you, Lily. All those years ago. I knew the second I saw you when you first came to visit me in LA. My life was perfect but I still felt that something was off, and when I saw you, everything made sense. I knew it was you that I *had* to have in my life. I just didn't know how. But now I do. You were all I wanted since I was eight, and that's not going to change because you push me away. I'll just keep pushing back."

She shakes her head and glances down, not giving me her eyes again. "It's time for us to move on with our lives." She pauses, but the pain in her trembling voice doesn't go unnoticed. "As different people."

I stop her dead in her tracks, prepared to enter the fight of my life. "Fuck that, Lily. You and me, we're meant to be together and that baby you're carrying proves it more than anything else ever has. I'll do whatever it takes to be a father to that baby and the man I know you deserve. Because I am. I'm the man for you. Always have been. Always will."

I turn, walking away, not waiting for her response and letting everything I just said sink in.

I've shown up every day but not to bug her about taking me back. Yes, some would call it stalking, but really, I'm just showing her in my own way that I'm not going anywhere. In the morning, I greet her with coffee in hand like I did when she was in college, and then leave, without saying a word, instead just letting her know that I'm here and will always be.

At night, when she arrives home from work, I bring her dinner so she doesn't have to worry about cooking and ensuring she's getting proper nutrition while she's growing our little miracle. Most nights I've cooked for her myself, but tonight I picked up her favorite take-out from when we were younger.

It's been years since I've eaten at the small wooden shack that somewhat resembles a Mexican restaurant. The walls are lined in the town's history and memories of sitting there countless times with Lily over the years brought an instant smile to my face. Maybe living back here won't be so bad after all.

As she pulls up to her parking spot, I'm already sitting on her doorstep with food on one side of me and a gift bag on the other. Every day I watch her eyes as they meet with mine, and at first, I'll admit, they were annoyed, but over time, I can see her wearing down. And today I even see a slight shift to her lips before she looks down, acting like she's dealing with something within her car.

I've brought her gifts of new clothes, books to read or anything I thought was fun to know about pregnancy. One time I even showed up with a masseuse to give her a pregnancy massage. Of course I offered first to be the one to massage her after I read all about what to do, and more importantly what not do to, but when she refused I hired someone.

Today though, this is the first time I brought a gift for our little boy or girl. I can't believe she won't find out the sex, but I have to choose my battles and that's not one that's worth it. I've been so wrapped up trying to get Lily back that today I went shopping just for the baby, and I can't wait to show her what I found. It's perfect!

Lily's eyes roam the bag of food and I watch as a face full of pure delight greets me at the door. "You didn't?" is all she says as she reaches down to grab the food, bringing it up to her nose and taking a deep inhalation through her nose to smell the greasy goodness.

"Of course I did. How could I possibly forget your favorite?" I say as I stand to give her a hug, which, for the first time, she willingly gives back, confirming I'm breaking down her walls.

"No onions but extra sour cream?" She looks up, surprised I'd remember her order.

"Yup, just like you like it." I smile brightly at her. "And here, I bought our little one a gift, too."

I take the food from her and hand her the gift bag. When she takes the two tiny onsies out, the laugh that comes from her melts my soul in a way I wondered if I'd ever feel again.

"In your dreams." She laughs as she turns the shirts around, showing me one that says Future Rock Star and the other that says Mommy's Little Rocker.

I smile big, lean in to give her a kiss on the cheek and begin to walk away. I can see that her walls are falling down and I don't want to push it more than I should. I can't screw this up.

Chapter 28

Will this be enough?
Will she finally see me for who I really am?
I'll pour my heart and soul into a song
Because I know our love will never be wrong

- Trevin Allen

Trevin – A month later

I t only took a month but my band was excited about the move, and they've all settled in San Francisco or the surrounding area. We're still going strong and discussing our next album, but first, we're shooting a special new song, just for her.

It's not your typical love song. No, I laid it all out there. Talking about everything in my life.

It's raw.

It's dark.

It's real.

It's me, because she's my gravity.

Even though Lily hasn't been pushing me away like she first did, she still hasn't taken me back, so her best friend, Morgan, has been helping to guide me on how to win her over.

She told me some of Lily's students found out about our relationship through our tattoos, so I plan on exploiting that bit of information to get her to listen to my new song. Every kid nowadays has a smartphone and hangs out on YouTube, Facebook, or Twitter, so I'm keeping my fingers crossed that this pays off.

We rented out a stage in my hometown and are going to perform the song then post it in hopes these students of hers take notice.

"Okay, we're all set up. You ready, Trev?" my camera guy asks.

I look around to the guys; they all nod in agreement and I take a deep breath. "Here we go. Let's hope this works."

"Quiet on the set. In five, four…" The cameraman mouths the remaining numbers then points to me as my cue to start.

"What's up, all you fans out there? If you're seeing this, please share, post, tweet, fuck…anything to help me get the attention of my girl. If you have Miss Lily Pace as your teacher, please show her this video. Much love to you all for your help."

The lights shut off for a second before a spotlight cuts through the room, lighting me up on stage. I strum the guitar strings a few chords before the rest of the band starts up.

I pour my heart into the song, knowing this is the most important performance I'll ever give.

The lyrics reminisce about my mom dying, me loving the rock star lifestyle with booze, girls and drugs, when I overdosed, and then the day Lily walked out of my life. I don't promise her I'll do better; I don't promise her things will change. I have to prove that to her, not just say it. This is all about pouring out my soul in a song—begging her for one more chance to prove I'll be the man she needs me to be.

Her simple man.

Without each other, we both will float away into darkness, because my life would be nothing without her. She'll always be my gravity. Keeping me grounded. Helping me be the man I want to be. The man I know I can be.

The lights fade to black as I sing the last lyrics about floating away.

Nothing but silence fills the air as the guitar strings come to a standstill. My head falls when I hear, "Cut" from the cameraman.

The guys all clap, cheering about how good the song sounded, but I can't move. This is it. It's my last chance to win her back. I fear there's nothing else I can do but hope it's enough, and it wrecks me to my core.

Gravity

Lily

This pregnancy is pushing me over the edge. I feel like I'm about to pop, and forget about sleeping. I've spent the last month trying to sleep on my recliner because I finally had to give up on my bed. I can't breathe if I lay on my back, my hips hurt if I'm on my side and breathing through my nose has become a luxury I hardly ever get.

There are only a few more weeks of school and I'm trying to make it till summer, but these might be my last few days. My doctor says she's positioned really low and there could be a chance she comes early, but no one ever knows for sure.

I'm having a baby girl. I wanted to wait and see in the delivery room, but decorating and getting ready for her arrival got the best of me and I finally broke down and asked at my last appointment. I was so excited to paint the room a light pink with the name Julie written in big, bold brush strokes over her crib.

I chose to name my daughter after Trevin's mom—nothing else felt right. When my mom suggested Julie, my heart grew twice its size, sending chills down my arms, and I knew that was it. I haven't told Trevin what I'm having though. I don't know why but I'm just not ready to.

I've told my parents everything about Trevin and they know he's the father. They don't understand why I keep pushing him away, but I've held my ground and they haven't pushed. Although, as we get closer to the date, my heart is yearning for him to hold me again.

I'm so scared. None of my friends have had babies. My mom and Morgan have helped as much as they can, but it's just not the same. I want to do this with him but I've pushed him away for so long. Though he still shows up every day, I'm not sure if I can take the plunge. How will I know if I actually want him back or if it's just my hormones talking?

I wobble down the hallway, unable to walk like a normal person anymore, only to be greeted by Mason. My student stands at my classroom door. School doesn't start for another thirty minutes and he's in my fifth-period class, so I question why he's here. Even more so when I see he's almost giddy as I reach out my hand to unlock my door.

"Ms. Pace, please tell me I'm the first one to show you?" he asks as he jumps up and down with excitement, holding his phone to his chest.

"Morning, Mason. I don't know what you're talking about, so yes, you're probably the first one," I respond as I open the door and wobble to my desk.

"Yes! Can you make sure you tell him it was me? Can you get me his autograph?"

Oh God! I'm afraid to ask what he's talking about. "What do you mean?" I ask, scared for his response.

"Look!" He holds out his phone and presses play on the YouTube video.

My heart sinks as I see Trevin standing on stage, and when he speaks, chills run down my spine from the sound of his voice. That same voice that always speaks directly to my heart. Lately, I've been playing Trevin's music through earphones attached to my belly. Every time I do, my heart hurts just as much as it smiles. I want Julie to know the sound of her father's voice. No matter what happens in the future.

I fall to my seat, listening to him as he asks his fans for assistance on getting this video to me.

Mason stands back and observes the mess I become as I listen to him sing about me being his gravity. Every part of the song fills me with painful memories, but also memories I helped him through, and memories of what made him who he is today.

And through it all, at every stage, I loved him more. Yes, I still walked out on him, but I never stopped loving him.

Instinctively, I wrap my arms around my belly, loving the little girl that he blessed me with. I reach for a tissue when I realize Mason is still standing there, watching me cry as the man I love sings his heart out for me.

"So, are you going to forgive him now? Wait, holy shit, Ms. Pace, is that baby his?"

I laugh through my tears at the awkwardness of sharing this moment with my student. "Watch your language." I laugh. "Here," I say and hand him his phone. "Thanks for showing me." I walk out of my classroom without saying anything else. I don't have a class first period, so I need to get out of here and regroup before I have to teach my students.

As I reach my car in the teacher parking lot, I see Trevin leaning against it, waiting for me to arrive, and I instantly fall apart, losing control of any ounce I had left.

I walk up, standing a few feet in front of him, and when he sees my tears, I watch as nothing but pain fills his eyes.

"Trevin…" I whisper.

"Shh…" He reaches up, wrapping one hand around my neck and pulling me into him, locking his lips with mine in a single, intense kiss.

We stand there locked at the lips until he releases to take a breath and goes in for more, opening his mouth and searching for any answer he can get from mine.

I hear the sounds of kids laughing in the background right before bolts of lightning rush through my body, sending sensations I've never felt wrapping around my belly, through my hips and around my lower back.

Confusion of us, of him, and my emotions run around in my heart until my head kicks in and I bring my hands up to push him away.

"Please, Lily…please don't do this. Let me be—"

"No, Trev…" I cut him off. "Oh shit, my water just broke!"

With our eyes open wide, we both start to panic. I stand still, holding my belly and trying to breathe through the pain. It rips my insides apart, and Trevin tries to comfort me while guiding me to the other side of my car to open the passenger door.

After he places me in the car, he reaches around to wrap the seatbelt around my belly, and crouches down next to me. "Are you okay? I'll get you to the hospital, I promise. I'm going to be here, Lily. I want to be a dad. I love you."

"Yes, Trev. I love you too, now get in the car and get me to the hospital!" I yell, pushing on him to get going.

His sexy smirk fills his face as he gets up, running to the other side of the car. The door flies open, and after he buckles, he looks around, reaching up to the ignition, the center console and his pockets. I watch as he starts to panic as I hand him the keys from my purse, holding them out to him just as another contraction rips through my body. I scream and double over in god-awful pain.

His hands are on me instantly, comforting me, rubbing my back as he says, "Breathe, just breathe. Come on, baby."

I glare up at him. "Drive."

"Oh yeah." He puts the key in the ignition and starts the car.

He peels out of the school parking lot and heads toward the hospital across town. "Hang in there, baby. You got this," he says as he rubs my leg back and forth before, yelling out, "Holy shit!"

"What?" I say shocked at his outburst.

"We're having a baby!" he says, hitting the steering wheel.

The excitement written all over his face brings a smile to my lips, even in the face of pain. I can't deny I'm beyond happy he's here with me. I have every answer I need in this moment, and I can't imagine having this baby without him by my side.

I reach out, intertwining my fingers with his. "We are, Trev. We're having a baby."

He pulls my fingers up to his mouth just in time for another contraction to rip through me. "Squeeze my hand, baby. I know you can do this."

"I'm scared, Trev. They're coming really fast."

"I'll get you there. Don't you worry. I'm here for you, Lilies. I'll always be here for you." We pull up to a light and he leans over to place a kiss on my forehead. "You're almost done." He looks at his watch. "In five, four, three, two…okay, it should start to get better now."

My head falls back as the pain subsides and I take a deep, cleansing breath. Once I can think again, I can't help but ask, "Why were you counting?"

"Each contraction builds, getting stronger and stronger for about twenty seconds and then it releases and will get better. So if you know you can last twenty seconds, it will help you get through the pain, knowing it's calming down," he states like he's an expert in the field of childbirth.

"Excuse me? And how do you know that?"

He shoots me my favorite smile I've missed so much before admitting, "I've been meeting with a midwife and taking private childbirth classes so I'd be ready when you went into labor."

"Trevin—" Happiness overwhelms me, but it's washed away quickly by pain ripping my insides apart.

Keeping my eyes closed, I focus on the feeling of Trevin's hand wrapped in mine, and his voice as he counts out the twenty seconds, knowing life is just the way it should be.

We pull into the parking lot, and after putting the car in park, Trevin races to the side and opens my door, helping me out of the car and up to the hospital.

Before we walk in, I stop him. "Wait."

"Please, Lily, don't stop me. I'm going to be here with you. There's no way I can miss the birth of our child."

"I'm sorry, Trevin. I'm so sorry I pushed you away for so long. I just want you to know I'm so glad you're here right now."

He pulls me close to him, kissing my forehead. "Me too, Lily Pad. Me too. Now let's go have a baby," he says, pulling me back and showing me exactly why I love this man so much.

A few hours later, we welcomed a tiny, seven-pound, six-ounce baby girl into the world. Right after she was born, they placed her on my bare chest as tears ran down Trevin's face seeing his daughter for the first time. He was by my side the entire time, and now we're waiting for them to finish her newborn screenings before we can get her back.

"Here, Dad," the nurse says. "You got a bare spot on that arm of yours for another tattoo?"

We both look at each other, wondering what she meant.

She laughs, signaling to him. "Come over here."

He lets go of my hand and walks toward our baby girl. My heart melts as

I watch his face fill with pride when he looks down at the miracle we created.

The nurse places an inkpad on the bottom of our daughter's tiny foot and reaches for Trevin's arm that isn't covered in a sleeve of tattoos. He holds out his arm, letting her stamp our daughter's footprint on the inside of his bicep.

He looks down at the small foot with five little toes then looks to me with a huge grin covering his face. "Looks like I need to find a tattoo artist in town," he says, keeping his arm out so it dries properly.

"Oh jeez," I tease.

"Okay, Dad, you ready?" the nurse says as she picks up our baby.

"What, um…really? I get to hold her?"

"Yes, silly. Meet your daughter," she says, holding out her arms and handing her to Trevin for the first time.

My heart soars as I watch his face light up with amazement when his arms wrap around our tiny angel.

"Do you guys have a name picked out?" the nurse asks.

Trevin looks at me, slightly panicked that he has no clue what our daughter's name is.

"Yes, we have a name." I look straight at Trevin, and with a gentle smile, I answer, "Her name is Julie."

His eyes fill with tears as emotions he can't hold back take over and he pulls Julie into his chest, letting out sobs he's trying to hide.

"Julie's a beautiful name," the nurse says as she walks to the whiteboard in the room, writing, *Welcome to the World Julie*, in big red letters with the time ten thirty-five am underneath it.

Trevin makes his way to my side, leaning down to kiss me before handing me our little bundle of joy.

She's so tiny, all wrapped up with her pink and blue striped hat. I unwrap the blanket just enough to pull out her tiny hand, wrapping her fingers around my pointer finger.

"I'm your mommy," I whisper. "And this crazy man next to me is your daddy." I laugh while glancing up at him. "Don't let him call you silly nicknames—it will last the rest of your life." He lets out a deep laugh. "But he'll love us to the end of days."

He gets up, saying, "You got that right," before locking his lips with mine.

Epilogue

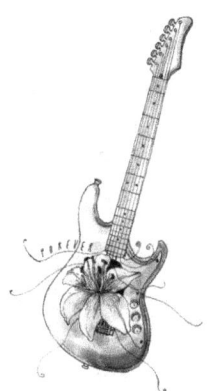

My girls are my life
I'll shower them with diamonds and pearls
Forever she'll be my wife
I'll always remember her baby curls.

- Trevin Allen

Trevin - Age 35

"**B**ut, Daddy, I can't do it," Julie whines as she gives me her best puppy dog eyes.

"Yes, you can, Julie Bean," I say, holding the bike steady for her to get back on.

"Just don't let go like you did when you taught me." I hear Lily laugh from the driveway where she's holding the camera, ready to capture Julie's first time without training wheels.

"No, Daddy. Don't let go!" Julie says, panicking.

"Way to go, Lily Pad," I jokingly shout over my shoulder.

I look back down at the beautiful little girl with long brown hair, watching me with wide eyes. I still can't believe I have a daughter. I don't get to be around for everything, but there was no way I would miss out on her riding a bike for the first time without training wheels. There's just certain things that are your right of passage as a dad.

After Julie was born, Lily, thankfully, forgave me for being a dumbass, and I've been working hard every day to prove I can be a rock star, a husband and a dad at the same time.

Escape Velocity took off after the Oz Fest tour, and we've headlined a few of our own tours since. We've also released three other albums with *Gravity* recorded in a different manner—the original, live, or acoustic—on each album.

But all my band's success is nothing compared to being a father.

My manager knows I can only be on the road for a few weeks before I have to take a break to head home to my girls. When I'm on the road, I Skype them so I can continue our nightly reading of Judy Blume's books—Julie's favorite.

"What does Mommy mean, Daddy?" Julie asks.

Lily walks out to join us in the street. "Did you know your daddy taught me to ride a bike?"

"You did?" Julie asks, glancing back at me.

"Yup, I did. And look at how good she is now."

"That's right, Julie. Your dad's a great teacher. And he won't let go."

I wrap my arms around Lily. "That's right, I'll never let go."

Gravity Playlist

Don't Take the Girl by Tim McGraw
  - Lily wants to learn this song when they start guitar lessons.

Simple Man by Lynyrd Skynyrd
  - The song Trevin's mom wants him to learn.

Comedown by Bush
  - Trevin plays this when sitting on Lily's floor.

Glycerine by Bush
  - The song that plays when they first kiss and later on when they are
    sitting on his car.

All Along the Watch Tower by Jimi Hendrix
  - Trevin plays this during his audition.

Paul Revere by the Beastie Boys
  - This plays on their car ride.

Songs that inspired Trevin's songs
Those Nights by Skillet
  - The song I envisioned Trevin writing about his past with Lily.

Let you Down and Without You by Three Days Grace
  - Songs I envisioned on Escape Velocity's album.

Forever by Papa Roach
- The song I envisioned Trevin playing for Lily while on the Oz Fest Tour.

Gravity by Papa Roach
- The song I envisioned Trevin playing at the end and what inspired this entire book.

Acknowledgments

To say I thought this book was going to be the death of me would be a huge understatement. I wrote it months ago but had to put it on hold when everything started finally happening with the non-profit kids science museum I was opening.

When I picked it back up, I felt like I was starting all over and without the help of Stefanie Pace and Jeannine Colette I might have given up. My other books are full of sex and twists and since this book had very little of that, I felt like the story had to be perfect. Stefanie pushed me through, I may or may not have wanted to hit her a few times in the process (LOL), but I can't thank her enough now that it's over. A huge thank you also to Sophia Scarlet and Autumn Gantz with Wordsmith Publicity for guiding me through my rough draft. Then lastly Kaye Blanchard and Grey Ditto for being my final proofreaders.

To my TWOT's, my favorite Secret Affair group, I'm so honored to be friends with you all. Having you guys makes this author journey worth it and it means the world to me that I can turn to you with anything and you are all there to help.

To Leddy Harper and Stephie Walls, I can't thank you enough for guiding me through, what felt like, word by word. Your guidance made the book what it is today and I'm forever in debt to you.

I knew I needed someone who hadn't been with me every step of the way to read it one final time for content and I'm so thankful I found Chelle Lagoski Northcutt with Indie Solutions. She was exactly what I needed to push me to the finish line and give you all what you hold in your hands now.

To April Wells, even though you probably talk to me because I'm the only one awake while you work your night shifts ;-), your friendship has meant the world to me. I swear one day we will meet for real and I look forward to the day.

To SueBee on Goodreads, helping a small author like me get noticed means more than you'll ever know. I'll never be able to thank you enough for your help.

Poor Megan at Designed with Grace who I'm sure wanted to hit me a few times due to the craziness over this cover, but at the end it was all SO worth it. I am so in love with this cover and you rocked it. Thank you for putting up with all my shit. Love you!

How could I ever leave out my own personal book boyfriend, turned cover model, my husband Chris. All of this may drive him nuts but in the end, I know he supports me and loves me more than any book could ever explain, and I'm more than lucky to have him in my life.

And lastly, to all the readers, blogs and everyone who helps make this indie world possible and my dreams come true. From the bottom of my heart, thank you.

About The Author

Lauren Runow is the author of multiple Adult Contemporary Romance novels, some more dirty than others. When Lauren isn't writing, you'll find her listening to music, at her local CrossFit, reading, or at the baseball field with her boys. Her only vice is coffee, and she swears it makes her a better mom!

Lauren is a graduate from the Academy of Art in San Francisco and is the founder and co-owner of the community magazine she and her husband publish. She lives in Northern California with her husband and two sons.

Sign up for her newsletter through her website at www.LaurenRunow.com to keep up to date about new releases.

She'd love to hear your comments and feedback. Please take the time to leave a review on Goodreads, Amazon, iBooks or wherever you purchased *Gravity*.

You can also stay in touch through the social media links below.

www.facebook.com/laurenjrunow
www.twitter.com/LaurenRunow
www.instagram.com/lrunow
www.goodreads.com/author/show/14168280.Lauren_Runow
www.bookbub.com/authors/lauren-runow

Join her street team Lauren's Law Breakers at https://www.facebook.com/groups/1628591530724682/

Want more books by Lauren Runow?
Check out *The Unwritten Series* and *Black Widow* that are both out now.

www.ingramcontent.com/pod-product-compliance
Lightning Source LLC
Chambersburg PA
CBHW061230170626
46809CB00007B/2590